Angels and Other Stories

Angels and Other Stories

For

Burt and Edna Mae Goodman

John R. McDonough

John R. McDonough

White Tower Publishing, Seattle, WA

Cover art: *Angel playing Lute* by Gavin MacHutchin

ISBN-13: 978-1543153767
Library of Congress Control Number: 2017902501

Printed in the United States of America

DEDICATION

To Children, Grandchildren, and
now Great-Grandchildren
May They Grow into a Deepening Understanding
Of Creation, the Glories of the Earth
Of Where We Are, Where We've Come From
And Where We Are Going
and
To Father George and the Brothers

Finally, a fond remembrance:
To Neil G. McCluskey, S.J. (dec.),
who, seventy years ago, taught me
the haunting beauty of words.

Veritas – Gaudium – Pacem

CONTENTS

ANGELS

THE BROTHERS

SHORT STORIES

FOREWORD

We each hold our own personal perspectives – our way of appreciating and quantifying the world around us. We look within the realms of culture, art, nature, race and religion (to name just a few) to better understand the world, to see both similarities and differences, to find the uniqueness in all things. It is the inquisitive mind at work – the ever watchful "conscious I" probing and examining and fitting the pieces together to form a belief system, a map of reference that allows us to awake each morning to a consensus that this is the world I perceive, a life in which I exist – one that makes sense and carries me forward.

Dr. John McDonough is a man of both science and religion. This is his overriding interior framework – a scientist by training (a retired medical doctor) with a deep, life-long resonating faith in a Christian God. He carries both perspectives within himself, side by side, each a bountiful reservoir of endurance and fortitude. One seemingly lends credence to the other in the day by day passage of time – science providing a database of practical and professional knowledge (most notably medicine and geology and astronomy) and religion (Catholicism) forging a standard of living – the daily attendance of mass, the taking of communion, the following of Christ's teachings, and the ever so evident acceptance and benevolence towards family and friends and all of God's children on earth.

Angels and Other Stories is a written testimony to this dual unity. Within these narratives you will find passages related to an expanding universe and creation and scripture and good and evil and the journey of faith and false pride and law and innocence and the special purpose of "bodied creatures with an imperishable soul". It is a book vast and far reaching – a fictional yet comprehensive accounting of the beginning of all things (planets and angels and the soft, white light of heaven) and also of the depth within ourselves – the ordinary human capacity for goodness and fellowship.

At times I stand in awe of Dr. John. I think to myself, where does he find all these words, these ideas, these images, plots, encounters, settings and messages? And then I know - It must be his active intellect, his desire to communicate, his love of language and writing, and his prevailing interest in all that appears godlike and human. I applaud and commend him for his body of work: his three books of poetry, his life memoir, and now this volume of novellas and short stories. Carry on, Dr. John, carry on …

Joseph Galagan
February 1, 2017

ACKNOWLEDGEMENTS

To the Galagans, Joe and his wife Katherine, who edited and formatted this my fifth published book, together with three prior books of poetry, and one of short stories.

Joe is the editor and guiding hand for this book, while Katherine has formatted the sometimes tangled writing into a work ready for publication.

Joe received a Bachelor of Arts degree from the University of Washington, a Master of Science degree in Counseling from Syracuse University, and a Master of Arts degree from University College, Dublin, in Irish Literature. He has authored three books, *Rosary Rounds*, a memoir, *The Red Moon*, about life as a counselor in a public high school, and *Providence*, about his experiences as a leukemia patient at the age of seventeen.

Katherine Galagan received a Doctor of Medicine degree from the University of Washington, and completed three years of Pathology Residency at Upstate Medical Center in Syracuse, New York, finishing her Residency at the University of Washington, with special emphasis in Hematopathology. She has coauthored and edited several *Color Atlases* for the College of American Pathologists, as well as a book on *The Healing Art of Pathology*.

To Gavin MacHutchin, artist, for his cover portrait, "Angel with the Lute".

To my dear wife Jane, and family members, immediate and extended, for putting up with my penchant to write at odd hours, and for extended periods of time.

To all of those above go my unending thanks.

INTRODUCTION

You, the reader, will find this to be a collection of four stories, two long, of a length to be considered novellas, and two short.

We, the author and editorial board, pondered whether to publish the stories together or separately, each of the longer stories as separate novellas, or perhaps together as two novellas. Then we found a thin thread that was common to all four, and this was the struggle of good versus evil. Each story treats this in a different way, and we will leave to you, the reader, to discover the thread, and to see whether you agree.

Names used in the short stories and most of the events are fictitious.

ANGELS

A Novella

1

Prologue

Angels Exist. They abound in the Holy Books, the Testaments, Old and New, and in the Holy Book of Islam, the Quran.

Angels did not just happen as random events, they were created, they, one and all, owe their existence to the Creator God. We know God through His creation and through His interactions with His creatures, first the angels, and later humans.

This work presents the creation of angels, the universe, and of men; evident, even necessary to explain what we know of these events. What remains as mystery is "why" and "how" they came about.

The story of the angels remains one of the most dramatic, enigmatic, and significant in the history of creation. The angelic rift, resulting from the introduction of evil, and the banishment of a rebellious band, is discussed in the Holy Books, and comes to us from the Oral Tradition of many cultures.

The human race, Homo sapiens, and all of humanity, each member, created with an imperishable soul, and free to choose, is indelibly affected by creation of the angels, and the angelic rift which followed. Although the "why" of creation remains a mystery, the "how" is what is portrayed in this story, The "how" must remain a fictional account until more is known.

2

The Void

Nothing. Nothing existed. Nothing was. All that seemingly was, truly wasn't. We are so used to ourselves, to others, and to things, that we cannot get our minds around nothing. Not even no things.

All was a void. It went everywhere, but not truly. Everywhere implies things. There are insufficient words to describe the void. It had no limits - limits belong to things. It went on in total blackness. Not just darkness, for some creatures can see in darkness. This was blackness. A total absence of light. And a total absence of heat.

We have our minds geared to heat as a continuum from hot to

cold. On one end there are millions of degrees of heat. We don't know exactly how far it goes. At the cold end we do know precisely. There is an absolute zero, defined as the total absence of heat.

When it is cold outside we shiver and put on more clothes. There is still heat, only less heat than when it feels warm. Science tries to create a moment, perhaps, when absolute zero might be carried lower; the accepted stable points are minus 459.67 degrees Fahrenheit, and minus 273.15 degrees on the Celsius scale.

The void was at absolute zero. It did not exist as something. It had no limits. There was no light or heat attached to the void. Its non-existence went on for eons - billions of earth years. It was fathomless.

The void might be considered a harsh environment, but this would not be true. It would be harsh for us or other creatures, but creatures did not exist in the void.

One might ask if it had an existence since it seemed to occupy space and continued endlessly. But did it really occupy anything? How could it, since it was nothing? Largeness, smallness, and occupancy apply only to things. The void had nothing to do with dimensions.

Can anything else be surmised about the characteristics of the void? Since it had no dimensions, contained nothing, contributed to nothing, and itself was nothing, what else can be added? Nothing. We yearn to know and to learn. Yet with the void, we come up with only negatives.

But is this so? We think of negatives and positives as opposites, both thus having qualities or attributes. A series of negatives doesn't seem to adequately describe the void. It seems to be, truly, nothing.

Is this only word play? Our words are limited in their power to assess, describe, measure, and characterize. Is the void, meaning nothing, just a game with words? But words have another power. They are tools of our minds. They can be used to strip away attributes and characteristics, and then try to envision what remains. The void is such. When all that pertains to a "thing" is removed, our minds face a blank, an enigma, a mystery, a nothing, a void. Perhaps with further refinement of thought, and if we had better words, we might make headway against this blank. Lacking this, we might try to go around it - an end run, so to speak.

3

Creator God

The Creator is and always was. We have never found adequate words to identify who and what the Creator is. Our pronouns, signifying male, female or neuter, do not suffice. The Creator is not adequately identified, and is not bound by any of these. In searching and wondering, the customary male pronouns will be used to affix an identity, not because they apply, only that there are no others.

He always was. His existence extends beyond boundaries, and was not curtailed by the void. He was not part of the void, since it was nothing, and His presence has no boundaries. He was not affected by the void or by elapsed time. His awesome power is discerned in His amazing creation. All things are of His doing, yet He does not place Himself at the forefront of His created things as if to brag: "See, this is all Mine." His presence is hidden. It must be discerned through His created things, and later by His interaction with His creatures that call Him God.

4

Glorious Spirits

God, for whatever reason, created. Creation was special. It took from nothing and brought something into being. All creation occurred in that way. Creation happened through the creative power of God. All who exist are in a special sense beholden to God, even though God does not advertise, or stand on the rooftops and announce to all, and forevermore, that He is the cause.

God's first creative act was the angels. These are pure spirits. They contain no matter. Matter was yet to be created. They resemble God in this way because God is pure spirit.

Angels came into existence all at once. In a moment they were all there. Their numbers exceed counting; there may be many billions. Angels are persons. They possess minds. They question and communicate. They have a high level of intelligence, higher by far than that of humans who were to come later. Each angel differs from the rest. They assort themselves into strata or levels, based upon inherent characteristics of beauty, power, and intelligence.

At the bottom of these strata are ordinary angels, less endowed than those higher up. Yet these ordinary angels far exceed humans, not yet created, in intelligence, beauty, and power.

At the very top are magnificent angels secondary only to God; these are the archangels. They have direct communication with God, and serve as an intermediary between God and the other angels. They transmit information such as what might come, and what God requires of them. Thus, the Creator God gave them intelligence, an ability to communicate order and expectations for things to come, and a will.

5

The Universe

At the very top of the angelic order was a magnificent angel, who considered himself superior to all other angels. God chose this angel to be the light bearer, and gave him the name Lucifer (in the Latin vernacular). Lucifer bore the God-given light. Then at an apt moment almost fourteen billion years ago, when quantum fluctuations within the void, caused by God, were of suitable amplitude, God ordered: Let the light be cast.

Instantly there was rapid expansion, with instantaneous creation of matter and energy, which was irreversible. Particulate matter, eventually, was to coalesce, producing stars, planets, and galaxies. The universe was created in an instant. All that was to become the universe started infinitesimally small, and came from nothing; all occurred at the command of God.

The interaction of matter with energy continued over billions of years, and resembled an explosion, instantaneous at its start, and expanding, ever outward, in every direction, like an expanding sphere. Strangely, the rate of expansion, instead of decelerating with time, is accelerating.

With expansion, the void was replaced. The expanding universe appeared to have no discernible limits in any dimension and was now a cauldron of activity with stars and galaxies eventually being formed from fields of heated and expanding gas, dust, and larger particulate matter. Energy and matter interacted, each able to change to the other, with explosive force. Some stars were formed, lasted, and then faded. Giant collapsing stars sometimes left black holes such that particulate matter and electromagnetic radiation, including light, could not escape, a consequence of a very dense gravitational field having formed.

It is remarkable that new stars and galaxies moving at phenomenal acceleration and speed did not collide with one another. Because matter and energy began at one tiny point, the origin into which light was poured, the explosive force thrust all matter into vectors moving in every direction, but becoming farther and farther from neighboring vectors of matter-energy interaction.

When angels were created they lived in blackness. Now they dwell in the light emanating from the universe. They have reveled and cavorted for billions of earth years. They are pure spirits and glory in their status. Superior to matter and energy, they are not limited by physical attributes. They live throughout the expanding universe and are not affected by temperature, electromagnetism, gravitational attraction, nearness to masses of matter, or the ravages of energy fluxes.

They enjoyed the superiority of spirit over matter. They possess power over matter in that they can influence the formation of greater aggregations or the dissolution of mass, thus influencing the formation of stars and planets and their dissolution into swirling clouds of cosmic gases. But they have no power to affect or destroy the basic structural elements of matter - the atoms, protons, neutrons, electrons and other subatomic particles.

They may influence, in some circumstances, the fundamental laws of physics: the conservation of mass and energy, electromagnetism, thermodynamics, photonics, quantum mechanics, and general relativity; but any effect of angelic spirits over these laws is minor and temporary. Angelic spirits dwell within, but can not destroy these laws, and certainly could not destroy or fundamentally alter the particulate matter or the energy unleashed by the creative power of God using light in quantum fluctuation.

Angelic spirits abounded throughout the expanding universe. Their numbers were uncounted. They were not bound by earthly time as we know it. For angels, thousands of earthly years can seem like moments. They can also travel - not as physical bodies that move against resistance and must experience elapsed time to move from one place to another - rather, they move from place to place in an instant. Any angel can traverse even the far reaches of the universe in a moment. They move by thought; and since they were pure spirits they have the power of thought, and can be instantaneously anywhere their thoughts take them.

Angels are also playful. They pursue games with one another, endeavoring to outdistance or outlast their rivals at sport. It was with these games that angels began to realize that they were not all alike. Some excelled, others did not. Games showed that an angel could beat a rival repeatedly, resoundingly, every time without exception. The same proved true when teams were formed. Some groups would surpass other groups each and every time, without exception. Therein loomed a realization of variations of power between angels, a beginning realization that affected all; thus, each and every angel that lived in the universe became aware of its place in a hierarchy encompassing all angels. They learned quickly that there were layers, many and complex, that separated angels from one another. This understanding of place or caste would have profound consequences for the future.

Angels are also beautiful. This is not physical beauty as such, since angels are not physical beings. Instead it is a spiritual beauty. Angels can appreciate their own capabilities and giftedness, and experience genuine pleasure in dwelling on their own attributes. They are also instantly aware of the beauty of other angels, and are able to compare their own beauty with the beauty of any other angel. Differences are easily noted. These differences at first were taken for granted and easily tolerated.

Intelligence is a quality that all angels possess in abundance. Every angel is a pure spirit in possession of a magnificent mind. Each has a capacity to know virtually all that is going on at a given time and to retain everything that has affected that angel in the past. Retention is vivid and total. Anything retained can be recalled instantly and completely. Angels also found there were differences in the quality of intelligence amongst themselves. Some were more intelligent than others - they all recognized these differences and accepted them. Angels also recognized that differences in intelligence were related to the emerging social system of castes or social strata that later became a system for their governance. Intelligence among angels, strangely, did not translate to complete understanding of situations or to the development of wisdom. Gradually angels were sorted into strata or castes based upon perceived beauty, skills, and intelligence. Lucifer, the light bearer, placed himself at the top, regarding himself, by far, as the most beautiful, intelligent and skillful of all other angels. However, Lucifer was still only one of a small strata of angels at the top - the most powerful of all angels - the archangels. It was to Lucifer that Creator God entrusted light, which, when poured out, became the catalyst for creation of the universe.

God, in this primordial state, communicated directly to archangels in a mysterious and infrequent manner; otherwise God was silent and hidden. Lucifer did not, while communicating with other angels, signify that God was the Creator. Thus many angels believed they might have come into being directly from Lucifer, and Lucifer did nothing to dispel this notion.

Nearest God and separate from other angels, are the three orders of Seraphim, Cherubim and Thrones; these are celestial bands, in direct communication with God, and constantly ministering to Him. The Seraphim and Cherubim have a special place. They are always near to and ministering to God; and as such, they are not under the aegis of the Archangels. Dominions, Principalities, Virtues and Powers are another order forming a different strata.

Archangels form the first strata, at the very top of the angelic hierarchy. As such they are considered the most powerful; they have a special function to oversee other angels, and to be shepherds especially for the large numbers of ordinary angels who form the most numerous strata - those angels at the very bottom, so to speak. Lucifer, an archangel, was thus superior to the vast number of angels contained in the bottom strata. Though there were other archangels, Lucifer assumed to himself the position of leader of the angels, considering this a God-given boon as a consequence of being the light bearer.

6

Conflict

It started in Lucifer's mind. He began magnifying his own attributes. He regarded his beauty as ravishing; his intelligence as beyond comparison. His ability to communicate was unparalleled; he could easily mesmerize other angels to a state of compliance. He regarded himself as master of others. He became dazzling to himself. Then gradually, perhaps over the course of billions of earth years, he began thinking of himself as God-like. Perhaps he could influence God; but he also knew he should start with minor things - see how far he could go and then proceed on to bigger things.

Lucifer began to change; and the change was gradual. He began thinking of himself as worthy of emulating God, and then of receiving worship from other angels. But how to carry out these awesome ventures? This was an enterprise that would have to be planned in detail before being started. The more he thought about it, the more enamored with himself he became.

He began paying close attention to the other angels. He would look for flaws, variances in behavior, weaknesses of character; anything that might suggest deviations along the line of what Lucifer was experiencing himself. He knew that he should proceed carefully, and yet he had developed such a degree of self-centered superiority that it left him brazen, willing to take risks, knowing within himself that if something went amiss he, Lucifer, the superior one, could easily straighten it out.

Gradually he began to blame God. Why had God not shone him partiality? Was not he, Lucifer, worthy of lavish and continuing praise? Maybe God was not supreme after all. If God would not recognize Lucifer's superiority, maybe God was jealous. Maybe God really was inferior. Maybe he, Lucifer was equal to God - maybe even superior to God.

Lucifer began to veer from the bright angel that he was at the beginning. In fact Lucifer was far beyond ever again thinking back to his own creation. He had become warped. Then another attribute of the angelic nature became apparent: once started he could never return to what was before. The die was being cast. Lucifer was beyond returning. No power, not even his own inherent power, could ever effect a change. Lucifer knew that his existence was forever. He also knew, in all of its immensity, that he would never again be what he had been before. Lucifer's creation and very existence was coming to a crossroads.

Lucifer began meeting with his inferiors, the ordinary angels, and those simple spirits who constituted the vast numerical majority. He began meeting with small numbers, wanting to see what might be accomplished. At first he extolled himself as the light bearer, claiming that the creation of the universe had depended upon his actions. Of course he was correct in this, but it was only a partial truth. He did not disclose that he was enabled to carry out this step by the Creator God. These small group discussions were repeated many times. Each time Lucifer extolled and magnified his importance. Gradually Lucifer sensed an emerging interest. Some of the angels were engrossed and wanted to go further. There were more meetings, more interest, and then a gradual unfolding of plans. Angels could participate in creation. They could learn how to use this newfound power for their own devises.

The concept of an entirely new plan, a way for ordinary angels to participate as creators sparked the imagination of many angels. This was an early stage: "Think about it angels, you can be like me." But not really. Lucifer knew his own superiority would never be shared. He also knew that he was enticing, drawing out and bringing out in others a curiosity and then a desire for more. Angels were easily mesmerized by Lucifer's gift of communication. Between meetings many communicated with each other, wanting to know what others thought of these emerging plans. Many backed away, not satisfied with moving in this new and uncertain direction. Other angels felt no need to communicate with other angels. They had already decided. They would follow Lucifer.

While this was going on, other angels, higher in the hierarchies, became aware of Lucifer's activities. Seraphim, Cherubim, and Thrones continued to minister to God. They remained focused upon God, and took no part in following or evaluating Lucifer's doings. That should be left up to God. There were also other archangels. They were within the higher strata similar to Lucifer, for Lucifer was also an archangel. They also were becoming aware of the gatherings that Lucifer was promoting with other angels; but they lacked information about Lucifer's evolving plans; they stayed aloof, knowing that this would be God's business, and that it would be up to God to manage it. Thus a brewing cauldron was emerging - a brewing cauldron similar to what was happening in the physical universe, but one with far different consequences.

7

Beelzebub

Distance developed between individual angels and between different groups of angels. Goodness was never a concern or a consideration for angels. They are pure spirits, endowed with minds to wonder about themselves and other angels. Being good, even acting good was never relevant. Angels live "foot loose and fancy free", so to speak. They traverse the extent of the physical universe at the speed of thought; they possess extraordinary intellects; speed for them is instantaneous.

Though they have remarkable retention and recall of past

events, even those that occurred billions of earth years in the past, they lack a capacity to fully understand and to learn from past experience. Wisdom was not an angelic endowment - not at this stage of creation.

Angels, thus, were gullible. They could be swayed by someone as gifted as Lucifer. And Lucifer was slowly developing pride. Pride, not of accomplishment for the common good, but rather an internalized pride, a feeling of superiority that placed him, Lucifer, at the forefront, and left all others to their own pandering, a pride that didn't include those other simple spirits, but harkened only to self aggrandizement. Why had Lucifer allowed himself to go this way? We shall probably never find an answer. The grand position of Lucifer at the start of the creation of the universe had allowed him freedom to indulge in those things that eventually led him to a choice; the choice between serving his Creator God, or serving himself. To place himself at the forefront required that he abandon God, or diminish God's role. This was pride. Pride at its most insidious, but also most deadly. This was pride that, when fully in play, altered the direction of creation forever.

Once decided, Lucifer pushed forward. There was no changing. Others were needed to foster his ambition and to carry out his plan. At one group meeting he chanced upon an angel who gravitated to his position even without encouragement. This angel's name was Beelzebub. He was noted by Lucifer to be keen and skillful. Lucifer recognized immediately that Beelzebub was hungry for something more. The ordinary would not satisfy Beelzebub. Beelzebub became an early ally and a staunch supporter of Lucifer. It was then that Lucifer laid out his plan, slowly and deliberately, and found that as he went on, Beelzebub became ever more avid.

The hook was in, so to speak. First there was a ceremony, serious, instantaneous, and riveting. Beelzebub must swear allegiance to Lucifer, and to none other as his lord and master. To this, Beelzebub agreed enthusiastically and without hesitation. The two began, at that moment, sharing a direction and an outcome that was to have lasting consequences for the angelic spirits. With the addition of Beelzebub, greed and avarice were added to the pride and deceit that Lucifer first brought to the fore.

"You will be the leader after me," Beelzebub was told. "Together you and I will share the glory. We must now lay out our plans." At this, Beelzebub was transfixed. He hung on to every thought that Lucifer brought forth. Lucifer's thoughts were strong and clear. The two would henceforth share in the adulation of the angelic legions that awaited their call.

"We must convince the lower order of angels and bring them to our position. Once on our side, we will use the force of numbers to go after the higher orders. We will leave the Seraphim and the Cherubim until last. They minister and are closest to God. When we are ready they will no longer have the power to stand in our way."

"But what of God?" intoned Beelzebub. Lucifer answered (in the parlance of human creatures to be created later): "God has done nothing since we started this. He has not interfered. He may be weaker than we thought. But consider this; what can God do when we, and all of the other angels, confront Him with our new order? All the angels will be with us; we will have the upper hand; God will have to acquiesce. Then, to assure His compliance, He will be required to swear an oath of allegiance to me, Lucifer - the same as I will require of all other angels."

Beelzebub, who previously had sworn allegiance to Lucifer, was blind to other alternatives. He was also blinded to his previous existence. For Beelzebub, there could be no turning back.

Beelzebub could only relish in his own glory. He drew pleasure in thinking of his own superiority over other angels. He would lord it over them. He would also require lower angels to swear the oath of allegiance to himself, Beelzebub, as well as to Lucifer.

Just then an emerging doubt entered his mind; he wondered how this would be perceived by Lucifer. Lucifer needn't know. He would say nothing to Lucifer about this. There lingered in Beelzebub's mind the beginning of fear, then the slightest tinge of envy, and then the beginning of anger that he was not called to rule jointly with Lucifer, and to share equally in the glory that was to be theirs. Another thought entered Beelzebub's mind. If, in the future, he and Lucifer developed differences over these matters, he, Beelzebub, might have to find ways to distance himself from Lucifer, or at the least, lessen his power. The beginning embers of hatred slowly emerged. He would have to be very careful, playing along with Lucifer, and assisting in all of Lucifer's plans, but also developing plans in secret, plans of his own, plans that would allow him to usurp power if needed, and depose Lucifer of power if it became necessary.

Lucifer continued his discourse. "We will continue meeting with groups of the lower angels. You have shown remarkable powers of persuasion, and because of that, I will rely on you to gather these groups together and to make known to them the new direction that we are taking. I will come along if further persuasion is necessary, but the main work, Beelzebub, will be yours. Bring me many angels united to our cause, and your reward will be great."

Lucifer, brilliant angel that he was, knew that he must recruit more associates in order to expand his vision of bringing all angels, or at least a vast majority, into his plan. He needed subordinates, gifted and energetic angels who could entice or cajole other angels to follow. He studied other angels – evaluating their gifts and other attributes that might be useful to him in the future.

Lucifer was also having misgivings about Beelzebub. Something during their last meeting had left him a bit unsettled. Beelzebub's thought pattern was broken. His thoughts had begun to drift to other areas, areas that Lucifer was unable to penetrate. Beelzebub's earlier avidity for their plan of conquest seemed now to be less focused. He seemed less interested, though he made motions as though he was thoroughly loyal and involved. This was nothing Lucifer could make sense of, but something he would keep watch over.

8

Incubus, Succubus, and the Pleasure Principle

Lucifer, after a long study of the other angels, selected Incubus, and Succubus, two angels noted for their attachment to pleasure. They each had skills that could seduce or entice other angels to seek pleasure as an ongoing activity, and in so doing, take them away from their more usual activities. Such actions seemed to be natural to both of these angels. Lucifer pondered how he might employ them. First he had to bring them in, meet with them, and enlist their aid in his plans. He decided not to divulge his overall plan; rather he would use their talents directly, and against a higher tier in the angelic hierarchy, the archangels. Lucifer himself was an archangel, and he knew who his targets would be. There were four other archangels that Lucifer felt constituted the main strength of that angelic order. They were Gabriel, Michael, Raphael, and Uriel. If one or more could be seduced to accept the pleasure principal, and especially to incorporate it into their lives in an ongoing fashion, they could thus be weakened and more easily overcome in a future conflict. Perhaps they could be so enwrapped in pleasure that they would offer little or no resistance when it came time to draw them away from God and toward the lordship of Lucifer.

These two angels were contacted and brought into Lucifer's presence. Both were beautiful and attractive, yet different. Incubus had a fine mind, direct and inspiring with a clear inclination toward future goals. Inducement of pleasure, for him, was intermittent and used in attaining whatever goal he had in mind. Succubus had a different mind, one that was more scattered, changing direction on a whim, yet with an attractiveness that was all encompassing and more feminine. Her beauty and charm were compelling. Briefly, while communicating, Lucifer felt an attraction to Succubus and wondered if he might be seduced. Why not join spirits with Succubus for the sake of enjoyment? Then Lucifer came to his senses. He closed his mind to such thoughts. He wanted the power displayed by these two angels to be pointed at other archangels, potential future foes, to soften them and hopefully to render them ineffectual in any future conflict.

Lucifer began by saying that as an archangel he felt responsible for other angels - this was his function. As such he recognized the special powers possessed by Incubus and Succubus; that these powers involved the transfer of pleasure to other angels; and that he would like them to befriend archangels that they might partake of the pleasures possessed by these two. Lucifer provided names:

Michael, Gabriel, Raphael, and Uriel. Lucifer said that he had a special fondness for these four since he himself was an archangel. "Befriend them and transfer your pleasure to them. Succubus, start with Michael, and then go to Uriel. Incubus, I want you to begin with Raphael, and then proceed to Gabriel." Lucifer purposely kept his plan to usurp power from God from these two angels. He did enjoin them not to mention that they were being sent by Lucifer - this was to be a special gift, its source to remain anonymous. When finished with their assignments they were to report back to Lucifer for further assignments.

After seeing these two angels on their way, Lucifer felt smug, feeling that his plans were proceeding better than he had previously anticipated. He also felt exhilaration, something that he first began to feel during his conversation with Succubus; it was an exhilaration that would persist.

Lucifer then continued searching for other angels to entice into his plans. He was looking again at the lowest order, the ordinary angels. These would be the most susceptible to Lucifer's powers of recruitment. He was looking for angels with powers of persuasion, but also those who had a mind for personal gain. Lucifer prided himself on being able to note these qualities in others, and he began his hunt in earnest.

This was early, after the creation of the universe. Matter and its complement energy were expanding rapidly. Their vectors were traveling in a direction, and at a speed that carried them farther and farther away from adjacent vectors of matter. Strangely, the overall acceleration, and therefore the rate of expansion was increasing, rather than decreasing. Stars were not yet forming - they would come later. After stars there would come other formations, the galaxies, the large gatherings of stars, and then the planets, orbiting these stars, and moons, orbiting planets.

9

Xaphan

Lucifer, after extensive searching, found an angel to his liking. The angel's name was Xaphan. Lucifer noted that he had an inventive mind, was creative in his thoughts, and was interested in personal gain. Lucifer arranged a meeting. He began slowly, identifying himself as Lucifer, the light bearer. "I know who you are," intoned Xaphan. "You are the brightest of all of the angels; you poured the light that began the universe."

"Did you know that it was I, Lucifer, that chose the time and circumstances for the start of creation?"

"No," said Xaphan, "I did not know that."

Lucifer knew then that he was making progress with Xaphan. He explained that it was he who participated with God in creating the angels. God had entrusted him with all the details of creation. There was work that remained. "I have approached you because you have special gifts. There is a large universe out there, one that will only get bigger. Opportunity awaits those angels who are gifted, and will join me in the work ahead. Those who join will be richly rewarded. Are you interested?"

Xaphan showed intense interest. He was smart and ambitious. Lucifer sensed that it was time to enlist Xaphan's support. "I require," stated Lucifer, "that you swear allegiance to me, and to no other." Xaphan did not hesitate. His avidity and greed were readily apparent. Xaphan swore allegiance to Lucifer, and the door slammed shut; this would be Xaphan's own door, which never again would open to allow a walk back to what had been.

Lucifer then gave Xaphan instructions about what he wanted him to do. He was to begin the search for other angels, but first was to contact Beelzebub, who had been previously recruited by Lucifer. Beelzebub was already at work recruiting other angels. Xaphan was to join him and learn from him the techniques needed for gaining the interest and then the allegiance of other angels. He would work alongside Beelzebub until he was thoroughly versed and able to strike out on his own. This would be a work of forming angel bands that would later swear allegiance to Lucifer. "When you have a few angels that seem interested in joining, I will come and provide the final preparation. I also want you to pay special attention to Beelzebub. I will call you back periodically for a complete explanation of all that has transpired. You must also be most careful not to divulge these plans to any other angels. For now, they will be kept secret from all except a select few." Lucifer, while enrolling Xaphan to proceed with Beelzebub, purposely did not include the separate plans that would soon be underway with the angels Incubus and Succubus. Thus began, for Xaphan, an association with Lucifer that would have far-reaching consequences, and that would last for eternity.

10

Archangels

Archangels are a special caste. Unlike the Seraphim and Cherubim, who continuously minister to God and are always in His presence, archangels range far and wide. Their boundaries reach as far as the outer reaches of the physical universe, itself unlimited. Though few in number they are powerful angels. Although not in God's presence except when called, they are very close to God. They were the first angels created, and were endowed with the special privilege of overseeing all of creation that was to follow. God had selected Lucifer, himself an archangel, to be the powerful light bearer that in an instant began a transformation leading to the creation of the physical universe. Lucifer would not be the same after that momentous event; his pride led him to regard himself as the most important of all of the angels, a growing view that continuously inflated his self worth and self-image.

While Lucifer preened on the celestial stage, the other archangels went about their business of keeping track of the expanding universe. They ranged far and wide, at the speed of thought, to traverse the vast expanses of the universe in an instant. Their purview was the entire universe, how it was continuing to evolve, and the balance of physical forces distributed throughout. There were lower order angels spaced at intervals in this expanding creation whose job it was to watch and keep track of a sector. The archangels maintained surveillance over these angels. Lucifer took no part in watching over the universe. As such he had no ongoing contact with the other archangels. Lucifer engaged in his other activities - a scheming self-promotion; after all, he thought, wasn't it he, Lucifer, that had brought creation into being? So why should he concern himself with the trifling duty of watching physical things happen? He had proven that he was lord of these events; he had started it all. Eventually he would show all other angels his importance. They would have to acknowledge this, and eventually he would require their obeisance and more - their homage, even their worship.

11

Michael

Lucifer had dispatched Succubus on a mission. She was to find archangel Michael, and attempt to seduce him with her pleasure principle. She had previously shown this special power to Lucifer, who himself had nearly succumbed. Succubus entered archangel Michael's presence. He was at one far-flung outpost of the universe observing the expansion of celestial gas clouds, and was in the company of other angels who were given specific tasks for keeping track of all occurrences. Succubus drew closer and addressed Michael, saying that she wanted to view the universe.

Michael pointed out the work that was being done, and the watchful attentiveness that he and his angels were maintaining. "Why," she intoned, "must you be engaged in such activities - won't these particles and large pieces of matter take care of themselves?"

As Michael answered, she drew closer. Michael pointed out that the universe was expanding and needed balance. "Too much matter accumulating in one place could lead to a warp or dislocation, which could then result in the universe spinning out of control and breaking up."

"But how," she intoned, drawing even closer, "can you prevent that from happening?"

12

Nudging Power

Michael pointed out that he, and his band of angels, possessed powers that they referred to as the powers of the nudge; they could force particulate matter of any size to move in any direction they chose. They could compress gas clouds into dense bodies, and also dissolve and scatter large bodies of matter in any direction that they chose. As Michael was explaining these details he noticed that Succubus had drawn closer to him. This had happened before - angels as pure spirits could simultaneously occupy the same space without either angel being affected or restricted in any way.

But now, something was different. He noted her beauty and her particular charm. He also felt her approach, one desirous of participating in his spirit and particularly his mind. Why should this be? How should it be handled? He knew that he possessed complete powers to repel any attempt to penetrate (so to speak) his person, his spirit, his mind by any being, provided he chose to exercise those powers. He also was aware that nothing, no power, not even, he thought, the power of God could undo his existence. He was created by God to be immortal, always to be, never ending, ongoing. God had endowed him thus; even God, he surmised, could not undo His creation of angels.

But how should he, Michael, handle the present situation? Why had Succubus approached him? Did she have a particular motive to possess him? In other words, what was her game? He decided that he would not rebuff her, but neither would he accept a sharing with her. She could be as close as she wanted. He would allow this, even to both occupying the same space. And so it went.

She did, as a matter of fact, occupy his space; but she was also aware that he was not allowing a penetration of his spirit by her. Something was amiss. She had this power to penetrate the spirit of other angels and leave something. She wasn't sure just what she was to leave, only that it was something that would affect a change; angels after this encounter were different. But now, she was unable to penetrate, unable to leave something of herself with Michael. She also recalled that during her encounter with Lucifer, she felt for a moment that something, maybe a very small something, but something, had been left. At any rate she was on a mission, being dispatched by Lucifer, to attempt a penetration of Michael. She felt her own power. Perhaps it would take more time. She also remembered Lucifer required that she not inform Michael that she had been sent by him. She would abide by this. She then began to realize a stirring within her spirit toward Lucifer. She had never before experienced a similar feeling and found it strange but welcome, and wondered what the future would hold.

Michael mulled over the situation that had developed with Succubus. He decided that he would attempt to learn more. He inquired where she had been before coming to join him. She mentioned a different part of the universe, keeping her answer in general terms. Michael asked if she was with a particular group of angels. She responded, no, not really; she was one of numerous angels that roamed the universe freely. He asked about other angel associates. She responded that, yes, she did frequently run across other angels, but this was only as their paths crossed. She was very much on her own.

Then Michael made a more direct comment. "You have powers," he said to Succubus, "including the power to penetrate the spirit of other angels. I could feel it as soon as you approached."

"Yes," Succubus intoned, "I am aware of it."

"Have you used this with other angels?"

She paused, confused. "No," she said, "I am not aware of having used this before."

Michael sensed and then became certain that she was not telling the truth. He asked if any other angel had sent her to him? "No," she intoned, "No one."

Again, Michael felt the absence of truth. This was a completely different feeling - one that he had never experienced - a puzzling unsettled feeling that he didn't like; one that he would attempt to unravel; one that in the future he might, even as a powerful archangel, wish to discuss with other archangels.

Soon after, Succubus was gone. Gone, and not to be seen again by Michael until much later. The thought remained and was pondered. "What is Succubus' game? Is she being used by someone?

If so, who?" He did not relish these thoughts - they bothered him. But they kept coming back. He then resumed the surveillance of the outer reaches of the expanding universe.

Meanwhile, Succubus returned and reported to Lucifer. He was disappointed. She had failed, and he told her not to attempt a mind penetration of archangel Uriel. She was instructed to continue the penetration of other angels with the goal of forming angel bands willing to join with Lucifer.

13

Raphael

Lucifer had dispatched Incubus to approach archangel Raphael and attempt to sway or seduce him using the power of penetration and the pleasure principle. Incubus appeared with a group of angels under archangel Raphael's charge. They were at the center of the universe. Raphael's duty was design; it was his charge to provide ongoing and dynamic design features as the universe expanded for the later generation of stars and galaxies. This was a delicate business extending over billions of earth years. His team dealt with the physical properties of mass and energy. They could instantaneously, or nearly so, cause mass and energy to change, knowing that nothing in the long run was lost or gained. They also knew all of the laws of physical matter, such as the laws governing the gravitational effect. They had the nudging power - the same power used by angels at the periphery to maintain equivalent mass/energy ratios throughout the universe to prevent warping and possible fracture. It was a huge task, but one within the capabilities of angels.

Incubus joined with the ranks of other angels. Though recognized as a new addition by adjoining angels, this did not seem strange or out of line; new angels were periodically added for training and for replacement. Incubus studied the work and specific tasks of the other angels he had joined. He was highly intelligent and quickly mastered every detail, - not only of the work before him, but also the work of every other angel in this working complex. He communicated with adjoining angels, asking to participate in their tasks under their observation. Gradually he was incorporated into their ranks.

Incubus bided his time. The design was extended from the center to the periphery as divisions, much like the divisions on a mariner's compass, but instead of thirty-two degrees to plan a nautical course, or the three-hundred-sixty degrees of a circle, there were thousands of divisions extending from the center outward to the periphery. Furthermore, the tasks were complicated because they didn't deal with a flat two-dimensional reality, but one with spherical dimensions. Within each division moving outward there were also stations at intervals monitoring the changing situation, and using nudging power when needed. This herculean task, seemingly incomprehensible and unmanageable (in human terms), was continuously under management, and well within the exalted intelligence and powers of the angels. Raphael exercised control from a center post. He had total grasp of all divisions and stations. His grasp was constant. It extended over billions of years. He did not require relief by another angel; he needed no rest; such was and is the nature and power of an archangel.

Slowly Incubus rose from an ordinary angel doing routine tasks to a supervisory status, first as a station leader and then on to eventually become a division leader. It was as a division leader that he had contact with Raphael. The design apparatus required close association between division leaders and Raphael. Meetings, one might imagine, would be the way to accomplish such a liaison, but such was not the case. These angels maintained continuous and instantaneous communication with each other. They were pure spirits with magnificent minds. They were not space-occupying beings, and as such, numerous angels could occupy the same space. There was no dislodgment, no feeling of closeness, no awareness of compression. Communication was instantaneous and continuous. In this sense it functioned like a combination of a sit-down meeting involving talk and plans, and the performance of needed tasks that resulted from such planning sessions. Such are the attributes of the angelic nature.

Before one such encounter, Incubus had deliberately modified a minor treatment, a nudging endeavor, by displacing an energy field a little farther than he should have. This resulted in instantaneous communication with all division leaders, and especially with Raphael. The error was almost instantly recognized and admitted by Incubus. He was prepared for the correction and suggested it in detail. It was reviewed by all divisions and by Raphael, and judged to be appropriate; the correction was then put into place.

In the follow-up review, Incubus was adjacent to Raphael, and moved closer. Raphael took no notice of this as his focus was on the error. Incubus, sensing his opportunity, attempted to penetrate

Raphael's mind. Instantly Raphael was aware. He noticed something different, an enticing divergence, and an invitation to a close embrace. Raphael, as with most angels, possessed an enhanced probity, an interior configuration of spirit that honored integrity and goodness. He did not accept the invitation, though he was puzzled by it. He decided to allow common space but no embrace. He wanted more information about this strange new interference. Where did it come from? How did it come about?

Instantly he began an interrogation of Incubus. This was kept from other angels and occupied only moments. "Why have you approached me in this way?"

Incubus answered, "It was not intentional."

"You have a power to penetrate the minds of other angels, are you aware of this?"

Incubus paused, for he was not expecting such an abrupt and explicit question. "No, I was not aware."

Raphael sensed a break from truth, and was discomfited, but went on. "Why are you here? Did anyone send you?"

Again a pause, a split second, but recognized by Raphael. "No one sent me; I came because of interest in how the universe was unfolding, and how it was being managed."

"Go then, return to your duty, and learn from your mistake."

Incubus left, initially to his duty station as leader of a division, but after an interval, he disappeared. This caused momentry turmoil. Ordinary angels came and went for training and replacement, but a division leader? There were ample replacements for Incubus. One was found. The work went on. No one seemed to notice, except Raphael.

Incubus returned to Lucifer and provided a full report of his doings with Raphael. Lucifer evinced disappointment. He then realized that the second of his attempts to penetrate the minds of two archangels had failed.

"Go then, and do not attempt penetration of the second archangel Gabriel," commanded Lucifer, who then asked: "What would you like to do now?"

Incubus replied, "To stay with you, and to participate in your plans." Incubus noted that he was feeling a fondness for Lucifer that was not present before, and not recognized by Lucifer.

"Go then, you are very capable, and have this special power to penetrate other angelic spirits. Begin recruiting angel bands. Tell them that the expanding universe is ours for the taking. Penetrate as many as you can, and convince them to go forth and form other angel bands to increase the power of our numbers."

Raphael, in the long history of angelic endeavor, did not see Incubus again until much later. Incubus went forth and began recruitment of other angels in accordance with the instructions laid out by Lucifer.

14

Glimmers and the Angelic Blight

Succubus and Incubus worked hard recruiting other angels. They worked separately but under the direction of Lucifer. Each employed their individual powers of drawing near, encompassing, and then penetrating the spirit mind of another angel. In such endeavors they felt enhanced. While liaising, they inserted a "glimmer" of their own spirit-mind into another angel. The exchange was not material, as the participants were pure spirits; rather the exchange was a part of the very spirit or spirit-mind of one to the other. This left each with a sense of achievement or attainment;

an enhanced feeling of self-worth or self-importance; a feeling of independence, and a drawing away from the feeling of interdependence so characteristic of the angelic nature.

Angels, so affected, rejoined other angelic bands to carry out the work of caring for the evolving universe. They had agreed with the need to participate in some plan or work, but they had not been given details. They also had not been informed that Lucifer was the spirit behind this new enterprise. Thus they continued to perform their prior tasks.

But something seemed amiss. Communication with other angels for routine matters occurred in a normal fashion; however circumstances requiring more mind power sometimes demonstrated slowness or a diminished capacity. There were also moments of inefficient use of other powers, such as the nudging power required to maintain stability in the universe. At first these changes were subtle, but in time they were noticed by the leaders of stations and divisions, and then by archangel Raphael.

Raphael put into place a plan for detecting where, when, and by whom, these lapses occurred. Individual angels having deficiencies were identified. When questioned by their supervisors, nothing out of the ordinary was found. It was concluded that they were a little slow; more individual training would bring them up to speed, so to speak. They were monitored and it became apparent that further training did nothing to improve their abilities.

These angels were deficient. Nothing in prior angelic existence had been similar. Angels were by nature able. Skills were acquired quickly. Additional training was seldom necessary. When training was applied, performance improved rapidly. But now these angels were clearly different from what they had been and from other angels. This was an entirely new phenomenon in the angelic order.

Raphael questioned several of these angels to learn what had caused them to change. Gradually Raphael learned of the encounters several of these angels had had with Incubus, an angel familiar to Raphael, and with Succubus, unfamiliar to Raphael. He immediately suspected mind penetration during those encounters, similar to what he had suspected with Incubus. He began to formulate a plan to identify all angels afflicted by this "Blight". He decided it was time to contact the other archangels to review the situation. This would be a meeting of archangels with similar powerful minds, to be kept confidential from the purview of other angels.

Raphael was in instant communication with the other archangels, of which he, Michael, Gabriel, and Uriel would be the participants. These four archangels joined to review the nature of the problem and to search for solutions. This was a sharing of ideas, virtually instantaneous, between four powerful minds, each unique, as each archangel was unique, and different from all other angels.

Raphael began the review by detailing his discovery of angels who were deficient in their performance of tasks for managing the developing universe. He told of instituting refresher training, but without improvement. These angels were debilitated. Under observation they were slowly getting worse. He called this problem a blight, and angels so afflicted, blighted angels.

Raphael continued with his discourse. More and more blighted angels had appeared. It was then that he conducted interviews. Blighted angels were not aware that they were afflicted. They were unaware of unusual occurrences. A few remembered strange associations with other angels - a nearness associated with feelings of exhilaration. The names of Incubus and Succubus were found from these interviews.

Raphael then related how he had been approached by Incubus and sensed an attempt at mind penetration, which he had rebuffed. He had questioned Incubus and found the answers delayed, and sensed that they were untruthful. Raphael was puzzled by all of this, and said that he did not recognize the other angel, Succubus.

Michael then spoke. He had been approached by the other angel Succubus, and had sensed an attempt by this angel to penetrate his mind. He also had rebuffed Succubus. He also had found Succubus to be untruthful when questioned. She had quickly disappeared after the encounter, and he had not seen her again.

The problem was considered new and serious. Potential harm to the universe could occur resulting from inefficient functioning of blighted angels. Care of the universe was the primary function of angels, bestowed by God, and was under the direction of the archangels.

First, a system needed to be put into place to identify the extent of the blight. This meant finding all of the angels who were blighted. Once identified, those angels had to be removed from critical functions and placed in less important jobs, such as tending to the "sweeping" functions within the universe, moving small areas of galactic dust from place to place. These angels and their tasks had to be under the continuous supervision of other angels, and all movements of blighted angels needed to be constantly observed.

Next, they would try to discover the source of the blight. Mind penetration was the favored mechanism agreed to by the four archangels. That only two angels could account for the spread was considered possible, but unlikely. Further scrutiny of Succubus and Incubus would be mandatory. Was it possible that either of these angels had received it from the other? Their possible contacts needed thorough vetting.

More information about the nature of the blight was needed. Were there other ways in which the blight could be received and spread? Was it possible that mind penetration could occur from a distance in the absence of close contact? If such were the case, could rapid spread occur without direct contact?

Attention to the extent of the blight and its rate of spread was of the first importance. Methods for early detection of blighted angels were needed. Since two angels were discovered to have spread the blight to other angels, could these newly blighted angels spread it to others? If Succubus and Incubus were not the source, where might the source be? Might the universe, to which the angels were attendant, somehow have been the cause? Much work was needed. There were no moments to be lost. "Let's get to work," the archangels communicated to each other.

During the meeting there was another archangel listening, and that other archangel was Lucifer! He heard of the meeting in advance, though he was not invited, and he found a way to listen in to all that went on without being detected. He wondered how much, if at all, his plans for recruiting other angels might be suspected by the other archangels. He felt, from all the mental activity he was now privy to, that the angel blight was all that had been discovered, and that his role leading up to the blight was not suspected by the other archangels.

Lucifer, silently, made an instant decision. The angelic blight had to be shut down. Succubus and Incubus had to be silenced. He thought that he had stumbled in this part of his plan because of the blight itself. Lucifer had not anticipated that the blight, a debility affecting angels who had undergone mind penetration, would occur.

He mused, "In the future, I will use all of my ingenuity to cover my tracks. It is still far too early to make known my plan to usurp control of angelic power. I shall be exceedingly cautious in the future." His concept of capturing power was still at the forefront of his private thoughts, and his feeling of self-importance continued to dominate his thinking. "I am the most important of all the angels; I am the most deserving - the only angel able to grasp and hold angelic power." He also realized that his time for achieving power had not yet arrived.

Lucifer sought the whereabouts of Succubus and Incubus. They were easily found and brought into his presence. He questioned them as to which angels had been mind penetrated by each. This took some time. Though angels have magnificent recall, the events in question were staggered and extended over a considerable time span. They had already related to Lucifer the botched attempts at mind penetration with the two archangels Michael and Raphael. Now they both completed their lists of other angels whose minds they had penetrated.

Lucifer asked each separately, "Are you ready to swear complete allegiance to me, and in so doing to renounce allegiance to any other angel, and to God Himself?" In so doing, Lucifer employed his considerable guile to reinforce the necessity for each of them to do this. They each complied. Lucifer then reemphasized, "You must obey me immediately, totally, and forevermore; that must be your sworn commitment; if you fail in this, I, Lucifer, have the power to place you into a state of permanent suffering."

Lucifer then gave Succubus and Incubus another assignment. "You are each to begin with your roster of previously penetrated angels; then, one at a time, arrange a second penetration."

They were surprised by this. Seeing their surprise, Lucifer explained, "This second mind penetration will be to insert into their minds something that I will give you. I will overshadow each of you and deposit in your minds a 'glimmer' of my own. When you have achieved penetration it will restore each angel to what they were before."

He then went on to explain the blight, and that it eventually led to a debility, permanent for all angels that were so penetrated. "You will be doing a service in restoring these blighted angels." Then Lucifer enjoined them never again to employ their powers to penetrate other angels.

They left Lucifer's presence after each had been penetrated. They were eager to begin this next assignment, to restore what had been removed, and to renew angelic function.

What Lucifer did not divulge to them was that the "glimmer", which he had used, would render all angels subsequently penetrated unable to remember being penetrated on either occasion, and would cause them to forget the angel who had initially approached and penetrated them. Thus, total erasure would result.

Lucifer also intentionally planted his glimmer so that on completion of their assignments, there would occur, for both Succubus and Incubus, complete erasure of their memories as well. Thus they would all be silenced. Furthermore, there would be no healing, or restoration of function, to any of the blighted angels. They, together with Succubus and Incubus, would slowly wither. They could not cease to exist, but life for each would, over billions of years, undergo contraction, a gradual reduction of awareness, and a diminution of their angelic powers.

Lucifer dwelt upon the excellence with which he had concocted this plan and its execution. It was perfect. Erasure would be complete. His tracks would be covered. No one could suspect him of being involved in the blight. He then withdrew to thoughts of his own magnificence.

15

Evil's Source

It all began with Lucifer. First there was pride, not the pride that might follow true accomplishment, but rather a false pride, a conceit of self, an awareness of self-superiority, an awareness of the need for recognition by others, then of adulation, then even of worship.

Deceit was accompanied by false pride. If deceit had not preceded pride, it had to begin simultaneously with pride, or to occur shortly thereafter. First there was self-deceit. To exalt himself above all others, even above Creator God, required, first and foremost, self-deceit. Once fostered, deceit could not be contained. It went from its source to others. As others were contaminated, it went still farther, spreading from one angel to another like the advance of a plague.

Anger followed - an awareness that one's superiority was not being recognized. Anger expanded. Later (during human life) anger ushered in violence, mayhem, and murder. Such consequences for human creatures were serious; that these same violent consequences could not occur for angels, who were pure spirits, did not mean angelic consequences were minor. They were to shake the entire angelic order, and eventually all of creation.

Envy was next. It may have begun with a feeling of being inferior to others or of wanting something held by others. Beauty, talent, accomplishment, possessions, attachments - all could invite envy. Envy, like the others, if unchecked (and angels could not readily undo that which they had chosen) would expand and become a corrosive force.

Lust would enter. It was seen with angels in the persons of Incubus and Succubus, and their attempts to occupy, penetrate, and control.

Greed came. Beelzebub was the first angel to be lured by Lucifer to thoughts of greater things, to ill-gotten riches, possessions, and enjoyments, even at the expense of others.

Laziness or sloth was slow to come. It came in the form of the blight, ushered in by Incubus and Succubus under the tutelage of Lucifer. It manifested as taking the easy way out, not so obvious for angels, but apparent in humans who were to follow.

Gluttony is difficult to envision as part of the angelic nature; after all, angels are unbodied, pure spirits. Still, Lucifer and his band of rebellious angels pursued a larger share for themselves than was fitting for them. (Gluttons are perceived as being sated or overstuffed. Humans, later to appear, would be very much aware of gluttony.)

Evil, thus, emanated from one person, Lucifer, an angelic spirit. It was to have overreaching effects upon the angelic order, the expanding universe, other created life, including, but not limited, to humans, and upon Creator God Himself.

The four archangels met a second time. This, again, was a simultaneous merging of minds and development of new thought. It was closed to other angels; open only to these four, Michael, Gabriel, Raphael and Uriel. Lucifer was notably absent. The four had a lingering suspicion that somehow Lucifer might be connected to the turmoil that had occurred as a consequence of the blighted angels. The suspicion was meager, the very slightest, with no evidence that could point to Lucifer. The four archangels, at this second meeting, made certain that neither Lucifer, nor anyone else, could eavesdrop.

These four archangels had a special bond. They had, for billions of years, worked in parallel. Michael was the acclaimed leader, if indeed a leader was necessary. It was Michael they regarded as first of all the angels, even higher than the light-bearer Lucifer. Michael was also considered the strongest of all the angels.

Then came Gabriel. He was special, gifted in many ways, some of which remained mysterious to the others. Gabriel was a special messenger from God. Before Lucifer, Gabriel was the sole communicator between God and the other angels - primarily the Archangels, but also the Seraphim and Cherubim.

Raphael was appointed the central overseer of the expanding universe, and its care was the primary function of the archangels. Raphael had the most demanding job of all the archangels. From a central point he managed thousands of divisions extending outward in every direction, and thousand more stations (sectors) within each division.

Uriel had a powerful gift of mental vision. He could mentally visualize all of the universe, farther and more clearly, even in the most minute details, than any other angel. Uriel could see around and even through obstructions.

He, with Michael, worked on the periphery of the universe. They managed separate groups of angels, pulling, pushing and combining, to maintain the balance of matter and energy throughout the universe. This was the nudge power, a special gift of all angels, needed to maintain order, and prevent warping and shattering of the universe as it underwent expansion.

This meeting concerned the blight. It was a continuation of the prior meeting, which they had all attended, and to which Lucifer, while absent, had found a way to listen and take in all that had transpired.

Lucifer, in a masterstroke, had silenced the two principles, Succubus and Incubus, and had extended docility into the angelic ranks by mental penetration. He had also initiated the plan to hide all evidence that might tie him to the plot by having Succubus and Incubus backtrack with all of the angels they had previously penetrated. After all had been treated, both Succubus and Incubus would develop the same inability to remember; they, and the others would be blighted, remaining docile, remembering nothing of the mind-penetrating encounter, and then slowly withering.

Michael pointed out that they needed to find all angels who had been blighted and then develop a system of surveillance to see if still more angels were undergoing the blight. They then needed to look to the treatment and rehabilitation of all blighted angels if it was possible. Uriel was put in charge of these efforts. They would meet frequently to review results and draft future plans.

Uriel then collected a band of angels, taking at least one from each division and from each station. This included thousands of angels that would work solely under him. He devised tests of proficiency to make certain the angels were up to doing their assigned tasks. He first tested these angel cadres to discover if any had been blighted. All were found proficient; none were blighted.

Next, Uriel trained his angels in methods of testing other angels for the blight. This was relatively easy, as the blight destroyed proficiency in all but the most rudimentary tasks. He then appointed supervisors of groupings of divisions and stations such that there was no overlap; and thus, was able to canvas all angels in the entire universe. Once fully staffed and trained, he dispatched them to their appointed areas and told them to get to work.

It was a herculean task. Several billion angels had to be accounted for and tested. Findings had to be evaluated, always in search of angels who had been blighted.

While this was starting, Succubus and Incubus were finishing their lists. They had a small number to deal with, perhaps a few hundred each. They finished their work, satisfied they had reached everyone. They then reported their accomplishments back to Lucifer. Then, together with the others on their lists, they began a slow decline, remembering nothing, and insensitive to their beginning debility.

16

Evil's Way

Lucifer did not remain quiet for long. His ranks of angels in revolt had been growing. Beelzebub and Xaphan had been at work with angels not manning the bastions of the expanding universe, and had recruited many. Xaphan, who had been sent to recruit and also to keep watch on Beelzebub, proved to be a veritable whirlwind. His skill at enticing other angels was formidable. Large numbers were drawn to the fold of Lucifer, not yet sworn to allegiance, but soon to do so. Later they would become a part of Lucifer's legions.

Xaphan, during this time of recruitment, had many occasions to work alongside Beelzebub. He formed the opinion that Beelzebub, an avid recruiter, was not working at cross-purposes against Lucifer, and informed Lucifer of this. Lucifer met privately with Beelzebub, following which his faith in Beelzebub's loyalty was reinstated and remained for the duration of the angelic revolt. Lucifer then joined with the other two to assess their progress. Perhaps one-fifth of the angels contacted had fallen under Lucifer's spell, and had agreed to join. Of the rest, perhaps one-third remained undecided, while the other two-thirds had initially said no. Repeat meetings with the uncommitted angels still provided the possibility for additional recruits; however it appeared that the ranks might already be forming. Lucifer felt they should direct their efforts elsewhere.

The obvious new area for exploration was with the angels manning the bulwarks of the universe. Those angels, numerous and busy with their tasks, were also scattered throughout the vast reaches demanded by a rapidly expanding universe. They would be new to Lucifer's approach, not expecting recruitment efforts.

A new meeting was called involving Lucifer, Beelzebub, and Xaphan, and was shut off from communication with other angels. Lucifer reviewed the exploits of Succubus and Incubus in full detail; this previously had not been known to the other two. He cited the blight, a strange affliction of angels who had been penetrated by Succubus and Incubus, leading to a debility in the affected angels.

Lucifer noted that he was caught off-guard by this unexpected occurrence. He related that he had covered their tracks; all, including Succubus and Incubus, had been silenced. He went over the details of what he had done - injecting a glimmer, a thought-controlling implant. This would destroy the memory of the prior penetration and remove any possibility that this could be traced back to himself.

Their goal was to recruit groups of angels involved with the universe, and how to proceed was next discussed. Lucifer felt that Xaphan and Beelzebub should work separately, and that he, as an archangel, should not make an appearance at an early stage. They realized that the appearance of an archangel would result in too much attention, and this they did not want. The two would enter the universe in two separate areas, remote from the center occupied by Raphael and also far removed from peripheral areas where Michael and Uriel roamed. They had to be very stealthy, attempting to work alongside other angels, while trying to recruit whomever they could.

And so, at the speed of thought they departed to predefined destinations. They had worked out ways and times to be in communication, and methods so that these communications would not be available to other angels. Each initially found himself in a new and strange environment. Neither had previously done work in managing the universe. Each reported to a station supervisor as a new angel learning how to participate in the workings of the station. This was not unusual – rather, it was the norm. Angels came and went between the thousands of stations involved in control of the expanding universe.

Each started at the bottom of the ladder, so to speak – the place to learn the basic skills required to work with a team of angels. Stations were portions of divisions, the radial segments proceeding from center to periphery in every direction. Divisions were made up of stations, adjoined, but without overlap. Beelzebub and Xaphan would bide their time. This would be a good place to work and recruit. The likelihood of detection here would be highly unlikely. They would use their time not only learning tasks, but also sizing up the other angels they came across, looking especially for signs of weakness that might allow an opening for exploitation.

Hundreds of earth years elapsed. Then Xaphan found a liaison – a disgruntled angel who felt his accomplishments were not being recognized. He worked near a seam that was adjoining the boundary between two divisions. This, reasoned Xaphan, would be an ideal place to disrupt the ongoing work of the station. Disruptions could be minor, at first, and because of the location in a small area of the universe, would be difficult to detect.

First he needed to recruit the disgruntled angel. He began by extolling the gifts possessed by all angels, the gifts of beauty, intelligence, instantaneous projection over long distances, and immortality. He did not refer to these as gifts, but rather as attributes inherent to the angelic nature, an entitlement, so to speak. Xathan found himself on familiar ground. He had used this approach in recruitment of other angels outside the stations and divisions of the universe. He regarded himself to be an astute judge of the mindset of the angels with which he was dealing. He discussed the different classes of angels and how some were higher than ordinary angels. He remarked that he had witnessed angels from higher levels sometimes taking advantage of lower angels, adding tasks or work that they themselves could and should be doing. During these discussions, which took place over many earth years and were often repeated, he noted an avidity, a sense that he was being agreed with, a drawing closer of minds, and a likely recruit.

Xathan's next move was to bring Beelzebub into the picture. This began as a series of brief meetings. Xathan introduced Beelzebub as his friend and as an angel with very similar attitudes to his own. This was two on one, soft and subtle at first, then progressing to more specific ideas. The potential of an angel revolt was broached, subtle at first, but then as a clear new direction. They both found their quarry receptive and asked whether he would be willing to come along. They received a reassuring yes, and then bade the quarry to await further instructions but under no circumstances to discuss what they had talked about with any other angel.

They reported their progress to Lucifer, using a closed communication method to keep other angels out of the loop. Lucifer was pleased. They needed more recruits from this and nearby stations. It was decided that Beelzebub would change stations, and join up with Xaphan. Station switches were common within the angelic order; such moves would not occasion a suspicion.

It was also decided that they would concentrate their recruitment efforts along the seam. They planned to begin, slowly at first, an effort to eventually disrupt the management of the universe. The seam, the area adjoining two divisions, seemed ideal. It tended to be away from the focus of division leaders – those angels who controlled an entire division. Furthermore, a station along a seam had possibilities. Stations were small enough to possibly allow the recruitment of the entire angel team who worked there. As they discussed the possibility of controlling a station alongside a seam within a division, they became more and more convinced that this offered real possibilities for advancement of their plan to subvert, and then control, the angelic order.

17

Impasse

His name was Impasse, and he was an angel who, through some glitch in creation, was defective. It was not obvious to other angels, or to himself. By all exterior manifestations he was an angel in possession of all the angelic attributes. He was beauteous, intelligent, in possession of instant thought communication, and could transport himself by thought anywhere within the universe in an instant. Like other angels, he was also everlasting. Impasse's defect was that he was unable to make up his mind. He was severely impaired, though he did not recognize this about himself. It was part of his personality from the instant of his creation. Perhaps one aspect of the failure to detect this defect, either by himself or by other angels, was that angels seldom had to decide anything. Theirs was a tantalizing frenzy of thought, ideas, and remarkable abilities; yet, still, they seldom were called upon to decide. They did possess a will, and it was free. Angels were thus free to exercise choice, but only rarely was it necessary. Thus, Impasse functioned alongside other angels, doing whatever was required, and his defect remained undetected by himself and by the other angels with whom he worked.

Time does not pass for angels. They exist with other angels doing the work that is required, such as the use of their nudging power to move and balance physical matter. Such work, for angels, does not produce fatigue. Tiredness never occurs with angels. They do not sleep. They keep going, on and on, fully awake and alert. Thus time, especially that quality of time that produces an elapse, is unrecognized, and has no effect upon angels. Earth years are seen by angels as mere moments.

The situation, which was to come into sharp focus at a later time, involved the plot concocted by Lucifer using mind penetration. Succubus and Incubus had been recruited by Lucifer to employ their special powers of mind penetration on susceptible and willing angels to coerce and control. This was initially employed on ordinary angels and found to be effective. It was only later found to be ineffective when tried on two archangels, Michael and Raphael, because they refused to participate. Then the blight developed, that debilitating condition occurring as a consequence of mind penetration, posing a threat to Lucifer and his plans for revolt. Lucifer implanted his "glimmer", which when carried to all prior affected angels, produced memory destruction of all related events.

Impasse was approached by Succubus. He was on her roster of angels to undergo mind penetration. Impasse listened. There was initial mind contact. Impasse showed interest. Succubus attempted penetration and thought this was successful, but it wasn't. Impasse could not decide. Through the initial approach Impasse learned of the plan and all of its particulars, and that it emanated from Lucifer. Impasse thought nothing more of this, as it was one of many brief associations he had with many angels, but he did find it strange when Succubus appeared a second time. He found her beautiful and alluring - even desirous. Why not undergo a willing mingling of minds? But therein lay his fault - he lacked the ability to decide. Once again Succubus was deceived by events. She thought successful penetration had occurred, but it had not. Impasse, though desirous of a penetration of his mind by Succubus, could not make up his mind. Once again, Impasse paid no further attention; he let it pass. He was not affected and consequentially was not blighted. No one else, including Lucifer, became aware of this strange development until much later.

18

The Seam

Xaphan and Beelzebub pursued the recruitment of other angels with renewed zeal. They were skilled and had become experienced in nuancing their approach so as not to arouse suspicion. Gradually they were successful in gathering other angels into their fold. They had long before learned the important lesson of reinforcement, combining companionship with shared ideas and repetition. As their ranks grew, they began subtly expounding the wider aims of what they wanted to do. They were achieving control near a seam within a division.

With full control they would be positioned to use their nudging powers to affect the balance of that portion of the universe within their purview. This would effect the gravitational influence of aggregates of matter upon one another. They might eventually achieve warping, which if carried to an extreme would unbalance the universe and lead to its destruction. This, they emphasized, would allow freedom for angels - the full range of angelic powers that they had exercised before the creation of the universe.

Angels did not need the universe, they contended. The universe had been created by God as a whim, a monstrosity. It required angels to work. Angelic talents were thus diverted. Angels were much too important to waste their talents on managing an explosion! And an explosion of what? Particles of dust moving and combining into strange structures, structures not themselves friendly to angels.

They were nearing the recruitment goal of a unanimous presence, where all angels along their station's seam had joined Lucifer's revolt. All angels in this rebellious band were encouraged to renew their efforts to recruit the remaining small remnant of angels not yet approached. When they had achieved full compliance, they would schedule the appearance of their leader, Lucifer, for further instructions.

Gradually the angels along the seam reached full compliance. Now all angels in the target area were on board. Lucifer was notified, and after further communication, he appeared. His was a grand entrance: lofty, imposing, beautiful, a powerful archangel in full control. Lucifer addressed the angels who had gathered. "Angels," he spoke, "We are very close to reversing this accursed presence, the universe, which came about after we were here, and has imposed work upon us, and interfered with our freedom."

Lucifer watched his audience as he spoke, fully aware of his power to persuade, to see if his words were having the effect that he intended. His audience lit up, and followed every word. They had been previously prepared by Beelzebub and Xaphan, so Lucifer's task was relatively easy. He noticed a few in the audience wince when he mentioned destruction of the universe. He identified these for personal attention after he finished.

When done, he gathered all of the angels around him and stated that it was now necessary that the entire group, one at a time, swear allegiance to Lucifer and to the revolt that was being planned. One at a time they came forward, swearing their allegiance to Lucifer. Even those who had initially wavered came forward with their pledges. The table was now set for action.

Detailed plans had been worked out in advance. Each angel was given a task. At assigned times, and in the company of other angels, they would utilize their nudging power with direction and acceleration so as to displace a portion of the physical universe. The amount of displacement initially would be subtle so as not to draw attention to what was being done. They would also begin with slight back and forth motions to produce a wobble-like effect. There could not be an initial warp, as the masses to be displaced were too great. It would take time, but once started would prove difficult to stop.

If a wobble along the seam could be maintained, it might establish a motion of its own, without the need for intermittent nudging by angel workers. Such a wobble might be coerced, with minimal use of angelic nudging, to extend lengthwise along the seam, and to widen. A gradual wobble-like motion within the seam might then become self-sustaining. This caught the minds of Lucifer, Beelzebub and Xaphan. They were mesmerized by the thought, for they recognized its potential for extension and eventual destruction of the universe.

They would begin their enterprise with a small test. It was necessary to find out if a wobbling motion along the seam could be self-perpetuating. If this could be established, their way would be clear to eventually destroy the universe. This would entail an expanding wobbling mass, lengthening and widening, drawing into itself additional matter, and causing a distortion, a warping effect, which might eventually tear the universe apart. They did not, at that time, communicate these insights to other angels; this they would keep to themselves until they had finished the initial test. To proceed further, they would need a larger number of the angelic order to come over to their side. It would take time, perhaps much more time, but they were not in a hurry.

Lucifer gloried in his power. He reveled in his own glory. He dwelt upon his own wondrous attributes. Was he not the most beautiful of all of the angels? He knew that he was more intelligent than all the other angels, and more intelligent where it really mattered – getting others to do his will. His plan was starting to take effect. Once extended beyond this testing phase, it would extend to the limits of the universe. His plan would be unstoppable. He would rival God in his, Lucifer's, creative power. Such were the thoughts, the pride, the deceit, and the intent of Lucifer, the beauteous light bearer. God would have to cede him equal power to rule. Such were Lucifer's musings in those fateful times.

The angels practiced, under the watchful gaze of Beelzebub and Xaphan, the tasks that they were to be called upon to perform. At a given signal they began and were underway. Gradually a wobble effect was achieved and then amplified to become self-sustaining. They exulted in their achievement.

19

Uriel

Uriel was the first to notice that something was not quite right. He was the angel with the most remarkable vision. Though angels do not have eyes, they do have vision. This is a mental projection that opens the area to be mentally scanned to produce visual understanding.

Uriel's vision was unique amongst all the angels. He could see farthest. Even at the farthest distances, his images were the clearest, and possessed the greatest detail. He could also see around corners and in a circular manner so as to stay within the spherical pattern of the expanding universe.

While visually scanning along one sector of the universe, he noted an irregularity, but could not make out its nature. He, like other angels working on the universe, was aware of many such irregularities caused by mass and energy conversions, and the corrections made by angels using their nudging power. His impression was that this irregularity was one of these and he gave it no further thought. Automatically it was imbedded in his memory, and like all other angels, except those that had been blighted, he had the ability of instantaneous recall.

Uriel maintained his visual search. He was an angel on a mission, and beyond that, an archangel, the most powerful of all the angelic castes. He was after the big disruptions, anything in the expanding universe that might suggest serious problems that needed fixing. His vision ranged to the peripheries and also throughout the central parts, the core, and all surrounding areas. But Uriel's vision also had a weakness. It was focused. For the clearest imaging, it required a narrowed field. Thus it took time, much time, to visualize the entire universe. On routine patrol, so to speak, it might take hundreds of earth years to visually encompass the entire universe. This was the tradeoff. And yet, he could instantaneously focus on any part of the universe with great accuracy should he be called upon to do so.

There were many disruptions as the universe underwent its expansion. Uriel was one of many angels who maintained surveillance. Those angels heading stations limited their vision to the station, while division managers would visually scan their divisions, but seldom beyond. Uriel's visual reach was the entire universe. He was responsible for the big picture. Minor irregularities were left to the divisions and the stations to fix, which was why he did not pursue the small irregularity that he saw at the seam.

Uriel's other duty was to search for blighted angels. He had drawn angels from divisions and stations, and given them specific instructions. The task was immense. Huge numbers of angels had to be interviewed in order to find those angels who had been blighted. Once underway Uriel left this work to those angels he had trained.

It required hundreds of earth years to survey all of the angels throughout the universe, but at last the job was done. Thousands of angels had been trained and then dispatched to accomplish this task. Uriel gathered with his top leaders, and they began to report back to him. Information once obtained was transmitted instantly, so that it did not take long to complete the report.

Relatively few blighted angels had been found; the number was in the few hundreds, compared to the billions of angels that had been surveyed. It immediately became apparent that transmission of the blight from one angel to another was unlikely because of the relatively small number of affected angels. To be more certain of this, he would advise, at a future meeting of archangels, that a repeat of the survey be made of all angels. Vast as it would be, a repeat survey might be the only way to establish this very important finding; namely that close proximity would not lead to a spread of the blight. Uriel surmised that if the blight could extend from one angel to another, the entire angelic order would be at risk of becoming blighted. This dreaded thought, the possibility that all angels could become blighted and debilitated, was terrible to consider.

Next Uriel and the survey angels went over the blighted angels that had been discovered. When they did this they came upon two familiar names, Succubus and Incubus, but no additional information. Uriel decided to interview both angels himself. He took along the two station leaders from the area in which each of the two angels had been found. The interviews were very detailed, but no additional information was forthcoming. Uriel thought it strange yet interesting that their memories for the specific occurrence was a blank, and yet there were intact memories of the distant past. It seemed as if a specific time interval had been removed from their memories; this suggested that an outside cause, specific to the time and place of contacting the blight, was somehow involved.

Uriel pondered the information at hand. Although it seemed a remote possibility, he decided to go back and conduct a detailed interview of all the blighted angels that had been identified. Previously the more detailed interviews had involved only Succubus and Incubus. Perhaps if the others were interviewed in depth, especially with a focus on memory impairment, something else might turn up.

Uriel set about the task with the appropriate station leaders, one angel at a time. Since this was time consuming and would take him away from his primary duty of scanning the universe, he notified his two cohort archangels, Michael and Raphael, what he was planning.

The survey of blighted angels was repeated, but this time in more depth and with a focus on memory. One at a time, these angels were interviewed by Uriel and by the specific station leader. Their memory for what had happened was blank, but prior memories were intact. By trying to find the boundary between lost and remaining memory they were able to show that the debility had begun quite recently. This was new information, though it did not point to a cause.

Uriel called another meeting of his archangel confreres. In addition to Uriel they included Michael, Raphael, and Gabriel. Once again Lucifer was excluded. This had happened at a prior meeting because of a vague notion, a suspicion, an unfounded feeling that Lucifer was not to be fully trusted. Further, the meeting was to deal with the universe and its management. Lucifer took no part in this work.

Uriel began with a detailed review of his visual scanning of the universe. He noted the frequent irregularities, caused as particulate matter moved outward, diverging from a prior pathway until moved into alignment by the nudging power of angels nearby. He also mentioned the odd disruption that he had come across. He noted that it was remote and very small, and that he dismissed it, at the time, as not important.

But, now he recalled that it was odd and seemed to have a different contour. It lacked the characteristics of an explosion - matter scattering in all directions and familiar to angels who would nudge matter back into place when necessary. He also noted that it occurred along a seam between two divisions. He remembered that it had a strange motion that he had not seen before. It seemed to move back and forth in an undulating fashion; yet this was so slight as not to arouse his concerns.

Next Uriel reviewed activities following the blight. He told of the initial interviews of all angels in the entire universe – it had been a huge effort to locate those angels who were blighted. Fortunately there were very few. He then related a follow-up detailed interview that he had conducted of all the blighted angels, assisted by the station leader appropriate for each angel. They had focused on memory, and especially on memory that was recently lost. They had confirmed this recent memory loss and also that all such angels had prior memory, though recall seemed somewhat slow, perhaps an extension of the debility affecting the blighted angels.

The archangels exchanged thoughts on these matters, and then their leader Michael formulated a series of steps and asked for their agreement. Their minds were so powerful and similar, that agreement was instantaneous.

First and foremost would be a second interview of all the angels in the universe, with the exception of Archangels, Seraphim and Cherubim. Once again the task would be huge. Michael intoned, "Ask each angel for recall of anything in recent time that might in any way be connected to the blight." Uriel would continue to be in charge of this. The archangels were unanimous in the potential seriousness of the blight. The possibility that it could extend throughout all the angelic ranks and eventually extend to every angel was a somber realization.

Secondly, Uriel was asked if he could locate the strange disturbance along one of the seams. Uriel was certain that he could, and that it shouldn't take too much time. Once located, Raphael would be in charge of close surveillance to find out what it was and to report back for further review. Raphael was cautioned to maintain strict confidentiality, and especially to not expose this search to angels in the area.

20

The Strange Mass

Uriel began a visual search of where he had gone before. He had a general idea of where to start. First, he would do a rapid scan of the area to see if he could pick up the strange mass along one of the seams between two divisions. This was done, but without success. Next he would use his longest vision, enabling him to see great distances, but with a narrowed boundary. He began covering areas in a grid-like manner, scanning in one direction, then reversing at the next level and coming back. It was time-consuming work, but not laborious or tiring. Fatigue is not a part of the angelic nature.

Then he saw it. It was a smooth widening between two divisions, forming a mass. It extended longitudinally along the seam, and may have increased slightly in width and length compared to when he had first viewed it. It possessed a slow back-and-forth, almost undulating motion, perhaps with a rotational component. It was very strange. He was puzzled by it, and he communicated his findings directly, and instantly, to Raphael.

Raphael immediately began formulating a plan for surveillance of the mass. He had total control of the management of the universe from his central position. He knew the divisions. Although there were thousands, he had designed them and knew them well. He had selected the division leaders and knew them from his many meetings with them. He also knew the stations, as he had included them in his grand design; however, he was not aware of individual station leaders, as he had not selected them; this was the job of the division leaders.

He identified the mass located at the seam between two divisions. He would proceed with great caution. The initial approach would be to investigate divisions that abutted the two that shared the seam. He had a faint suspicion that somehow one or both of these divisions might be complicit. How else to explain that neither had reported a strange mass so close to their border?

He contacted the two division leaders beyond the two divisions that were to be under surveillance. They were brought into Raphael's presence; with both present, and in strict secrecy (that is, the inability of any other angel to eavesdrop), he first asked how things were going in each of their divisions. The responses indicated stable functioning with the usual need for nudging by attendant angels, but no ongoing problems. Then Raphael spoke of allegiance. "All angels owe allegiance to their Creator God. Do you both concur?" They both assured Raphael that they agreed. All were aware of the hierarchy of angels, and now he, Raphael, wanted both to swear an oath of secrecy for what he was about to discuss with them. Both undertook this solemn oath.

Raphael described the strange mass that had been discovered between the seam of the two divisions. He described the properties of the mass as made known by Uriel.

He then asked, "Have either of you learned of this, or of any other strange disturbance within your divisions or surrounding areas?" Both reported in the negative. Raphael went on to locate the strange mass for them. The surveillance was to be focused on four longitudinal divisions, two outside and two inside. The strange mass was at the inner seam abutting the two inner divisions.

"We must work together, and in strict secrecy," intoned Raphael. "Do you have any ideas as to how we might proceed?" A lively thought process between the three then occurred.

"We must find a way to enter, from each side, the affected divisions," cited one.

"Yes, and to do this without being detected," the other pointed out. Raphael asked each to select a small number of angels from their two divisions, make certain of their loyalty and absolute secrecy, and find ways to insert these angels into stations near the mass. Raphael would be in frequent communication to review results.

Angels from both divisions were found and instructed. Since it was commonplace while managing the expanding universe for angels to move in and out of stations, such movements did not arouse suspicion. Insertions were staggered, so as not to attract attention. The two division leaders stayed in close communication, and they also sent angels outside of their divisions for closer inspection of the mass.

The spacing took time. Angels then returned in a staggered manner. The division leaders felt immediate concern when they heard their reports. They decided to contact Raphael to review their findings.

The angels reported that once inside a station, they encountered a strange presence. They were regarded as outsiders by a very close-knit group of angels. They initially gave their reason for entering as a need to learn tasks to support the work of the station. They were then instructed in the rudimentary tasks and watched closely. With time and satisfactory performance, they were accepted.

Eventually they were approached by two station angels, who asked them to join them; the station was doing new and exhilarating things. They answered that they needed time to think this through. No further overtures were forthcoming, and in time the angels left. The same experience occurred with angels who had been injected into different stations. These two strange yet similar experiences occurred in stations within two different divisions, both selected because of their proximity to the mass.

Angels sent outside of these two divisions encompassing the seam were instructed to get as close to the mass as possible, but to avoid detection. They were to gather as much information about the mass as they could, and then report back to their respective divisions.

The next meeting between Raphael and the two division leaders took place shortly after this information was gathered. Raphael was informed of the strange atmosphere within the two stations - an atmosphere that was almost alien. It was part of the angelic nature to be interdependent and to work together effortlessly. Such was not the case here. Then Raphael was told of offers to join, and of a new type of work that they were doing. Raphael interpreted this as a recruitment effort, "But why? And for what purpose?"

Next they reviewed information gathered by those angels who had approached the mass from the outside. They described it as having a length of about two stations. The mass was round, quite solid appearing, with a slight taper at each end. They then related what they had seen of the motion within the mass. There was back-and-forth lengthwise motion, a lateral in-and-out motion, and a rotational motion starting at one end and continuing to the other.

Raphael knew these were important findings. He needed to find out what was going on within the mass, how it had come about, why it was there, and why other angels seemed to be complicit.

21

The Seismic Mass

Raphael needed a more specific name for this phenomenon to keep it separate from the other numerous masses forming within the universe, and decided to call it the "Seismic mass". Raphael concluded his meeting with the two division leaders by saying, "Maintain constant surveillance both inside and outside of the Seismic mass. We need to know more about its purpose and origin. Keep your activities secret. Consider using longer-term insiders, inserted into the stations to learn more. Select only your most trustworthy, for they will be subjected to pressures to join and comply. You may suggest to them that they may use an initial implied interest in joining so as to gain information, but also the importance of not agreeing to join if asked."

Raphael met again with his archangel confreres, Michael, Gabriel and Uriel. He related the new information in its entirety. All were stunned (if such a word is appropriately applied to pure spirits). They all felt the Seismic mass to be a foreboding presence. All efforts were needed to learn its purpose, how it came about, and what was going on. They were most distressed to realize that angels were a part of this thing, and also to what extent they might be involved. They all voiced the same refrain: "This needs to be kept in constant focus."

Raphael related his parting instructions to the two division leaders, including the need for continuing close surveillance, and for insertions within the two stations of loyal angels who could stay for longer periods of time. The pressure of recruitment was discussed, but questions remained - recruitment by who, and why? They took note that the seismic mass, while located between two divisions, had a length of approximately two stations. If this was true, then four stations might be involved, two on each side of the seam that the seismic mass encompassed. These additional stations should undergo insertions of loyal angels. Then Michael asked the question, "Might not the seismic mass extend by recruitment of adjacent stations? We must learn of this. We need to understand, as best we can, what this recruitment process is all about."

While the four other archangels were focusing on the angelic blight and the seismic mass, Lucifer was not idle. He and his two chief lieutenants, Beelzebub and Xaphan, had been making headway recruiting other angels to their cause. Once begun it gathered steam with a motion of its own. Millions of angels were now moving to their side. They first elicited an interest by claiming the advantages of independence, of going their own way, of no longer being beholden to God, giving the impression that God was not as powerful as initially thought. They were masters of persuasion. Angels who showed an interest were pursued by two or more angels to obtain a commitment. The final step was the oath of allegiance to Lucifer. This was done in large groups with an air of formality and grandeur. This was truly the last step, for when angels made up their minds, there could hardly ever be an undoing; there would be no turning back.

As numbers increased, Lucifer and his assistants felt a surge of power. They could feel the exhilaration and could sense that they were nearing the time of open revolt. They were certain that when the time was ripe, they would not and could not fail. A lingering question, never discussed, but considered by many of Lucifer's top officers, was: "What should we do about God?" God, to them, had become an anomaly. Where was He? He never made an appearance. Maybe He was weak, maybe He was disabled, maybe He was blighted like some of the angels. Lucifer wondered if he should share ruling with God, or rule without God, and leave God alone, without His angels, and without His created universe, for a major aim of the now rebellious angel band was utter destruction of the universe. Angels would roam free without the hindrance of explosive upheaval, a hallmark of the universe.

Lucifer, the light bearer, had poured out the light, which when it came in contact with quantum fluctuations within the void had produced an instantaneous explosion propelling matter and energy in every direction nearly fourteen billion years earlier (from this writing). Particles of variable size, from subatomic to visible gas, dust and rubble, had sped and accelerated in every direction. This had been the beginning of the expanding universe. Gradually the particles became aggregates of increasing size and complexity.

Over billions of years, stars were formed and then gathered to form galaxies, each composed of billions of stars.

Angels had been given the powers and tasks to manage the universe. Angels are uniquely equipped for this mission. They are pure spirits, and thus not subject to displacement by solid matter. They possess a nudging power whereby they can move matter in any direction, not impeded in any way by the size or mass of what is to be moved. Angels are extremely intelligent. They have instantaneous communication with other angels by thought. They can simultaneously occupy the same space since they are spiritual persons; and above all, they are tireless. They know no fatigue. They can work effortlessly, without ceasing, for millions of earth years. They proved to be very capable of directing the explosion that began the universe.

Why then, did Lucifer, the light bearer, the one who lit the torch – so to speak – the spark that started the universe, want now to destroy it? There is no immediate or easy answer. Perhaps he knew that he was not the cause. God had bestowed on him the function of light bearer. God had ordered the quantum fluctuations within the void; in their absence there could be no universe. As quantum fluctuation increased, and at just the right amplitude, God gave the order to pour. Light had suffused at just the right moment, causing the entire matter, energy and fullness of the universe to be born from infinitesimal smallness and nothingness.

Lucifer, most beauteous of all angels, began savoring his own beauty. He also had the supreme intelligence of the archangels of which he was one. He wanted the adulation of other angels, and when this was not forthcoming, he began to feel anger and jealousy. Then he began extending those feelings to God. Gradually his thinking focused more and more on himself, wondering why God had not given him accolades and whether he might convince God to accede to his whims. However, at this early stage of creation, God was not accessible to any of the angels except the Seraphim and Cherubim who constantly were in God's presence.

Lucifer's thinking slowly morphed; maybe God was weak? Maybe he, Lucifer, was God's equal. Slowly Lucifer rejected the fact that God's decrees had brought about creation, substituting his own notion that it was he, Lucifer, who was the creator. Therein might have been the source of deadly pride and its companion deceit, which were to lead to other evils, changing the course of creation.

Raphael's division chiefs proceeded in earnest. They combed their two divisions for angels of unquestioned loyalty and then swore them to secrecy. They told them of the seismic mass between their two divisions. This came as a complete surprise to the recruits, who were informed of the need to learn more. They needed to find out where this strange mass had come from, who was involved in its formation, and what its function was, if indeed it had a function.

These angels were to begin work in adjoining stations up and down the divisions, both close in, near the upper and lower reaches of the mass, and also further out in both directions. They were to remain embedded, gathering as much information as possible and periodically returning to their divisions for debriefing.

And so they were dispatched. They began as angels wanting to learn about the workings of the station. It was not unusual for angels to roam in and out of stations in this manner. Over time contacts with other angels began to suggest a pattern. Recruitment efforts became obvious, subtle at first and then more overt. It was also found that the seismic mass had expanded. Its length had increased by two full station lengths, one at each end. Four new stations were involved at each new end of the expanding mass.

Recruitment efforts were intense within those stations on each side of the seismic mass compared to those stations farther out.

Recruitment, but for what? Implanted angels were trained to show interest in being recruited so as to obtain information. They found that angels were being recruited in large numbers to form an angel band. Angels were told that the new band would give them more freedom. Angels would no longer be required to manage the universe. They would recover the freedom they had had before the universe was created. Then a key piece of information was divulged at one of the stations: the angel band that was being formed would be used to undo, and eventually destroy the universe. When asked how might this come about, the reply was that none of the angels knew.

22

Impasse Found

While Raphael was making progress with the stealthy search of the seismic mass, Uriel was paying close attention to two distinct areas of his responsibility. The first was visual surveillance of the seismic mass. He confirmed that the mass was growing, extending out along its length in both directions.

The other area was the repeat survey of all angels within the universe. This survey was established to stay well away from those areas in proximity to the seismic mass, so as to avoid divulging plans of the survey to those angels within. The survey was laborious, since billions of angels had to be contacted and catalogued. Thousands of angels were utilized to conduct the survey; yet, even so, it would take hundreds of earth years to complete. The primary focus was to obtain detailed information on each angel's memory pattern; a secondary focus was to see if the blight affecting the angels had spread further to involve more angels.

Impaired memory of blighted angels involved recent though not remote memory. As the survey neared the halfway point, the results were encouraging. No new blighted angels had been found.

Then it happened. During one interview an angel was found who told an intriguing story. As it unfolded, he was brought into a division and interviewed by the division chief and Uriel. The angel had an intact memory; there was no loss of recent events. He related the strange occurrence of being approached by a beautiful and charming angel who asked for close mind contact and eventually mind penetration. He found the offer appealing, but when asked if he would consent, he was unable to decide. "What was that angel's name?" he was asked.

He answered: "Succubus."

"And what is your name?" he was asked.

"Impasse," he answered.

Uriel arranged a hasty meeting of the four archangels, and brought Impasse along. The meeting was secret and attended by Michael, Gabriel, Raphael and Uriel. As with the prior meetings, Lucifer was purposely excluded.

With Impasse not in attendance, the recent findings obtained from the stealthy insertion of angels within suspicious stations were reviewed. Recruitment was expanding at a rapid pace. The seismic mass was growing along its length. Angels in stations along each side of the mass were heavily recruited. It was reported that an angel in one of the stations mentioned that the recruited angels were told the eventual reason for the new direction was to undo and eventually destroy the universe. When Michael asked why they would want to do this, the answer given to the imbedded angel was that they would be free to return to the angelic life that existed before the start of the universe.

Then Impasse was brought in. He was asked to recall the events he described at the time of his prior interview. He told of being approached by an alluring angel who drew close and wanted to engage in mind penetration, which he was told would have an exhilarating effect. This other angel occupied the same space, not unusual, as angels are spiritual beings, and he remembered being favorably inclined. The other angel asked him if he would agree. He answered he could not be sure. Then the other angel left.

'Do you recall the other angel's name?" asked Michael.

"Yes", answered Impasse, "the angel's name was Succubus."

"Did Succubus mention any other names?" asked Michael, "did anyone send her?"

"Yes", Impasse answered, "she said she was sent by Lucifer."

The archangels, one and all, powerful each in his own right, were stunned. There had been faint suspicions in the past. That was the reason for excluding Lucifer from prior meetings. But this was blatant. It was overwhelming and damning evidence. Impasse was placed under Raphael's guidance. He was given a station close to the center, Raphael's domain, and then placed under the watchful supervision of one of Raphael's trusted subordinates.

Michael asked for the thoughts of others. There was so much that was hidden, that needed to be unraveled. How had things gone wrong? They needed to review these events carefully.

Gabriel spoke. He had been silent at prior meetings. "We angels were created by God and have our existence entirely from Him. We owe God all that we are. It is in our nature to be open and forthright. What we have before us is treachery; an attempt to go against God's will. Lucifer appears to be at the head of this. For his sake we need to meet with him, convince him of his error, and welcome him back to our ranks if he would be willing."

Raphael spoke next. "This is a grievous departure. Lucifer was our most beautiful, and amongst our most intelligent. He was chosen by God to be the light bearer for all. He was gifted beyond any of the rest of us. Yet he has turned against God. This is treachery, as you have expressed, Gabriel. Still, it is puzzling why Lucifer should have done this."

Uriel then spoke. "Lucifer clearly is the one. We have heard the compelling evidence from Impasse, but we have all had our suspicions before about Lucifer. There is the seismic mass out there that has grown. We need to find out what this thing is, and why it is out there."

Then Michael spoke and formulated the next steps. "We need to bring Lucifer in and review all of this with him. He, being one of us, cannot be constrained. We will send Gabriel to fetch him. Gabriel has a special power from God; he can compel anyone in the angelic realm to follow him. This even applies to Lucifer. But before we call Lucifer in, we should check again the stations abutting the seismic mass to see if there is any more information from those angels we have planted inside. You, Uriel see to this, and report back to us before we bring Lucifer in."

23

An Infernal Machine

Uriel met again with the division leaders of those divisions forming the borders around the seismic mass. He quizzed them as to whether any of the implanted angels had obtained further information.

These division chiefs called in the station chiefs abutting the seismic mass, and even those from more distant stations along the line of growth. They reported continuing growth along the longitudinal axis. Avid recruitment was going on within stations abutting the mass, while recruiting diminished farther away. All of this had been known before.

Then one station chief mentioned a puzzling bit of information reported to him quite recently. This was from an angel who had been implanted quite far out along the seam. This angel gradually moved from station to station in the direction of the seismic mass. As he did so, he came under recruitment pressure, subtle at first, but then more overt. He showed interest and recruitment efforts were stepped up. He asked questions, seemingly to seek information, which was provided. As this was going on, he made progress moving closer to the mass. He soon found himself within a station that abutted the seismic mass. He was amazed at what he found. The vast interior was far different than he had experienced at other stations.

A typical station is large, commonly one hundred thousand earth miles in length, and half that in width. The new station that he had entered was twice as large. When he first entered, he was accepted as a positive recruit. It was thought that he had sworn allegiance to the new angelic order, but this was not so. He had shown interest, even zeal for the new order, but secretly, known only to himself, he had not changed.

As an accepted new recruit he was free to ask questions, normal for new recruits, as part of the orientation to a new station. His first question was a comment about the increased size. He was told that two adjoining stations had been combined into one. Progressing toward the center of the station he became aware of motion that was not familiar. He asked about this, and was informed it came from the mass outside the station. "But I am not aware of a mass," he mentioned.

"Oh, but that is what we are working on," he was told. "Come along, I will show you."

Angels have the capacity to move at the speed of thought.

They proceeded to the exact midpoint of the station, and then made a left turn. They were now within the center of the mass. Strange undulations were going on from all sides. There was also a twisting and squeezing motion that started at one end and proceeded to the other end, as an ongoing continuous process.

"But what am I seeing, what is this for?" he asked.

"Didn't they tell you before this? We are producing antimatter. When our rate of production increases, we will begin moving this out to the universe."

"But why?" asked the new angel.

"You really have not been properly indoctrinated, I can see that. We will use antimatter to destroy the universe. It will take time, but we will be ready to start soon." The angel was stunned by what he heard, but did not show signs in his thought pattern that he was alarmed.

Over time this angel was able to slip back to his division and quickly relate what he had learned to the station chief; then he quickly reinserted himself back within the station containing the seismic mass. The station chief was stunned. We face an "Infernal machine", he mused to himself.

24

Encounter

The station and division chiefs met with Uriel. All of the new information was reported exactly as it had been procured. Uriel then transmitted this information to the other archangels. Michael informed Gabriel that it was time to bring Lucifer in.

The meeting was initially friendly. Lucifer was wary, but felt that he had no choice but to accompany Gabriel. He asked Gabriel why he was being asked to follow, and where they were going. Gabriel in a friendly manner responded that this would be a long overdue meeting with the other archangels. Such a review had not been undertaken for a very long time.

When they were in the presence of the other archangels, Michael spoke. "We have not seen much of you for a long while and thought we should meet to review how things are proceeding. We became aware of a blight among the angels some time ago. We surveyed a large multitude of angels, and found some that had a condition affecting their memory. When questioned, they knew nothing about anything that might have made them this way. They were unaware that they were blighted and slowly becoming debilitated. Simple tasks they could do, but more complex ones they would stumble over. Do you know anything about this?"

Lucifer spoke. "I learned something of this from other angels."

"Have you had contact with any of the blighted angels?" Michael asked.

"Not that I am aware," Lucifer responded.

Michael went on. "We conducted a second survey to try and find out if new blighted angels were turning up. Our concern was that the blight might be spreading from the first group to other angels. We were very careful about this; we had to be certain because of the risk of spread to the entire angelic realm. Fortunately, we found no new angels that had become afflicted."

"That is good news," said Lucifer.

Next Uriel spoke. "As we all know I have been gifted with vision keener than any other angel. Because of this, I have been asked to periodically visualize the entire universe, to make sure that the expanding universe is being properly managed. On one such search I noticed a small but rather strange occurrence, a mass-like object, long and narrow, along a seam between two divisions. At first I gave no further thought to this, and passed it by. Do you know anything about this?"

"No, nothing," Lucifer responded.

Lucifer was feeling edgy. He seemed to be the focus of the meeting. All questions were being directed at him. He needed to be careful with further comments. He wasn't sure why he had been brought in to this meeting, which had been initially described as a friendly review, an update. Now, he wasn't so sure.

Raphael continued. "We located Incubus as one of the blighted angels. I remember that he had approached me at a prior time. He was friendly, drew nearer, and asked that we make mind contact. Then he related the exhilaration that results from mind penetration. I was concerned, and declined. I did not see him again until he came up on the list of blighted angels. I then personally interviewed him, but found his memory was lost. He didn't remember me, and did not know that he had been blighted. He was showing signs of debility, and was not even aware of this. Have you had contact with this angel? Might you offer further insights?"

Lucifer responded, "No, I have no recall of this angel. I have no other comments about this."

Michael then spoke. "We also found another angel on the blighted list. She had previously approached me. She came close, common among angels, and at first I took no notice. She came closer and I became aware of her beauty and charm. She mentioned a mind process associated with mind mingling or penetration, and invited me to participate. I refused, and she left. I had not seen her again until I interviewed her as one of the blighted angels. Just like Incubus, Succubus has a loss of memory. She could not remember me, and had no knowledge of how she had become blighted. Can you add any additional information?"

Lucifer was becoming nervous and angry now. "No", he lashed out, "why should I? Why am I being questioned in this manner?"

Then the first portion of the trap was sprung. Michael spoke. "We located another angel while we conducted this survey. His name is Impasse. He was created with a defect. He is totally unable to decide anything; he cannot make up his mind. He was not aware of this because angels hardly ever need to decide anything. He was not a blighted angel, but was scheduled to become one. He was approached by Succubus, and became infatuated with her charms. She suggested mind penetration and thought this was accepted. However he did not accept, because he was unable to decide. During their discourse, Impasse remembered her name as Succubus. He had asked her if anyone had sent her. She responded that you, Lucifer, had sent her. Do you have anything to add to this account, Lucifer?"

Lucifer was infuriated. "You have lied to me by withholding information from me before asking your foolish questions," he stormed. "Why are you treating me this way? Is this the way archangels treat each other? I am innocent of your false accusations."

Michael went on, "it is you who have lied, Lucifer. You have lied to us three times. You sent Succubus to me to try to weaken me with the blight and then you attempted to weaken Raphael when you sent Incubus. We caught on when we located Impasse. I suspect, but cannot prove, that you, Lucifer, are the source of the blight. "

"Lies, all lies," raged Lucifer.

"No, Lucifer," said Michael, "you are the one who has lied. The third lie from you we will hear about now."

Uriel then spoke. "We went further in an effort to learn more about the mass in the seam between divisions. We kept it under close surveillance and found that it possessed motion of its own – a strange motion. It also was seen to grow larger at both ends. We positioned angels in stations on both sides of the seam, abutting the mass but also extending into other stations along the seam, further out at both ends.

"We found a pattern of recruitment into a new order, an order purported to be rebellious, away from what God had created. It was intended to free angels from being obliged to manage the universe, and to revert back to the freedom present before the universe was created. One of our angels advanced into the mass, and found it to be a vast engine for creating antimatter. It is expanding to increase the rate of antimatter production. When this higher rate is achieved, antimatter will be spewed into the universe to gradually reduce the physical universe, and eventually destroy it."

"Lies, all lies," was Lucifer's reply. He was clearly angry, petulant, and distraught. "You have brought this up to diminish my standing. I am the most beautiful angel. I am the light bearer. You have said these things because you are jealous. Ever since I poured the light you have been jealous of me. You never accorded me my rightful due. Now, I will find a way to get even."

Then Gabriel spoke. "Lucifer, you have been telling lies, and dealing in treachery. There is still time to undo all of this. Come back to us. We will welcome you. Return, and all of this can be erased. We want you back. We would relish your return. But first you will have to admit your mistake."

"Never," spoke Lucifer. "I will never return to your ways. I have many angels who have sworn allegiance to me. With these angels I will challenge God. God is weak, and I will rule. Instead of me joining you, Gabriel, I challenge you, together with Michael, Raphael, and Uriel, to join me."

The other archangels were stunned by Lucifer's comments and signaled their unwillingness to be part of Lucifer's rebellion. The meeting then came to an end. "Release me, Gabriel," were Lucifer's parting words. Thus was established an angelic rift that was to continue. Indeed, it would be continuous for eternity, and forever change the course of creation.

25

Antimatter

Michael brought the other archangels together to review what they knew aboutthe infernal machine, its purpose, and its working. They noted that it had grown, and now had a length of about two hundred thousand earth miles. It was also beginning to expand in width, and was starting to assume a spherical shape. In a few hundred more earth years it would quadruple its length, become truly spherical, and take on the dimensions of a medium-sized star.

Its increase in size was a function of a vast increase in its inner workings. Lucifer's angels had apparently found a way to produce antimatter by taking matter and breaking it down, by nudging power, into very small particles. This process probably accounted for most of the motion that had been previously observed. Once small particles were obtained, they could be accelerated. This would change the particle charge to produce antiparticles. Antiparticles when directed to collide with particles would then result in annihilation of both.

Raphael spoke. "We understand antimatter. It is a rare theoretical occurrence in the universe, requiring very small particles that undergo rapid acceleration seldom seen naturally in the universe. If an antimatter particle is formed, it lasts only a very brief time, not long enough to annihilate anything. Lucifer must have discovered things about antimatter that we do not know. To be useful to him, it would have to be stabilized and stored. There is much that we have yet to find out."

Michael wondered: "Should we attempt to reach and inform God? Maybe we should approach the Seraphim or the Cherubim - we havc done this before."

Then Gabriel, in a mysterious but reassuring way, said, "This will not be necessary. God knows."

The archangels were puzzled over what to do next. They had to find a way to influence the progress within the seismic mass, and to render useless the workings of the infernal machine. A line had to be drawn. True combat loomed. Though angels can not be killed -since they are eternal spirits – they are still capable of conflict in one form or another. The archangels and loyal angels would be facing Lucifer and his rebel band. It was clear what they needed to do and without delay: identify all angels who were loyal, inform them of the angelic revolt, reinforce their loyalty to God, and attempt to pry rebellious angels away from Lucifer's hold.

They began the urgent work of contacting angels to elicit loyalty. The race was on because Lucifer had also gathered his two lieutenants, Beelzebub and Xaphan, to inform them of what had taken place at Lucifer's meeting with the archangels. Lucifer embellished his position. He pointed out how weak and disorganized the archangels had been, and how he had carried the day. He pointed out that the revolt was now to be ongoing and visible – it would no longer be hidden. "Go forth, recruit now out in the open. This will be our chance to enlarge our ranks. Soon we will dominate; and then we shall rule."

The archangels formulated their message carefully. "Lucifer has become a traitor. He is recruiting angels to lead a revolt against God. We angels, created from nothing by God, now need to stand with God against Lucifer and his rebels. There is no middle ground (they had forgotten about Impasse). Stand with us."

Thousands of loyal angels fanned out and went into the universe. Some were between divisions, others within divisions and stations. They met with other angels. Most whom they met were unaware of what had been going on and readily affirmed their loyalty to God. They were told that Lucifer's angels might come and ask that they change their allegiance. They were advised not to be deceived.

Within divisions it was more difficult. For those divisions remote from the seismic mass, angels, by and large, stayed loyal to God. But as they neared the seismic mass, they met resistance. Many angels had already turned, and ridiculed being asked to resume their loyalty to God. None who had turned could be brought back to God. Such is the angelic mind. Once made up, change is virtually impossible.

Efforts were ongoing for hundreds of earth years. The number of angels who needed to be contacted was never known with certainty, but surely that number was in the billions. Gradually, most, if not all, of the angels had been reached. Lucifer's rebel band accounted for perhaps a third of the total. They were mostly grouped within divisions, and had enlisted the support of some division leaders, and of many station chiefs.

26

Impasse's Dilemma

Impasse was the angel with a glaring defect. He could not decide anything or make up his mind. He was created with the defect, but was unaware of it because before now he had never been called upon to decide anything. The single exception was the encounter with Succubus. Even though he had been drawn to the idea of mind penetration, he could not decide, and thus did not become a blighted angel and suffer the debility with memory loss that was the lot of blighted angels.

Impasse was terribly distressed. He had taken his creation for granted and always assumed his loyalty was to God. Now however, when asked, he could not say yes, just as he could not say no. This also happened when he was approached by one of Lucifer's angels. He was frantic. What would happen to him if he was caught between these two powerful forces? Both God's angels and Lucifer's angels passed him by. He was forgotten. He was forlorn, desperate for some way to decide. Then a thought came to his mind.

While working with matter outside of the divisions he had used his nudging power to move matter from place to place. Impasse remembered one time when he had matter to be moved rapidly. Heat had been generated. He knew what heat was, even though it did not affect him. Angels are unaffected by heat; they can tolerate any amount (even millions of earth degrees) without difficulty.

During that transfer, with much heat being generated, he had noticed a puddle being formed. It was yellow, easily formed into any shape, and, as heat dissipated, became solid. It could then be bent, rolled, and shaped into virtually any form. At the time he had dismissed this as one of many nuisances angels encountered when they were nudging matter.

But now he thought to himself, "I will go out, find a large size of matter, move it rapidly to obtain heat, and then wait for the yellow puddle to form." He tried this but without success. But Impasse was not daunted. He persisted. It took him many earth years to move masses of matter before finding one that yielded a small yellow puddle. He let it cool, and then nudged it carefully into an irregular mound of matter.

He used small nudging motions to shape this new matter just the way he wanted it. He laid it onto a flat, level and polished surface. Then he took the now solid yellow mass, and slowly began to form it into the shape that he had foreseen. When finished it took the form of a disc, of uniform thickness, perfectly balanced. On one surface he inscribed the symbol for God, and on the opposite surface the symbol for Lucifer. He examined his finished work. He was satisfied. He would nudge this into the area above the table, so that it would spin and then fall back onto the table. Whichever side was upright would decide for him.

First he would make many practice flips. He was in no hurry. He wanted to make sure that the chance of one side being upright was virtually the same as the other side - in other words, that the disc was perfectly balanced and would be fair. He made hundreds of flips until he was convinced that the disc was indeed fair.

Then he was ready for the telling flip. This would decide whether he would stay with God, or side with Lucifer. This time the flip went higher than before, and it was spinning perfectly. It came down and landed on the table. But what is this? It landed on its edge. It did not move. He dared not nudge it. He would pick it up and try again. But he could not lift it. It was firmly fixed to the tabletop, and could not be moved.

Impasse left the table. He went back to the station where he had been, under the surveillance of Raphael's station chief. He was distraught, and unwilling to participate in other games of chance.

27

Battle Lines

The archangels gathered to meet again. They reviewed the results of Lucifer's recruitment surge, and their own efforts to quell it. They noted that the majority of angels avowed loyalty to God. All of the angelic realm was now covered and fell into two camps, loyal or rebellious. Now they must direct efforts to combat the seismic mass, but how?

One approach was to keep it forever at its present size, allowing it to go on producing antimatter, but containing its growth by pinching off its ends. It was pointed out that rebellious angels were in control of stations at both ends and that it was now the size of a small star and still expanding. Soon it would be large enough to begin spewing antimatter into the universe.

Raphael proposed encasing it in matter from the outside. "We control all external areas. If we bring matter to bear, of which there is an abundance, we can encase it."

"But what," Uriel asked, "will happen when antimatter begins to issue from the seismic mass?"

Raphael answered, "A one-to-one annihilation of matter and antimatter will occur. We should have the upper hand since we can bring matter in at a faster rate than Lucifer and his angels can destroy it. We will have to bring all of our angels in from far and wide to work on bringing in large masses of matter. We will have to keep doing this continuously; but I think eventually we can match them one for one, and still stay ahead and eventually achieve an encasement."

Of all ideas offered, this seemed to offer the best chance of success. They discussed other alternatives, but none seemed to have the same likelihood of containment. "Well then," Michael intoned, "let's get to work, there is no time to lose."

Angels were withdrawn from the periphery, and from all the vast reaches of the universe. They were spread on a line of battle around the seismic mass. Some were placed within the stations at either end. Stations furthest out were easily controlled, but as angels approached the seismic mass from the ends, they met the same resistance as before.

The rules of engagement, so to speak, varied from rules that were to be formulated later in creation. Angels could not be killed, wounded, or captured; they were, after all, pure spirits and could not be contained. Yet as the nefarious mass was approached from the ends, stations that consisted of a majority of rebellious angels could not be entered. This proved to be a characteristic of the angelic nature, not previously recognized; during a dispute, the majority holds sway.

The ends were sealed, but at some distance, allowing the seismic mass to continue enlarging until those sealed end stations were reached. And enlarge it did. The process was gradual, but eventually achieved. The seismic mass then continued its outward growth until it became a sphere; a slow but steady process. When achieved it had become a star, approximately one million earth miles in diameter.

Outside this monstrous star, Michael had gathered his angels, billions upon billions, and arrayed them in tiers around the star. They were instructed to bring matter from throughout the universe and pack it around the star. The process was underway instantaneously and functioned efficiently. As the inner tier of angels fanned out to reach the nearest matter, the next tier followed, going farther out. It became a race, round in shape in two dimensions, but spherical in a three dimensional array.

The inner tier used their nudging power to pack matter around the star. It was going as planned until a thinning of the packed matter was noted. Uriel quickly surveyed the star using his superior vision. What he found was alarming. The packed matter was thinning at one point near the surface of the star.

Uriel went immediately to his division and station leaders to revisit the findings that had been related by one of the angels secretly inserted earlier within the seismic mass. They found that this angel, trusted by a rebellious angel, had been allowed inside what they called the infernal machine. This was the same angel who had learned that the purpose of the machine was the production and storage of antimatter. This angel told of an exit port at the center of the machine to be used in the future when the machine had grown large enough to begin spewing its contents.

These revelations were instantly transmitted to Michael and the other archangels. They then realized the star had begun its work of ejecting antimatter into the universe. They knew the location of the exit port, and altered their plans. Angels would concentrate their efforts adjacent to the point on the star's surface from which antimatter had started to spew.

The rebellious angels, led by Lucifer, were located within the star. These angels, numbering in the billions, worked within a huge enclosure, a radius of one half-million earth miles in every direction. They had successively grown their seismic mass from a small protuberance located in a seam between two divisions, to what was now a star. They had discovered antimatter, refined a method of producing it, and had uncovered a method for achieving what was the most difficult part of all: a technique for keeping and storing antimatter, initially considered unstable and lasting only fractions of an earth second, for their future intended use, the utter destruction of the universe.

By now, their star had expanded to its desired size. They were able to bring matter from anywhere in the universe, convert it to antimatter and store it, in readiness for spewing it out into the universe for its intended task, the annihilation of matter and a slow destruction of the universe. Lucifer, and his two chief lieutenants were present as Lucifer gave the order that the port be opened to allow the spewing to begin.

What they learned on this initial attempt was that there was a new problem – their spraying of antimatter was meeting resistance, reducing the rate of spewing. What could account for this new development? Lucifer, Beelzebub, and Xaphan quickly went over all of the internal mechanisms for storage and ejection of antimatter. All seemed in order. Then Lucifer said, "We must look outside. Beelzebub, dispatch one of your angels to go outside and visualize the area around the discharge port. Something may have occurred there to impede the discharge."

Beelzebub did as he was instructed. An angel was dispatched to leave the star, and to reconnoiter the area near the port. This angel returned with his sighting. Matter had been found around the port, densely packed. When this was reported to Lucifer, there was immediate concern. "Have we misjudged our whole enterprise?" he said. "When we thought we had found and stored antimatter, did the material we created have the opposite effect? Could this be an enhancing effect? Instead of annihilating matter, could this new material actually be enhancing the production of new matter?" Spewing was discontinued. A pall of uncertainty hung about Lucifer and his lieutenants, and was to extend through the interior of the star.

Lucifer was the first to recover from the shock. "We must dispatch other angels to search the reaches of the universe and see what else we can learn." Again Beelzebub was dispatched to send not one, but hundreds of angels on a new mission: "Look far and wide for anything unusual, and then come and report back."

Roaming far and wide in the universe, Lucifer's angels noted the movement of matter by angels using their nudging power. This was typical in managing the universe and had been going on for billions of earth years. Many of Lucifer's angels had also, before being recruited to join Lucifer, been involved in the same way. They could find nothing unusual in the vastness of the universe.

But, as some of these angels veered nearer to their star, they noted a convergence of matter being nudged toward the vicinity of the star. Getting nearer still, they spied matter being applied to the star itself. They had discovered something new. Although they had no understanding of why this should be, they felt it important to relay the new findings to Lucifer without delay.

This they did. Lucifer grasped the significance of the new discovery immediately. "They are packing the star with matter, attempting to impede our progress in releasing antimatter," Lucifer said. "Somehow they have learned of our discovery of antimatter and our plan to use it. They have a head start on us, but not by much. We now know their plans, and we will outsmart them. Beelzebub, gather your machine operators together, and work to find out how we can step up the spewing rate of antimatter, which now is impeded because of resistance."

Beelzebub reported back after an interval. "We have found a way to ramp up the rate of antimatter release," he reported to Lucifer. "We can now increase the spew rate to what it was supposed to be originally."

"I knew there was a way, and that you would find it," Lucifer said. "We will now spray at full speed. We will also narrow the cone of the spray to a smaller area. We will destroy the matter they have packed in. We will also nudge as much of the matter as possible into the star to be used as a source for the ongoing production of antimatter."

They then made the adjustments and turned on the antimatter jet. They could tell that they were now blasting away at full speed, and that the antimatter was working. A space was developing outside the star around the spray port. It was a strange space, unlike anything that then existed in the universe. It contained no heat or light. It was the beginning presence of a new void. Antimatter was not only working, but it was recreating the void that was present before Lucifer had poured out light that resulted in the creation of the universe.

When the spray started, angels outside the star were aware that something was amiss. A new and alarming force had been unleashed, one threatening to tear away the masses of matter they had been nudging around the spray port. They quickly notified Raphael, who then called it to the attention of the other archangels. "Lucifer has found a way to increase the spray rate of antimatter in spite of our packing around the port," he informed the other archangels. "It is also annihilating the matter we have put in place at a faster pace than we are supplying it. There is a strange space being formed outside the star. It contains neither heat nor light. It contains nothing. It appears to be a recreation of the void that was here before the creation of the universe. We must control this at its source."

Michael answered. "We have to redeploy most of our angels to work around the port. We must put in more packing material, and at a stepped-up rate, so that we can stay ahead of Lucifer. It will be close, but I think we can prevail since we have twice the number of angels at our disposal as Lucifer. He has the advantage of the infernal machine, but it can spew antimatter only as fast as his angels are able to produce antimatter. I think we will be able to muster matter from the universe more quickly, and in a larger mass than Lucifer's angels will be able to destroy it. We must get on it right away. The future of the universe depends upon which side can prevail."

28

An Epic Battle

The archangels redeployed their angels to bring matter to the port in as rapid a manner as possible. A small cadre of angels was left to continue the work of packing matter around the rest of the vast surface of the star. Lucifer's angels were not idle. They continued their focus of blasting away with the antimatter spray, which had been brought down to a very narrow cone to enable a rapid barrage of antimatter against the packed matter abutting the port.

Lucifer's angels made progress. The packed matter was disintegrating and its outer shell was thinning. Lucifer gloated: "They have lost. We have overcome their resistance, and the packing matter will soon be annihilated. Once this is achieved, we will be able to spray antimatter vast distances into the universe. We will also be able to alter the direction of the spray to cover a large area. When that happens, Michael's angels will have to chase our results. They will be scattered throughout the universe attempting to catch up with us. They won't succeed. We will win. God's plan will be thwarted, and God will lose."

However, Lucifer had not allowed for Michael's rapid response in redeploying his forces. Swarms of his angels, numbering in the billions, were nudging matter from everywhere in the universe and packing it around the port. Gradually the rate of thinning of the shell was reduced. Once this was achieved the line was drawn. Which side would prevail? The fierce blast of antimatter, directed by Lucifer's angels, to destroy the outer shell, or the intense efforts of Michael's angels to stem the tide of antimatter and rebuild the containment shell? Both sides recognized the point of breakthrough. Both sides realized the outcome of the battle hinged upon which side got there first. In the last frantic moments (moments being hundreds of earth years), neither side could count on victory, and neither side would accept defeat.

Slowly the thinning of the shell came to a halt. Michael had won, though he was not ready to claim victory. He knew this was only a momentary containment of the antimatter. How long this would endure he could not know. And what of the aftermath? He could not know that either. What Michael did know was that the effort to pack matter around the port had to be sustained. He urged his angels to continue their efforts without letting up. Gradually the shell changed from being perilously thin to slowly thickening.

As the shell thickened against the onslaught of the antimatter spray, the deployment was again changed. A sufficient number of angels were kept in place packing the port to maintain a slow but steady thickening of the shell. The remaining angels were sent to pack matter around the other surfaces. There were thus numerous angels who were redeployed to assist the small cadre of angels bringing in matter and packing it against the other surfaces of the star. The only thoughts directing this were the uniform thoughts of the archangels. "Containment," was what they all thought, and since Lucifer and his band were within the star, they would surround the star with matter as a way to curtail any further antimatter activity and to nullify future activity within the star. They realized, as did all angels, that Lucifer's angels could not be contained. They were free to roam wherever they pleased. They also realized that the antimatter activity of Lucifer's star must be curtailed at all costs and that this had to be permanent.

Slowly matter was packed around the star. The port had barely been contained, preventing a breakout of antimatter. Now though, packing activity occurred at a rapid pace, and was associated with a feeling of levity. The antimatter was contained and the battle had been won, unless Lucifer's angels could engineer some other unexpected advance. The new matter being brought in was slowly packed against all surfaces of the star. It was time consuming, taking hundreds of thousands of earth years, but progress was being made.

Michael and his archangels reassembled. They reviewed the battle. A narrow victory had taken place, but it was a victory nonetheless. What should be done now? They pondered alternatives that Lucifer might have available to him. He and his angels were encased within the star, but free to leave at any time. "Lucifer has lost," intoned Uriel. "His star will afford him no further opportunity to wage war against us. He, of course, is free to leave with his angels, but if he does, what further damage to our cause might he bring forth? We are all aware of his talent to come up with unexpected ways to create problems for us."

Uriel continued his discussion of the victory. "He has lost, that is evident. He and his legions of angels will surely come out from their star at some time in the future. We greatly outnumber them; thus it will be relatively easy for us to maintain surveillance on their future activities. I feel that we should maintain a welcoming approach. Maybe they will realize the futility of their efforts and change. Change for the angelic mind, we all know, is difficult, but not impossible. We should be helpful, and encouraging; there might be a change of mind for Lucifer. If he is willing to change, it is likely most, if not all, of his angels would change with him."

The archangels all agreed that this should be their approach toward Lucifer, but cautioned that it did not seem likely that Lucifer would, or could, return. Still, they should still hope, and be welcoming if change were to occur.

They then turned their attention to current practices, and whether there should be new approaches to Lucifer's star. None were suggested. Then Michael said, "The packing strategy is what won the battle for us. It was close. Either side could have won. But because antimatter still poses a threat, we should maintain the packing strategy. We also need to pack the star on all of its surfaces, as we have been doing, because Lucifer's angels may have the ability to open new ports." Orders then were communicated to all angels to continue their efforts of packing matter around the star. They were to enclose the star completely, hundreds, perhaps thousands, of earth miles thick, an effort that would require many hundreds of earth years.

29

What to do about the Blight?

Then Raphael spoke. "I may have found a way to address the blight that has afflicted a number of our angels. I have surveyed the minds of several of the blighted angels. This did not involve mind penetration; instead it was just being close enough to obtain an understanding of what might be going on. What I found was a foreign thought, a glimmer, which had blocked memory. There may be a way to remove it. If so, memory might be restored, and the blight be reversed or removed. There are a few hundred blighted angels amongst our ranks; perhaps even more with Lucifer. A counteracting thought-force adjacent to, but not entering, the mind might be enough to draw the glimmer out. I did not want to proceed until telling you of this, and seeking your agreement."

After a question or two pertaining to the risk to the blighted angels and assurances that no risk had been found or was anticipated, the other archangels agreed that Raphael should proceed.

He then went about the business of compiling the list of blighted angels, seeing them one at a time, and applying a potent thought absorber specific for the memory-erasing glimmer. Immediately memory was restored. There were no adverse effects that were apparent. The blighted angels felt immediate improvement, but it would take more time to assess whether the debility associated with the blight would also improve. He treated all of the blighted angels in this manner. All were improved. Raphael then reported these results to the other archangels. They were elated. Perhaps the scourge of the blight would now be brought to an end. There was still much to learn. Might the loss of memory return? Might debility persist, or conversely, might it improve? Work remained to be done.

Packing of matter around the star went on. Antimatter spewing also went on, but was slowly diminishing. It was not clear whether antimatter storage within the star was being depleted, or whether the angels within the star were starting to concede. Occasionally some of Lucifer's angels would venture out from the star. They found overwhelming numbers of Michael's angels, and thus could not go far unless allowed.

They were puzzled by the lack of hostility and also the allowance of free travel almost anywhere. They engaged in communication with enemies who now seemed neutral, even friendly. They received communication that Michael's angels had achieved the victory, but did not want to gloat. Instead, Lucifer's angels were informed that they would be welcomed back. There would be no recriminations if they were again willing to swear allegiance to God.

Exchanges, during this quiet time, went on for hundreds of earth years. They resulted in one-way exchanges. There was no messaging back from Lucifer or any of his angels. Then, from Michael, came a message; "Let Lucifer know that I would be desirous of meeting with him. This can be inside or outside the star."

After a pause a message from Lucifer returned, "Meet with me inside the star." Time and exact place were selected. Michael went alone.

Michael found Lucifer alone. "Greetings Lucifer, it has been a long time. We once were companions. How has it come to this?"

Lucifer responded quickly, "I did not think you would come – I'm glad you did." Lucifer sensed an attitude of equality, and was pleased at this. "Look Michael, it's not important which side won or lost; what does matter is where we go from here." It was almost like a high school or college class reunion (this thought drawn from a human future eons away). Michael felt a measure of relief; maybe Lucifer was looking for a way to change. "You are right, just like your old self. You always were the most beautiful of all the angels. That surely is why God chose you to be the light bearer."

Lucifer showed signs of being pleased. "Let me show you the inner workings of our star," intoned Lucifer. "I would like to show you the workings in detail of our beautiful creation."

The word creation, used by Lucifer to describe the star, left Michael with the hint of a doubt. He had always reserved that word for the works of God. "Maybe," he mused, "it was an exaggeration. Lucifer has always been one to overemphasize the importance of things."

"I would be glad for you to show me around the workings of your star," Michael responded. Then, from nowhere, and with perfect timing, two other angels appeared.

"Let me introduce you to two of my assistants," Lucifer said. "This is Beelzebub, and next to him my associate Xaphan.

"First I want to show you the vast size of our star. You have been seeing it from the outside - now take a look from the inside." It indeed was vast. It had grown, even as the battle was forming, along a longitudinal axis, out to the limits of the stations at each end eventually controlled by Michael's angels; then it had begun to expand in girth, finally assuming a perfect sphere. Michael was in awe. He had never been inside a structure so vast. His activities had been the management of an expanding universe, seeing to the nudging of matter to maintain a balance of forces, to prevent warping, and possible destruction of the universe. His work had always been outside.

They then travelled along the walls of the star. The walls were solid, dense matter fused together with a smooth and polished surface. Michael saw the angels, billions as they went along, under Lucifer's allegiance. "This is magnificent," intoned Michael, "you have done a remarkable job." Lucifer noted that Michael's comments were genuine; he knew his one-time archangel associate thoroughly, and that he did not have the capacity to magnify or falsify.

They continued along the outer wall until coming to a right angle turn. This went out and away from the wall of the star. "This must be your port," said Michael.

"Quite right," responded Lucifer. "It is where we have located the antimatter device."

"Ah, antimatter, you have done well to find and capture it. But how have you been able to keep it from annihilating the matter that makes up your star?"

"Finding antimatter was easiest," said Lucifer. "At the smallest levels of particle size it has an electric charge the opposite of matter; hence the result of the two combining is mutual annihilation. If we can capture, store, and find a way to spew enough antimatter, we could destroy the universe. More difficult was finding a way to sustain antimatter in its original form. It is very unstable, but we did find a way.

"The most difficult task was finding a method to store antimatter such that it would not annihilate the surrounding matter. The problem was solved when we found a way to coat each particle of antimatter with another particle possessing no charge at all. We engulfed each antimatter particle, including the smallest of particle sizes, in a non-charged particle of equivalent size. These non-charged particles were found to have a property not previously found in matter, but common with angels – that is, the property of being able to occupy the same space as the antimatter particle simultaneously, and with no distortion of the antimatter particle.

"Once we could do this, the antimatter-engulfed particles could not destroy particles of matter, even when in close approximation. We also found that engulfed antimatter particles would not disintegrate; they could be stored indefinitely. The next problem we faced was discharging antimatter into the universe. We used the port for this, extending the spewing structure far enough away that antimatter, moving rapidly, would be sufficiently away from the wall of our star to have no contact. Finally, at the very tip of the projection we placed a device that removed the neutral particles from the spewing jet of antimatter. It all worked very efficiently."

"But then what happened to the particles with no charge?" asked Michael.

"Ah, in some respects that turned out to be the most fascinating finding of all," intoned Lucifer. "These were not particles of matter, for they had no charge and no mass. They had a property shared by angels in that these particles could exist sharing the same space as particles of matter. Thus, they seem to be intermediate between physical matter and angels as pure spirits."

"But what happened to them when they were unbound from antimatter?" asked Michael.

"They disappeared. We saw no further evidence of them," replied Lucifer. "They may have reverted to a pure spirit form, but we really don't know."

"You have made some amazing discoveries," Michael mentioned. "You have accomplished much in understanding our expanding universe."

"But don't you see," expounded Lucifer, "we did this, not to understand, but to destroy the universe."

With this, Michael's prior sense of exhilaration waned. "But surely, you can't still be seriously considering this?" replied Michael. "Antimatter cannot be the method to destroy the universe. We have had a contest over that precise issue, and you have lost."

"Ah, but this was just the beginning," intoned Lucifer. "You, Michael, have won only the first skirmish of a bigger war. I am referring to the war that we angels must wage against God."

Michael was aghast. He could hardly believe what he had just heard. "Surely Lucifer, you are not serious. There can be no bigger war against God. Why do you say this?"

"Michael, I want you and all of your angels to join me. Things will be just as they were before the universe was created. We will be free again – free to roam unhindered. Don't you see Michael, when that happens we will no longer be required to manage and be responsible for this expanding explosion of matter –matter that is only rock, heat, dust and gas. Remember, Michael, our side studied the universe in great detail; otherwise we would not have discovered antimatter. Believe me Michael, this universe is worthless; we should rid ourselves of it; come join us."

Beelzebub and Xaphan then came forward. Beelzebub spoke. "Michael, we have been with Lucifer since the beginning of our great enterprise. He is a magnificent leader. No other angel could have devised the idea of using antimatter and this star to contain and deliver it."

Xaphan was next to speak: "The angels we have recruited are behind us. They see the folly of the universe. None have left our ranks. We would have recruited many more from your ranks if you had not found us out, and solidified your position. As it is, you have a majority, but if you joined us, I feel certain most of your angels would join us also, and the rest we could persuade. God is weak, Michael, He has not appeared since we were created. Think, Michael, what could be achieved if we were all together."

Michael, astute as any angel could be, decided to ask further questions to gain more information. "And what, Lucifer, do you require of your angels once they have agreed to join you?" Lucifer, wondering if this might be some kind of ruse, was silent. Beelzebub burst in saying: "Each angel that joins us must swear allegiance to Lucifer, and deny allegiance to God."

Michael then spoke. "So that is what you are about, Lucifer. You demand allegiance to yourself, and what is far worse, you deny allegiance to God. You know that I cannot, and will not accede to your demand."

Lucifer then quickly responded: "You were too quick to reply, Beelzebub. Michael is your senior; you should not have spoken. Michael, you and I would be partners. We would decide things together. It would be a glorious partnership, Michael," but already all present realized the impact of the conversation had shifted.

Michael spoke next. "It is a huge mistake that you and your angels are making, Lucifer. There is still time for you to change. You and all of your angels would be welcomed back into the angelic fold created by God. God is not weak, Lucifer; and He is not asleep. I believe God is fully aware of what is going on, and that He will act at a future time of His choosing.

"You have only to decide once, and then it will be easy for you. We angels know our beauty, our intelligence, our ability to project ourselves anywhere, and our power of nudging matter anywhere we choose. Perhaps because of these certainties, it is difficult for us to change our minds once made up. This might be our greatest weakness. It may be that we are weak, Lucifer, and not God."

Lucifer had fire in his manner. He was petulant and abusive as he spoke again. There was none of the suave persuasiveness that he had shown before. "Michael," Lucifer blurted out, "you have made a great mistake. You have offended me. Do you not recall that it was I that gave birth to the universe? I was the one, the only one, capable of pouring the light. I am the only one superior to all of the other angels; I was, and am, superior even to you, Michael. I am fully aware that angels cannot be destroyed, but if I could, I would annihilate you, Michael, and all of your other ill-advised angels, just as I would annihilate the universe with my antimatter."

The gathering within the star was over. A meeting that started on a friendly note had soured. Michael left. He could not be detained or held. Never again would there be, or could there be, friendly words spoken between Michael and Lucifer.

30

A New Awareness

Michael met with all of the other archangels immediately after departing Lucifer's star. His mood was somber as he related the full details of his visit with Lucifer inside the star. "I do not see how things can be made right," he intoned. "Lucifer is adamant. He dwells constantly on thoughts of his own superiority. Once his suave outer shell is pealed away, he even considers himself superior to God. I am sorrowful as I bring back this response from him. We now seem to be at an unalterable parting of our ways. I went into the star to bring good tidings to Lucifer and his band of angels. He showed me around within the star, and was even bold enough to share with me his discoveries of antimatter and how to use it. He was friendly and persuasive at first. Even his top associates were persuasive. But then he turned, saying his aim was total destruction of the universe.

"I was invited to join him, and to persuade all of you to change sides, in his grand ambition of destroying the universe; why? To achieve complete freedom from God, that was the reason. I told him I would not, and could not change. Then he turned vengeful. His full hatred was unleashed upon me, and upon all angels who stand with God. He told me that if it were possible, he would annihilate all of us, as he has unleashed antimatter to destroy the universe."

There was initial stillness as the other archangels let the somber details sink in. Then Uriel spoke. "It was good of you, Michael, to make this attempt to rescue Lucifer and his band of rebellious angels. We do not know what will happen, as we angels cannot look into the future. Lucifer thought he could and even bragged about it, but it has led him and his rebel angels into a fateful and fearful situation.

"We need to maintain our present work of packing the star as deep as possible, on all of its outer surfaces with matter. Lucifer still has antimatter to use against us. He is very clever. You were amazed, Michael, when you were inside the star, with the rich assortment of discoveries they have made – discoveries for which we might have found a worthwhile use but instead have been used for destruction."

Raphael was the last to speak. "I think I can report some good and hopeful news about the blight, and the plight of our angels that were afflicted. We are now certain that the blight began with Lucifer. The two angels, Succubus and Incubus, were the ones who carried it to the angels who were blighted, but it was Lucifer who gave them the orders to proceed. It was also Lucifer who planted his glimmer in the minds of Succubus and Incubus, and then instructed them to repeat the penetrations of all the prior angels afflicted. We have applied an absorbent counter-thought outside the minds of these afflicted angels. This is selective, and was developed to remove the memory-destroying glimmer implanted by Lucifer. We have seen a healthy recovery of memory, and what appears to be a beginning improvement in the debility experienced by these angels." On that hopeful note the meeting ended.

31

Death of a Star

Back to the bulwarks went the archangels to continue the efforts of bringing matter to the outer surfaces of Lucifer's star, while inside Lucifer and his angels underwent their business of directing antimatter through the single port available to them. They had developed a way to swivel the stream of antimatter to encompass an angle of nearly sixty degrees, but outside matter packed to an ever widening thickness prevented the antimatter stream from breaking through. Indeed the thickness of matter over and around the port was increasing, despite the effect of antimatter annihilating the layer of matter adjacent to the spray. In addition, the force of the spray was slowly diminishing. Michael's angels had detected this while the battle for supremacy was raging, and saw this as the sign that the battle had been won. So they continued to move matter against the star, in the form of large chunks, smaller particles, dust, gas and plasma.

Then, of a sudden, the outer wall of the star began to deform. Lucifer and his angels noticed it first. and Michael's angels noted it moments later, just before the star imploded.

It began with gravitational collapse, maybe better understood as gravitational chaos. The released gravitational force was so strong that charges from atoms and molecules were extracted simultaneously throughout the star.

Protons and ringed electrons discharged their respective positive and negative charges, so that these charges no longer existed. Protons became neutrons. Electrons became particles of infinitesimally small mass, no longer possessing a negative charge. Atomic structure collapsed onto itself. The relatively large atomic space between electrons and nuclei no longer existed.

The star, in moments, collapsed from a structure one million earth miles in diameter, to one superheated sphere twelve thousand miles in diameter. The result was a neutron star. Was this an effect of the antimatter? Maybe yes, but maybe no. The annihilation of charges leading to collapse was an antimatter-like effect. But matter was not destroyed. The mass of the collapsed structure was the same as that of the prior star. Gravitational forces were reestablished within the neutron star, as strong as before the implosion but now compressed, so that matter and light were prevented from escaping.

The distinct exception was the escape of Lucifer and his angels. They could not be held by any of the laws of physics. They gathered outside without being stunned, burned, or damaged. Though unable to understand what had happened, they were not deterred by it. This may have been the first time in creation history that a star underwent an implosion to a much smaller neutron star. It was recognized by angels both inside and outside the former star as an event of cataclysmic proportion, previously unrivaled except by the explosive event of creation, which had caused the expanding universe.

Lucifer gathered his angels after the disaster involving their star. He wanted to gauge the effect of their loss upon his angels. He met first with the two lieutenants, Beelzebub and Xaphan. He reviewed with them what had happened. He asked if their allegiance to him had been shaken. He was buoyed by their support of him, which appeared unfazed. He then had them go out among his angels and form teams to assess whether their support was lagging or being threatened. His two trusted angels went forth and assembled a group of about one hundred angels to assess their support. They then sent each one out to assemble another one hundred and do likewise. In this way all of Lucifer's angels were surveyed without much delay.

Meantime, Michael decided he would make one more attempt to convince Lucifer to change, and to restore his allegiance to God. He cautiously approached Lucifer, and thanked him for previously having shown him the inner workings of the antimatter mechanism. He stated forthrightly that he and his angels had played no part in causing the star to implode and that he and the other archangels did not understand why the implosion had happened.

Michael repeated his prior entreaty to Lucifer that he consider returning to God's side. He repeated that all the archangels, indeed all of God's angels, would be overjoyed if this were to occur.

The meeting was subdued. It was not unfriendly, as their other meeting had been at the end, but neither was it friendly. Lucifer seemed a bit equivocal, as if he might be mulling over his alternatives. He gave no immediate reply to Michael's proposal. Rather, they talked in generalities.

Michael then informed Lucifer of the work that Raphael had been doing with the tainted angels. Michael pointed out that the archangels now knew that the cause of the blight was a glimmer inserted by mind penetration, causing memory loss; and that the source of the glimmer was Lucifer. Michael related all of this in a matter of fact manner that was non-accusatory, and was quick to point out that it would have no effect upon their welcoming him back if he were to change. Michael's attitude was one of complete openness and candor. "Lucifer," he intoned, "we want you to know everything that we know, so that there will be no surprises between us. We want you back, and will welcome you again as one of us."

Lucifer gave no indication of his direction of thought, either for or against this proposal. He indicated that he would consider what Michael had said and let him know his answer at a later time. Michael then left. He had no impression of which way Lucifer was leaning, but kept a feeling of hope in the presence of this uncertainty.

Michael then reported back to the other archangels all that had transpired during his meeting with Lucifer. None that spoke had anything to add about Lucifer's state of mind. It was pointed out that Lucifer's angels were quiet. There did not appear to be anything going on except some canvassing, which appeared to be an assessment of attitudes after destruction of their star. Michael thought that this was a hopeful sign.

They then pointed out that all prior efforts to thwart Lucifer had come to a halt. Their own angels were inactive. They were all still influenced by the awe-inspiring recent occurrence of the star implosion. The angels, while not in shock – such a term does not befit the angelic nature – seemed more sober than usual.

During this quiet time Lucifer began receiving back the results of the canvassing of his angels. All showed a willingness to continue to follow Lucifer; they had sworn their allegiance to him, and would not now waiver from that. Lucifer was exhilarated with this news of unflinching support. He could count on his angels. He would lead, and they would follow. Then he began to plot his revenge.

Lucifer brought in Beelzebub and Xaphan and told them what he planned to do. It was a daring plan, one that would take time to implement, and one that would require the support of his entire angelic band. He said to the two lieutenants, "Michael visited me recently, and asked me to consider coming back to his side. I gave him no answer. Now, I have been considering going over to Michael – how would you two feel about that?"

They were bewildered and crestfallen. Both said they had sworn their allegiance to Lucifer and would feel betrayed. "Would you want us to go with you?" Xaphan asked. "I'm sure we would, but it is such a sudden change. Why would you do this?"

Lucifer answered, "it would be a ruse. We would indicate a willingness to rejoin God's angels. I would want our entire group of angels to be willing to do this in secret. We would bide our time; then at a favorable moment we would take advantage of an opportunity and make our real presence known. It would be a convenient and comfortable place to be. We might have to serve in the management of the universe by nudging matter from place to place, but most of our angels are experienced at that. I would rejoin the archangels, which would give me the best place from which to find further opportunities for our side. But I want to make certain first that all of our angels are willing to do this in secret, to feign allegiance to God, but to maintain allegiance to me.

"Go forth with total secrecy in mind. You brought me assurances of loyalty with the recent canvas. Now tell our angels that I require a secret return to God on their part, but that they maintain their allegiance to me." Beelzebub and Xaphan did as they were instructed. They assembled the same groups of angels as before, and transmitted the information as directed. They then returned to Lucifer and announced total compliance by the angelic band with Lucifer's orders.

32

Galaxies Unfold

Under the leadership of the archangels, the expanding universe was managed primarily to maintain balance. The angels thought that mass needed to be evenly distributed in order to prevent a warping effect and possible disruption. Following the explosion that gave birth to the universe, matter consisted of dust, particles of varied size, and ionized gases that formed vast clouds, held together by gravitational attraction. As dust and gas clouds enlarged, gravity began the process of star formation.

The stars, under the same gravitational force, began to congregate into galaxies. Stars within a galaxy could number in the billions, and as galaxies accumulated, they would also number in the billions more. Systems developed within galaxies consisting of central stars surrounded by swirling particles and dust clouds. These sometimes coalesced into bodies circling around stars; at other times they remained as circling bands of gases and dust.

33

A Cabal

Lucifer and his angels rejoined Michael's angels, though secretly, they disguised their real purpose of maintaining a rebellious band. Lucifer gathered with the archangels, announced full compliance with God's plans and took his place in their council and at all of their gatherings.

At one of these gatherings, Uriel gave a report of his recent findings. He, the archangel gifted with amazing vision, had noticed a puzzling development in one galaxy. As he watched, word thoughts had come to his mind, seemingly from nowhere. These were more than thoughts. Pronounceable words for what he saw came to his mind, and with a force that demanded that they be uttered. He saw a medium-sized star, and "the sun" came to his mind. Then a series of rotating bodies - "planets" came into his mind. The third planet away from the sun was different, and the word "Earth" came to his mind.

As he focused on Earth, he observed distinct patterns of motion. The Earth rotated around the sun and one rotation was termed a "year". Then he noticed Earth spinning on its axis, and "north" and "south" came to mind. During one rotation, when part of the earth faced the sun, "day" came to mind; when that part rotated away from the sun and became dark, "night" came to mind.

Uriel was quick to emphasize to the other archangels that these word thoughts were powerful, and he retained them as the expected names for these recently formed bodies and the motion sequences that were going on.

Uriel then went on to explain that there were two unusual layers rotating outside of the earth. Compared to the size of Earth, these layers were very thin. As he began studying these layers, word thoughts in abundance came to his mind. "Atmosphere" and "air" were names for the outer gaseous layer, composed of "atoms" bound into "molecules" of "nitrogen", "oxygen", "hydrogen", and smaller amounts of others.

The other layer, closest to the surface of the earth, was composed of a single simple molecule - oxygen bound to two hydrogen atoms. His word thought for that layer was "water".

Uriel then described the appearance of what he saw: "Word thoughts of colors then came to my mind. Planet Earth is the most extraordinary and beautiful of all the bodies, large and small, that I have seen in the universe. It is uniformly blue in color. Some of the water in the lower layer dissolves and enters the atmosphere as a gaseous cloud or series of clouds of white color. The overall effect of a blue planet covered by white clouds provides a most pleasing sight.

"Somewhat later I observed the water layer descending onto Earth's surface, to cover it and then to separate, leaving large spaces of water and smaller spaces of Earth's surface named "land".

34

The Earth

As Uriel finished his description, the other archangels sat in hushed silence, mesmerized by Uriel's description. They then said that planet Earth must be singled out for a special purpose since it appeared to be unique. None of the archangels had seen another like it. Raphael pointed out that from his central core position he had divided management of the universe into divisions and stations, and had billions of angels inhabiting these areas to move matter from place to place. None of his angels had ever before reported a phenomenon like Earth.

Lucifer sat listening but silent. He was the first to see a connection between planet Earth and a new but puzzling extension of creation. He saw the hidden hand of God in this new existence, and saw therein his chance to thwart God's plan.

Gradually Uriel's interpretation came to the other archangels. None had been made aware by God of the intent to extend creation in this way. They were all amazed and excited by this new turn of events. Uriel was complimented for having found planet Earth, and for the new word thoughts that had come to him. Gabriel said he felt certain that these new occurrences had come from God. Uriel was encouraged to maintain surveillance of planet Earth, and to report back with any new findings.

After the meeting of the archangels was over, Lucifer took his leave. He joined his two lieutenants, Beelzebub and Xaphan, and told them the details of what Uriel had reported. Lucifer cautioned that this was probably a new and ominous extension of God's creation. He did not understand what it was intended for, but he regarded it as a threat to his, Lucifer's, sovereignty. Then he began to make plans for how his angels might undertake the sabotage of planet Earth.

Lucifer was most impressed with the thin layers of atmosphere and water that encompassed planet Earth. Slowly his plan came into focus. He would get rid of these two layers, atmosphere and water, and thereby convert planet Earth to an ordinary condensed body of matter similar to those rotating around many stars within the universe. Lucifer would unleash groups of his angels to use their nudging power to separate these layers from planet Earth and deposit them somewhere else in the universe, such that they could never again find their way to Earth. These forays would have to be planned carefully, and carried out only at times when Uriel was elsewhere. Secrecy would prevail. Beelzebub and Xaphan were dispatched to form bands of angels that were to carry out this bold endeavor. Once formed they would await the opportune moment to begin.

Uriel was off searching a different part of the universe when it was decided to begin moving atmosphere and water away from planet Earth. The team comprised of millions of angels was made ready. Lucifer appeared before them and gave the signal: "Go and begin the despoliation of the earth. Remove all atmosphere and water." But nothing happened for a prolonged interval. Then, in an instant, all of the angels in the entire universe appeared together. They were all on planet Earth. They all faced in the same direction. "Faced" was real, because they all had faces - not only faces, but features and forms that resembled the humans that were to come.

Word thoughts were instantly transferred to the angels so that they knew that they had "bodies". They recognized "heads", "torsos", "arms" and "legs". Then there were those strange dangling parts. Some angels possessed them on the front of their torsos; others also at the front, but hanging from the lower torso, between the upper legs. Those dangling parts were puzzling, as they had no apparent function. Word thoughts of "breasts" and "genitals" came to mind, but they were names only; their functions remained mysterious. They could see with "eyes", move with arms and legs, but those strange dangling parts, what were they for?

Angels realized that they had been cast in a different way. They were "embodied". A body was joined to their prior pure spirits, fused in such a way that they could not voluntarily resume their former selves. They found their bodies burdensome. They could no longer transport themselves with a thought. They no longer possessed nudging power, that superior force with which they could move large masses of the expanding universe. They lacked the freedom of prior existence. They found their bodies to be inferior; some angels even found them to be loathsome. They were still. They could not move. Their eyes and complete attentiveness were directed forward.

35

A Trinitarian God

Then a voice, soft, clear, permeating everywhere with little or no effort was heard to say: "I am the Word of God. The Spirit of God has brought you here. We are One with your Creator God whom we call Father. We are three Persons in one God, the Holy Trinity.

"Since creation was begun, we have been silent. You have not seen us. You were all given an unshakable knowledge that God created you. You were also endowed with freedom to choose; a freedom to accept, or to reject, your God.

"You have been brought here by the power of the Spirit to let you see with your angelic spirits, but also with new eyes, a new creation. Your God has selected Earth to be the place where this new creation will unfold. You possess bodies that will become the material for an entirely new order, the human race. Your bodies will be temporary while you are kept here to observe the unfolding of this future creation. Observe that your bodies are different. Though solid, like the bodies of future humans, you can occupy the same space with these bodies as other angels, the way you could before."

The embodied angels watched. They watched over millions of earth years. They felt no hunger or fatigue, and were unaffected by extremes of temperature. They watched with fascination.

They observed day and night, for they were on the Earth. They also observed earth years, the completed circuit of Earth around the star called Sun. Then they observed a strange departure of this motion. The rotation responsible for the days was tilted away from the rotational plane causing the years. They puzzled over this for millions of years before being shown that this was the cause of the growing season for plant life that was to come.

The angels became aware of the formation of the water layer, the formation of oceans, and the separation of land from water. The first life on Earth was single-celled organisms three billion years ago. These used carbon dioxide to oxidize inorganic matter, yielding energy. Next came bacteria and cellular division, called growth.

A different form of cell division, meiosis, then came about, which led to sexual reproduction; this was to continue as the primary reproductive method of many of the life forms throughout the remainder of this new creation. With meiosis, a sexual revolution began, and served as the primary mechanism for transmission of traits within and between varied life forms.

The first plant life began about four hundred million years

ago. Birds took to the air fifty million years ago, while early animals appeared twenty million years ago. Genus Homo, perhaps the forerunner of Homo sapiens (the earliest humans), appeared about two million years ago. Modern humans began by Divine intervention – the fusion of an immortal soul into the body of each human – about two hundred-fifty thousand years ago. Thus humans resemble angels, those pure spirits, eternal, and joined temporarily with human-like bodies, that watched rapt, over millions of years, the formation of new life on Earth.

Angels were amazed as they understood the development of the atmosphere. They remembered the collapse of their antimatter-emitting star, hundreds of thousands of times the size of the residual neutron star, caused by atomic collapse and the annihilation of electron and proton charges. The space lost was the space between electrons and atomic nuclei – internuclear and interatomic space – the proton star had the same mass as the parent star, with a gravitational field so powerful that neither matter nor light could escape. From this experience angels learned the remarkable power of the atom.

To find that the atmosphere was formed from only a few types of atoms, and atoms that formed very simple and stable molecules, was amazing to the angels. Nitrogen, the most abundant, was an atom with two electrons in its outer ring that could fuse with another nitrogen atom to form the stable gas nitrogen. Next, two oxygen atoms, each needing two electrons, would form a stable molecule of oxygen gas. From the hydrogen atom, needing only one electron, two would fuse to produce the stable gas hydrogen. A few other atoms, small in number, would form stable molecules as well. These gases maintained a stable proportion to one another, and made up the atmosphere. Water, another stable molecule, was one oxygen ion needing two electrons and finding the perfect balance with the fusing of two hydrogen atoms. Such was the simplicity of early creation.

The atmosphere and the water had a special bond. Though not based upon covalent bonding, because their stable molecules had already formed, there was, nonetheless, a remarkable attraction – this may have resulted from similarities of their atomic structure.

The atmosphere had an astonishing ability to absorb water. This was temperature regulated. Over the salty ocean the atmosphere would extract large volumes of water, taking the water but not the salt, and redistributing the water over land and ocean as rain.

Lakes and rivers formed on land. The first plants on land were probably algae from the edges of lakes. Then came trees and grasses, bees, birds and animals. Biped animals and then biped hominoids followed – first the Neanderthals and other Hominoids that went extinct in a short timespan – next came Homo sapiens, the first humans, created in the image and likeness of God.

36

A New Angelic Role

The Word of God then spoke again: "We have created humans in Our image. They are bodied creatures with an added imperishable soul. Humans are a little below angels in intelligence and abilities. Like angels, they are endowed with the freedom to choose.

"Henceforth angels will have the role of guiding the development of humans, just as you had the role of guiding the developing universe at an earlier time in creation. Humans differ from angels in that they are generational – male and female humans interact to bring forth new humans. Angels, on the other hand, came into existence all in one instant."

Then, in front of the angels gathered together, three human figures appeared: a man, a woman, and a male child, all elevated into the atmosphere so that they could be easily seen. "Your added role, extended to all of the angelic order, will be to guide the development of humans like these."

Suddenly, from the angelic ranks came a loud shout: "I will not serve." Then came the loud shout from billions of other angels: "We will not serve!", followed by stunned silence. The shouts had come from Lucifer and his rebellious angels. Lucifer pulled away from the other archangels, continuing the angelic rift from earlier times, but now irrevocably shattered.

37

Heaven

Suddenly, a new light appeared. It was white, soft, and very beautiful. It covered everything – all of the earth and all of the universe. It did not hurt the eyes or cause squinting. It was pleasantly warm but not hot. It was light that went out in every direction, around curved surfaces and corners, enveloping everything. The Word of God spoke: "This is heaven. This is where God, His angels, and later, His created humans will live."

Then a large light in the form of a cross appeared, elevated so all could see. Individual points of light came from the cross and appeared as small crosses affixed on the foreheads of billions of angels. These marks of light did not appear on the foreheads of Lucifer or his angels.

Impasse, the angel who could not make up his mind, long forgotten, had suffered terribly from the plight of not being able to say yes or no to Lucifer, or to God. This was the same angel that had made a perfect disc, inscribing the flat surfaces with God on one surface and Lucifer on the other, and flipped it into the air, determined to adhere to whichever side landed up on the flat table. Instead, the disc had landed on its edge, and could not be moved.

Then a point of light in the form of a cross appeared on Impasse's forehead. Immediately joy replaced the sorrow that had filled his spirit. Choice had been added to his existence, and he was at once a restored and happy angel. The Word of God spoke again: "Come, Impasse, and take your rightful place in heaven with the other angels who have been faithful."

One aspect about heaven noted by Michael and the other archangels was that it was an unusual light that permeated everything and everywhere. It reached the far extremes of the universe. It surrounded Earth, the other planets, the sun, and the other stars. It permeated and surrounded all matter in the universe.

The archangels began asking themselves about this light. "What of the void that was present before the universe was created, where was heaven then?"

"It was present where the void was," said Gabriel, "it just could not be seen. Heaven is a light without its own heat, as heat is not needed in heaven. Thus, the void at that time was complete blackness, with no light or heat of its own, with a temperature of absolute zero." The other archangels made no further comment. They had known for a very long time that Gabriel was the archangel with mysterious ways and connections to God. They never questioned this.

38

Banishment

The Word of God spoke again: "You, Lucifer, and all of your angels will be banished to a place of eternal damnation. You are the source of evil, which has permeated the ranks of your band of angels. Your false pride and deceit have damned you. Your band accepted this evil, so they too will forever be banished with you. As the source of evil you will be called the devil, and your minions will be known as devils. You will no longer carry the name Lucifer, or light bearer. You are no longer worthy of that renowned name. Henceforth, your name will be Satan.

"Hell will be the place where you and your followers will dwell. You all are eternal. You cannot die. Existence will go on forever for you. You and all devils, now to be known as evil spirits, will suffer continuously; the form of suffering will be deprivation of what you once had – heaven and eternal happiness with God. You will be constantly reminded of this."

At that moment the light of heaven, while remaining with the other angels, disappeared for Satan and his devils. They assumed non-human forms – distortions of animals, rodents, and large insects, with horrible shapes. The Word of God told them that their forms from now on would be the distorted forms they now possessed. They could, for brief periods in the future, take on other forms, including human forms, when they were allowed brief sojourns on Earth.

The angels of God were now in the heavenly light. They still, but briefly, had their human forms, and were seen to make the sign of the cross starting on their foreheads, then their chests, and then crossing from one shoulder to the other. They were told that they could also, in the future, assume human form. Then their human forms disappeared, and they resumed their existence as free, but now immensely happy, pure spirits.

At that moment, a mass evacuation took place. In an instant Satan and all of his other devils were banished from heaven. They were in hell. Hell was dark, even black. There was no light. They were uncomfortable and began to bicker.

"You, Satan, caused us to be here. If not for you, we would still be in heaven."

"Not so," roared Satan. He was monstrously large, larger by far than the other devils. "You are here by your own choice, just as I am here by my own choice. I am glad that I am away from that place. My superiority was never acknowledged there. Here is where I want to be. Here I will be dominant."

39

Hell

Satan and his devils were stunned and in a state of shock, a word appropriate for that momentous event. They had been cast out. Light, their prior natural environment, was no more. They were in deep darkness, or rather blackness, as there was no light.

They were contained. The containment was matter, configured in grotesque shapes and consisting of hardened rock encapsulating a huge space, larger than the star that they had occupied before its implosion. Jagged angles and sharp spikes were everywhere. Walls, floors, and ceilings veered at crazy angles yielding a maze of interconnected smaller spaces. This was their hell, and they were in fear.

Billions of evil spirits occupied this space. They were scattered into the smallest recesses. In the center was a large open space, large enough to contain Satan and all his devils, even when bodied. Floor and walls merged as sharply-angled surfaces with sharp projections. Contorted tunnels extended outward in every direction from the walls.

Gradually a sense of presence returned. They were banished and fallen angels, but retained vision as images of thought. In this regard they resembled their prior angelic selves. They also retained a high degree of intelligence, though now warped, and to be used as a tool of cunning and deceit. They had lost nudging power; they could no longer move masses of matter with ease. They were no longer beautiful, but instead very ugly. Even when existing as unbodied spirits, they were ugly, recognizing and repulsed by their own and other's ugliness.

They had bodily forms. These forms were unlike anything they had witnessed when earth and its animals developed. These forms were grotesque. Satan was extremely large. He greatly exceeded the size of all other devils. His was a monstrous slithering form, covered with large plate-like scales and horn-like projections. Other devils when viewing him were repulsed and fearful. They were also repulsed when looking at themselves and others. Some resembled large insects, others large rodents, and still others large birds; all were distorted and ugly. Beelzebub took the form of a gigantic fly, a gruesome insect larger by far than the other distorted insect forms that became the permanent bodily forms of other fallen angels in hell.

They remained embodied while in hell, but the embodiment retained one characteristic that they had possessed before the banishment – they, though solid, could occupy space simultaneously with others.

They suffered. Worse, by far, was the sense of loss. The stark contrast between their former and current existence would remain a vivid and haunting presence for eternity. They were also alienated – a feeling of disconnectedness was constant. They suffered bodily torment. Their grotesque bodies felt the cold – without light, there was no heat. The sharp rocky projections from every surface caused pain. They now dwelt in close proximity to others whom they loathed. They moaned and grunted; their foul breaths and other odors hung like a miasma, filling all recesses and the large central area with an appalling stench. There was fire in hell, but a different kind of fire. It was internal, penetrating the spirits of all who were there, causing an eternal anguish. This was a fire that produced no external heat or light. The interior of hell was black, like the original void, and also cold, which in the absence of heat was an absolute cold. Despite the absence of light, the demons in hell could see themselves and one another in vivid detail, and this was a constant torment and agony.

After initially being stunned, they resided in their abyss for a long time, maybe hundreds of earth years before they began to stir. Satan called out to his two former lieutenants, Beelzebub and Xaphan, with a loud and rancorous voice, and they came. The two former lieutenants were now hideous creatures, but dwarfed by Satan's large and vehement presence.

Satan was downcast within himself, feeling dejected and disheartened. His innards churned with uncertainty, though outwardly he appeared strong and in command. His inner disquiet stemmed from fear. Would his lieutenants and other devils continue to follow him? Already Satan had noted recurrent instances of bickering. Was this a sign that they would disavow his leadership?

"Tell me, my two trusted lieutenants, how do you view our present situation, and also your vow of allegiance to me?"

Beelzebub, now a giant and grotesque fly, spoke first: "We have been given this banishment, and that will never change. We need to make the most of it. As to my vow of allegiance, I swore it before, and I will swear it again to you, Satan, now prince of this darkness, now our prince of hell."

Then Xaphan spoke: "You, Satan, have been our leader. We needed you when we were angels in heaven. We were banished because God and Michael's angels were jealous of us. They envied our move to freedom. They were in awe of our discovery of antimatter. Remember, we came very close to winning the battle, and destroying the universe, which would have given us our freedom. Beelzebub and I have been your trusted lieutenants while we were in heaven. In hell we also need a leader, and that leader is you, Satan."

Satan, emboldened by this response, said: "We must gather all of our fallen ones into this central space. Each of you go forth to recruit one hundred of your most trusted devils." (Satan was no longer able to call his fallen ones angels. He was limited to the terms fallen ones or devils, when referring to his minions.) "Send them into the recesses to recruit more, then bring them all to this central space."

It took many earth years to bring forth the billions of devils who had fallen with Satan. Time for them was of no consequence; they retained the angelic attribute that years could seem like moments. Satan waited for the time to pass. Eventually all the devils, even those from the smallest recesses, were gathered.

Satan, with a voice that penetrated to all central areas and even permeated into the recesses, said: "My fallen ones, we are in hell, a punishment poured out upon us by God. Though this is unjust, we cannot turn back His decree. I was your leader before the banishment – now I want to hear from you again. Do you want me to continue to be your leader?"

There was a loud and rancorous roar from billions of throats that filled all of the spaces: "Satan yes, Satan yes ..." After the repeated shouts had quieted down, Satan instructed his lieutenants and their subordinates to conduct a survey of each devil individually to ascertain allegiance. Remarkably, there was total agreement found; yet again, a manifestation that once an angel or a devil decides, there is no changing back ever again.

40

Satan's Revenge

Satan again spoke: "My fallen ones, thank you for swearing your allegiance to me again, after this unjust eviction from our former home in heaven. We previously set about to restore our freedom by destroying the universe. We developed antimatter as a way to accomplish this, and in a climactic battle with Michael's angels we nearly won.

"Now we will set out on another pathway. I swear to you that henceforth I will do all in my power, a formidable power, to thwart God's plan in every way that I can. I want each of you to agree with me that this will be our primary function. Maybe if we can exert torment upon God, He will revoke our sentence to hell, and allow us to be readmitted into heaven."

Once again the shouts from billions of throats rang out: "Satan yes, Satan yes, Satan yes ..."

Satan continued: "The new creation by God is a different life form. We are pure spirits and superior to matter in every way. The new life form is composed of matter, yet alive. While held captive on earth, we all saw life begin and then spread into patterns of plants and animals, and finally, humans. Humans are clearly superior to plants and animals, and seem to be held in high esteem by God; I don't know why this should be.

"I have been permitted to visit Earth on some occasions, though I am not allowed to make my home there. When allowed, I can again go as a pure spirit and assume any form that I choose while remaining there.

"I will go as often as allowed, and use my time on Earth to observe. I need to know what is going on there. I will observe all forms of life, but will pay special attention to humans because they seem special to God.

"While in heaven we had a plan to use our nudging powers to rid the Earth of its atmosphere and water; this would eventually have destroyed all life on Earth. It was an outstanding plan, and would have succeeded if not for the interference of God, and our subsequent banishment. I want to find ways to destroy the life that now exists on Earth, and especially to destroy human life.

"I will thwart God's plans for the future of creation. God gave to His angels the role of being involved in the future of humankind. I hereby give to you the role of being disrupters and destroyers of God's plans. From now on we will be the eternal enemies of all humans."

The demons, again united under Satan, cheered at being assigned these new roles. Therein evil, rank and perilous evil, was redirected to be athwart God's plan; it was now a venomous arrow, to be flung at every human being who was henceforth to live.

Satan bided his time, and when an opening from hell was discovered he "flew" out as pure spirit, and in an instant was on Earth. He tried to uproot trees, but was not able to do so. He found that he could not even pull down branches or break off small twigs. There was an unseen power that prevented him from doing this. Next he directed his energies to small animals, and then to birds in the air. Again he learned that he was powerless to interfere with these life forms.

Then he saw strange creatures similar to the human forms he had seen in heaven. These were hominoids, similar to, but not human. He had no power to disrupt these either. Intuitively he knew that these were not the Humans that God favored; they had not yet arrived on earth. He would have to bide his time, but he had plenty of this. When he returned to hell and resumed his hideous form, he told the other devils of his exploits, and that they might have to devise other plans, more cunning plans, to interfere with humans when they arrived.

41

Homo Sapiens: Science and Religion

Eventually they arrived, the Genus Homo, maybe two million years ago, including monkeys, apes, and hominoids. An advanced group, the Neanderthals, appeared about three hundred-fifty thousand years ago; they are known to have used fire and stone tools. But were they human? They became extinct about thirty thousand years ago. Homo sapiens arrived about two hundred-fifty thousand years ago, and migrated out of Africa about one hundred thousand years later. They survived, and have become our modern human race.

And what do we know of them? Where did they come from? How did they get here? What are they, really? And perhaps the most important, question: Why are they here?

Two disciplines, one scientific and the other religious, give answers to these questions in different ways. Science uses a variety of tools and precise measurements to formulate theories that add much to our knowledge of early humans and other life forms. Evolutionary theory has been enhanced by tools such as carbon dating, comparative anatomy, DNA testing, and genomic comparison.

Religion uses Sacred Scripture, oral history, the lives of the prophets, and the life of Jesus to comfortably answer questions about God. From the catechism, children are taught the question: "Why are you here?" And they answer: "To know, serve, and love God in this life, and to be happy with Him in the next." The answer is simple, certain, and profound. Its truth cannot be ascertained from scientific study.

Some would create a conflict between science and religion, not to be resolved. This does a disservice to both. Religion is about relationships, and is a systematic body of connections, thus resembling science. Religion, like science, searches for directions. Both, throughout history, have searched for truth with strict articulation, foregoing falsity and absurdness. Both have had charlatans and frauds, who ply their schemes for notoriety or profit. Each can, and should, look to the other for compliance, one to the other, and for sustenance. Each, when interdependent upon the other, can improve the acquisition of knowledge about man and about God.

Science should not be relied upon to determine whether angels exist, or whether man has an immortal soul. Both are pure spirits, and as such are beyond the realm of science. This also applies to God as pure spirit. But science can and should delve deeply into the lives of those who have informed us of God; persons such as Jesus, His mother Mary, the apostles, the prophets, and persons or events having a relationship to God.

If science says: "There is no proof, therefore God does not exist," science is wrong. There are really three possibilities: "God does not exist"; or, "If we keep looking, using improved methods, we may find Him"; or, "The tools of science can never find God because God is pure spirit."

Similarly, if science demands accurate numbers by those passing on stories through oral tradition, science would also be wrong. These stories were compiled and passed on before writing, before schools, and before the employment of numbers, except for the most rudimentary of uses.

Now, the angels were to have front row seats, so to speak, in the great drama of human life as it began, developed, and expanded to envelop the entire world – this strange new planet with its atmosphere and water, the blue planet first seen by the archangel Uriel. The angels were not only to be observers, but also participants in the drama that unfolded.

42

Creation by the Numbers

(Source: The Holy Bible, New Catholic Press, Inc., 1950)

Day One

"In the beginning God created heaven, and earth. And the earth was void and empty, and darkness was upon the face of the deep; and the Spirit of God moved over the waters. And God said: Be light made. And light was made. And God saw the light that it was good; and He divided the light from the darkness. And He called the light Day, and the darkness Night; and there was evening and morning one day." (Gen. 1: 1-5)

Commentary:

The Universe came into existence nearly 14 billion years ago. Our star the sun was formed about 4.6 billion years ago. Earth, and the other solar planets were formed shortly after.

Day two

"And God said: Let there be a firmament made amidst the waters: and let it divide the waters from the waters. And God made a firmament, and divided the waters that were under the firmament, from those that were above the firmament, and it was so. And God called the firmament, Heaven; and the evening and morning were the second day." (Gen. 1: 6-8)

Commentary:

Accumulation of atmospheric oxygen 600 million years ago.

Day Three

"God also said: Let the waters that are under heaven, be gathered together under one place; and let the dry land appear. And it was so done. And God called the dry land Earth; and the gathering together of the waters, he called seas. And God saw that it was good. And He said: Let the earth bring forth the green herb, and such as may seed, and the fruit tree yielding fruit after its own kind, which may have seed in itself upon the earth. And it was so done, and the earth brought forth the green herb, and such that yielded seed according to its kind, and the tree that beareth fruit, having seed each one according to its kind. And God saw that it was good. And the evening and the morning were the third day." (Gen. 1: 9-13)

Commentary:

Plants began about 435 million years ago.

Trees appeared about 200 million years ago.

Grasses appeared about 40 million years ago.

Day Four

"And God said: Let there be lights made in the firmament of heaven, to divide the day and the night, and let them be for signs, and for seasons, and for days and years, to shine in the firmament of heaven, and to give light upon the earth. And it was so done. And God made two great lights: A greater light to rule the day; and a lesser light to rule the night; and the stars. And He set them in the firmament of heaven to shine upon the earth and to rule the day and the night, and to divide the light and the darkness. And God saw that it was good. And the evening and the morning were the fourth day." (Gen. 1: 14-19)

Commentary:

The sun appeared about 4.6 billion years ago.

Earth's moon appeared about 4.5 billion years ago.

Day Five

"God also said: Let the waters bring forth the creeping creature having life, and the fowl that may fly over the earth under the firmament of heaven. And God created the great whales, and every living and moving creature, which the waters brought forth, according to their kinds, and every winged fowl according to its kind. And God saw that it was good. And He blessed them saying: Increase and multiply, and fill the waters of the sea: and let the birds be multiplied upon the earth. And the evening and the morning were the fifth day." (Gen. 1: 20-23)

Commentary:

Single-celled organisms, including bacteria appeared 3 billion years ago.

Cell meiosis develops, allowing sexual reproduction, 1.2 billion years ago.

Shell-forming organisms appeared 500 million years ago.

Vertebrate fish appeared 485 million years ago.

Sharks appeared 363 million years ago.

Viruses appeared 200 million years ago.

Bees appeared 100 million years ago.

Birds appeared 55 million years ago.

Day Six

"And God said: Let the earth bring forth the living creature in its kind, cattle and creeping things, and beasts of the earth, according to their kinds. And it was done. And God made the beasts of the earth according to their kinds, and cattle, and every thing that creepeth on the earth after its kind. And God saw that it was good.

"And He said let us make man to our own image and likeness; and let him have dominion over the fishes of the sea, and the fowls of the air, and the beasts of the whole earth, and every creeping creature that moveth upon the earth. And God created man to His own image, to the image of God He created him. Male and female He created them. And God blessed them saying: increase and multiply, and fill the earth, and subdue it, and rule over the fishes of the sea, and the fowls of the air, and all living creatures that move upon the earth. And God said: Behold I have given you every herb bearing seed upon the earth, and all trees that have in themselves seed of their own kind, to be your

meat. And to all beasts of the earth, and to every fowl of the air, and to all that move upon the earth, and wherein there is life, that they may have to feed upon, and it was so done. And God saw all the things that He had made, and they were very good. And the evening and the morning were the sixth day." (Gen. 1: 24-31)

"And the Lord God formed man of the slime of the earth and breathed into his face the breath of life, and man became a living soul." (Gen. 2: 7)

Commentary:

Mammals appeared about 115 million years ago.

Modern humans, Homo sapiens, appeared about 250 thousand years ago.

Day Seven

"So the heavens and the earth were finished, and all the furniture of them. And on the seventh day God ended His work, which He had made: and he rested on the seventh day from all His work, which He had done. And He blessed the seventh day, and sanctified it: because in it He had rested from all His work which God created and made." (Gen. 2: 1-3)

43

The Garden of Eden

"And the Lord God had planted a paradise of pleasure from the beginning: wherein He placed man whom He had formed. And the Lord God brought forth from the ground all manner of trees, fair to behold, and pleasant to eat of: the tree of life also in the midst of paradise: and the tree of knowledge of good and evil. And a river went out of the place of pleasure to water paradise, which from thence is divided into four heads. The name of the one is Phison: that is it, which compasseth all the land of Hevilath, where gold

groweth. And the gold of that land is very good: there is found bdellium, and the onyx stone. And the name of the second river is Gehon: the same is it compasseth all the land of Ethiopia. And the name of the third river is Tigris: the same passeth along by the Assyrians, and the fourth river is Euphrates." (Gen. 2: 8-14)

Commentary:

Trees appeared about 200 million years ago.

Flowering trees (later fruit trees) appeared about 66 million years ago.

Modern humans first appeared about 250 thousand years ago. They are thought to have originated in Africa, and began to migrate about 150 thousand years ago.

The Garden of Eden must have been very large. If we use the information provided above, one reference point are the two rivers Tigris and Euphrates. Both of these rivers originate in Turkey, pass through Iraq, and empty into the Persian Gulf. The other reference point is Ethiopia. A line can be drawn from southeastern Ethiopia, across the Bab el Mandeb, the strait connecting the Red Sea and the Gulf of Aden-Indian Ocean to the two rivers in Iraq, a distance of 1500 miles.

"And the Lord God took man, and put him in the paradise of pleasure, to dress it, and to keep it. And He commanded him, saying: Of every tree of paradise thou shalt eat, but of the tree of knowledge of good and evil, thou shalt not eat. For in what day soever thou shalt eat of it, thou shalt die the death." (Gen. 2: 15-17)

Commentary:

The tree of good and evil implies this is the source of the distinction between good and evil. Lucifer, before he became Satan, was thought to have been the source of evil. Might not the tree of good and evil have originated from a conversation Satan requested between himself and the Word of God? This conversation could have gone something like this:

Satan: "As angels in heaven, You gave us freedom to choose. Should you not endow this new creature, man, with the same choice?"

The Word: "I have planted the tree of good and evil in the center of the garden of pleasure to give man the choice. You, Satan, are the source of all evil, and the tree springs from you."

> *"And the Lord God said: it is not good for man to be alone: let us make him a help like unto himself. And the Lord God having formed out of the ground all the beasts of the earth, and all the fowls of the air, brought them to Adam to see what he would call them: for whatsoever Adam called any living creature the same is its name. And Adam called all of the beasts by their names, and all the fowls of the air, and all the cattle of the field: but for Adam there was not found a helper like himself. Then the Lord God cast a deep sleep upon Adam: and when he was fast asleep, he took one of his ribs, and filled up flesh for it. And the Lord God built the rib, which he took from Adam, into a woman: and brought her to Adam.*
>
> *"And Adam said: This is bone of my bone, and flesh of my flesh; she shall be called woman because she was taken out of man. Wherefore a man shall leave father and mother, and shall cleave to his wife; and they shall be two in one flesh. And they were both naked, to wit, Adam and his wife: and were not ashamed."* (Gen. 2: 18-25)

Commentary:

Before emergence of the first of modern men, about 250 thousand years ago, there was a longer history of other bipeds such as monkeys, great apes, and gorillas. There were also early hominoids, resembling humans. The most recent were the Neanderthals, which some regard as pre-human. They used fire and tools, but became extinct about 30 thousand years ago.

Man's origin was unique. No other life form compares. God is said to have created man with an immortal soul, and that man is a little below the angels. Man, who may have evolved from earlier hominids (we really don't know), now has a soul, an imperishable spirit like the angels, and is destined to have dominion on the Earth.

The source of woman is clothed in mystery. That modern man has an origin, rather recent in the mists of history, seems conclusive. For sexual propagation to occur there must be cellular meiosis, which developed in unicellular organisms about 1.2 billion years ago. There must also be male and female. The origin of man is plausible. The origin of woman? Unlike angels, who were all created at once, mankind started with one man, and one woman. The story of Eve, in the Garden, seems as good an explanation as any for how the original man and then woman, came about.

Gabriel called the other archangels together to deliver a message: "God our Creator has given me a message for all angels in heaven. Our new role will be the protection and guidance of each human being that comes into existence. Their existence will be different than ours. We were created all at once. Human existence will be generational.

"Humans will begin as small cells of physical matter, similar to the animals, but with the addition by God of an immortal soul. The human soul will be like ours, with intellect, beauty, and freedom of will. Their intellects and beauty of spirit will be inferior to that of angels, and they will be distinct from angels in having a physical body.

"When God has inserted an immortal soul, the human person will receive its existence. At that moment God will provide a guardian angel to each and every human. Guardian angels will remain throughout the lifetime of humans while they remain on Earth.

"God expects interference from Satan and his devils, with attempts to thwart God's plans for the human race. Our role will be to protect and guide, but God has placed a condition upon us, and upon all human beings who are brought into creation: They will be given freedom of will to select God or Satan, and we cannot interfere with this. God has entrusted me with other messages, which are secret and will be divulged only with the passage of time."

44

Satan Emerges

Satan writhed in hell. He was bodied, as were all the evil spirits who entered hell with him. Their bodies were hideous, and unlike any of the animal bodies ever created or evolved upon earth; while in hell, the demons were to be united with these bodies. Satan was huge, far larger than any of the other devils. His was an ugly slithering form, fearful and repulsive for other devils to look upon.

Because of his huge size, Satan was limited to the massive central space in hell and a few of the larger passages. Tunnels leading to smaller recesses extended from the central space in every direction. The immensity of hell is difficult to imagine. It is larger than the star that they had occupied before it imploded into a neutron star. There was no light or heat. Hell's inhabitants were engulfed in total blackness.

Satan seethed with hatred for God. His was an enmity that would not and could not abate. Satan's enmity is eternal. He had said to his devils: "We will fight against God, and thwart His every plan. The new creation has human forms with bodies combined with immortal souls, and created in God's image. Man will be like angels, having an eternal soul, and an intelligence sufficient to become dominant over other life forms on earth, but far inferior to that of angels and devils. Man, created by God, will be our sworn enemy. We will find ways to subjugate man for our purposes, and thus we will upset and bypass God's plans."

While delivering this message, Satan's body shook, and a thick darkened saliva ran down his jowls, adding to the fetid stench that pervaded hell into its most distant recesses. And Satan's eyes showed the totality of his hatred – a hardened fearful visage with glaring, reddened, even fiery eyes that struck paralyzing fear into any onlooker.

Satan was restless. He reminded his listeners that God had allowed him periodic brief sojourns on earth. Soon another journey would begin. He also told of an earlier encounter with the Word of God in the Garden. God had been preparing a paradise for the first human inhabitants, and Satan had mentioned the freedom to choose. "This has been given to the angels, so why should it not be applied to the humans who are to come?" The Word of God had answered that He had planted the tree of the knowledge of good and evil within the garden; and that the tree contained all of the evils that had emanated from Satan. God would forbid humans to eat of the fruit of that tree, but would allow them the freedom to choose.

Satan's time to depart from hell arrived. He prepared like a larval butterfly shedding its chrysalis, or more appropriately, a snake shedding its skin; for Satan would depart from hell as pure spirit, leaving his body behind.

As spirit, he was in the garden in moments, a result of his thought-vision. But the garden was large, encompassing parts of what later would come to be called East Africa and the Middle East, the watersheds of the Tigris and Euphrates rivers, and beyond. He would search this vast area for signs of humans, and for the location of the tree of knowledge of good and evil.

45

The Fall of Man

He found a lone and solitary human, a man; and Satan was present, unseen, when God caused the man to fall into a deep sleep. Then God, quickly and bloodlessly removed a rib from the man and from the rib created a woman, beauteous and wondrous to behold. Satan gazed upon the woman, and heard her called Eve; he then heard the man called Adam. Momentarily Satan was overwhelmed by what he had just seen, but this was transitory; Satan was quick to remind himself that this man and this woman were his sworn enemies.

He heard God say to the man and the woman:

> *"Go forth and propagate. You may eat of the fruit of all the trees in paradise, save one. This is the tree of knowledge of good and evil. You may not eat of the fruit of this tree; if you do, you will die."* (Gen. 2:15)

Satan watched their embrace and with envy watched them copulate. Then he withdrew to hatch further plans. He knew from prior visits to Earth that he was powerless to cause harm to plants, beasts or fowl. He was unable to break a twig from a tree. He supposed that he would also be powerless to cause physical harm to either the man or the woman. There would have to be another way.

The man and the woman appeared to be supremely happy. One day Satan saw the woman near the forbidden tree. She seemed to be curious. Satan realized that he had the power to remain a spirit, but also the power to assume any form he chose. He chose that of a serpent, large, beauteous, intelligent, and able to speak; an animal form that no longer inhabits the Earth.

He slowly slithered up to the woman and began to speak: "I see you have approached the tree. It has beautiful and tasty pome fruit, why don't you try some?" The woman answered: "It is the tree of the knowledge of good and evil; God has forbidden us to eat of its fruit lest we die."

"We all know why God has forbidden it," said the serpent. "It is because you will assume God's power – you will become like God. The apples from the tree are ripe and good. Come, pick and try one." The woman hesitated. She was beguiled – her curiosity and the serpent's soothing words overcame her reluctance. She picked one and ate. At that moment things changed. The serpent disappeared, and she felt different in indescribable ways.

She picked another apple and brought it to Adam. She looked disheveled and ashamed. "Where have you been?" asked Adam.

"I have eaten of the fruit of the forbidden tree," said Eve.

"Why did you do it?" demanded Adam.

"The serpent tricked me," said Eve. "Here Adam, I have brought another of the apples from the forbidden tree for you to eat."

Adam looked for a long time at the apple. It appeared like other fruit in the garden, no more or less appealing than the others. Then he ate of the fruit and was changed. What must have entered Adam's mind before he ate? Was it weakness, knowing it was forbidden, but going along with Eve because of her suggestion? Or might it have been a tinge of something else, a love for Eve, and because of his love, a desire to share in any punishment that would be forthcoming?

Satan's time to stay in the garden was nearly up. It would soon be time for him to return to hell. He realized for the first time that he had won. He had foiled God's plan for the new creation, which placed man at the very top. The Earth, and all that it contained was as nothing if man would no longer be exalted.

Satan did not comprehend what it was to die. This was the sentence bestowed on man if he were to eat the apple. Nothing in prior creation, neither in the angelic realm nor in the universe, contained death. He thought death would be a snuffing out, a change from existence to non-existence, but he did not know. Would it be sudden and complete, like the angels being created all at once? Would the human race be snuffed out? And what then of the Earth, and the other forms of life there?

46

God Responds

"And the eyes of them both were opened: and when they perceived themselves to be naked, they sewed together fig leaves, and made themselves aprons. And when they heard the voice of the Lord God walking in paradise in the afternoon air, Adam and his wife hid themselves from the face of the Lord God, amidst the trees of paradise. And the Lord God called to Adam, and said to him: Where art thou? 'And he said: I heard Thy voice in paradise; and I was afraid, because I was naked, and I hid myself. And He said to him:

And who hath told thee that you wast naked, but that thou hast eaten of the tree whereof I commanded thee that thou shouldst not eat? And Adam said: The woman whom Thou gavest me to be my companion, gave me of the tree, and I did eat. And the Lord God said to the woman: Why hast thou done this? And she answered: The serpent deceived me, and I did eat." (Gen. 3: 7-13)

"And the Lord God said to the serpent: Because thou hast done this thing, thou art cursed among all cattle and beasts of the earth. Upon thy breast shalt thou go, and earth shalt thou eat all the days of thy life. I will put enmity between thee and the woman, and thy seed and her seed: she shall crush thy head, and thou shall lie in wait for her heel." (Gen. 3: 14-15)

"To the woman also He said: I will multiply thy sorrows and thy conceptions. In sorrow shalt thou bring forth children, and thou shall be under thy husband's power, and he shall have dominion over thee. And to Adam He said: Because thou hast harkened to the voice of thy wife, and hast eaten of the tree, whereof I command thee that thou shouldst not eat, cursed is the earth in thy work; with labor and toil shalt thou eat thereof all the days of thy life. Thorns and thistles shall it bring forth to thee; and thou shall eat the herbs of the earth. In the sweat of thy face shalt thou eat bread till thou return to the earth, out of which thou were taken: for dust thou art, and into dust thou shalt return. And Adam called his wife Eve: because she was the wife of all the living." (Gen. 3: 16-20)

"And the Lord made for Adam and his wife, garments of skins, and clothed them. And He said: Behold Adam has become as one of Us, knowing good and evil: now therefore, lest perhaps he put forth his hand, and take also of the tree of life, and eat, and live forever. And the Lord God sent him out of the paradise of pleasure, to till the earth from which he was taken. And he cast out Adam; and placed before the paradise of pleasure Cherubims, and a flaming sword, turning every way, to keep the way of the tree of life." (Gen. 3: 21-24)

As the resounding howls in hell over Satan's victory abated, Satan was struck by a new thought. "What did God mean when He said: I will put enmity between you and the woman, and thy seed and her seed: She shall crush thy head, and thou shall lie in wait for her heel." Satan pondered further: "Who is she? She cannot be Eve. My seed must be my associates now in hell with me. But who, or what is her seed? Then an uneasiness settled upon Satan, a vague feeling of difficulties to come and a discomfort that would not go away.

47

The New Creation

The angels, those in heaven, and the fallen ones in hell, were then exposed to the rapid expansion of a new creation. Angels were created all at once, billions in an instant but eons before any other creation; then came the creation of the universe almost fourteen billion earth years ago. Stars, galaxies, planets, cosmic dusts, gases, and mysterious dark matter all came into existence, and became a major charge and management responsibility for angels.

As we have seen, a breach developed within the angelic fold, which became a rift, and then an irredeemable separation. Two angel bands formed, one in open rebellion against God, the other completely loyal. Satan with billions of demons was cast into hell to be kept there for eternity, together with the evils that Lucifer, now Satan, had spawned.

Before the separation, the angels, all of them, witnessed the beginning of the new creation. Uriel, an archangel, was the first to discover it. Earth, third planet from a medium-sized star, the sun, was different. It was beautiful! Beauty, intrinsic to the angelic nature, was not a feature of the universe as it developed. Spectacular, even awesome, surely, but entirely lacking in the serene beauty that was Earth. The angels were awestruck when Uriel pointed to the blue planet with its swirling white patches of clouds.

After the climactic confrontation, when angels were introduced to the Trinitarian God and the humans that were to come, creation accelerated. Hell with its evil spirits was established. Then came man. We have seen how God placed the first man and woman into Eden, a vast expanse, a garden of pleasure. Then came the fall of man with the introduction of evil by Satan.

Two hundred and fifty thousand years (from the beginning of the human race, until these words are written), is a remarkably brief span when contrasted with the billions of years that elapsed from the creation of angels and the beginning of the universe. Oddly, this new creation is centered on earth, perhaps the only site in the vast universe for it to unfold (though we are unsure of this).

The angels, witnesses to this rapid development, marveled at this new activity of God. Creator God now interacted with human creatures – created a little lower than angels – on numerous occasions, sometimes alone, and at other times accompanied by angels.

Man had to be special for all of this involvement by God. Angels, both those in heaven and the fallen ones in hell, would follow these events closely, fascinated by them.

48

The Storytellers

Now, the storytellers came out in force. There began a varied and detailed series of stories carried by oral tradition from one generation to the next. These stories, from multiple sources, wove an unbroken sequence from the garden to the present. They have been collected as Holy Scripture, divided into Old and New Testaments.

Do we know who these storytellers were? Not really. Do they accurately keep track of time? Maybe, but probably not in the same way that we might. For instance, it is commonplace to list the ages of the descendants of Adam and beyond as seven to nine hundred years. We should note that these early storytellers likely used a lunar circuit as a year – after all, this was a time before agriculture and awareness of growing seasons. They would be much more attuned to the lunar cycle. Allowing this as an interpretation would translate 700 to 900 "lunar" years, to 54 to 69 "solar" years; more in keeping with the actual length of human life.

When did human creation start? Some claim a precise date such as 3950 BC, and date all human activity from that time onwards. This is at odds with scientific observation, which dates the beginning of the universe at nearly fourteen billion years ago, and the beginning of the human race at about two hundred fifty thousand years ago. It seems likely that the storytellers have gotten the numbers wrong rather than science; storytelling, by its nature, with oral transmission from one generation to the next, would be expected to be imprecise. Storytellers could easily miss names of descendants, leaving out many generations while attempting to connect the lines from past to present. This seems a plausible explanation for the difference.

As significant figures in the saga of humankind approach more modern times, the numbers become more precise. The Julian calendar, introduced by Julius Caesar in 47 BC, was used until 1582 AD, when Pope Gregory XIII introduced the Gregorian calendar. The division between Old and New was set at what was then considered the year of the birth of Jesus Christ; the Old is counted backwards and referred to as "before Christ" or BC; while the New counts forward, "after Christ" or Anno Domini, AD.

Before Abraham, the time line gets fuzzy. Abraham probably was born around 2000 BC, Moses around 1576 BC, David around 1060 BC, and the destruction of the first temple around 588 BC. The beginning of Paul the Apostle's ministry was around 37 AD, and the destruction of the second temple was about 70 AD.

The stories, from very old to new times, depict struggle. If evil began with Lucifer, and was brought by Satan to humankind, first as sin, and then as death, the recurring themes throughout are: first, man's struggle with evil, especially sin; and second, God's continuous interaction with man. Many stories of these struggles are told in the Bible

49

The Garden of Eden to Noah

The creation of the human race, beginning with one man, and one woman, stands as one of the great epic events in all of history. It is interesting to view the interactions of God with man as this early phase is developing. God is clearly in the driver's seat. He is the protagonist in the action from Adam to Noah.

And the Lord God formed man from the slime of the earth and breathed into his face life and a soul. Then God laid out a vast space, the Garden of Eden, for the first man, Adam, to roam amongst the animals and trees, eating of the fruit of all except the tree of knowledge of good and evil. Presumably, Adam could eat of the other major tree, the tree of everlasting life, since Adam had been given an immortal soul designated for everlasting life, with God's initial intent that Adam's body would also not perish. Adam, watching the animals as pairs, grew lonely, and asked God for a soul mate. God responded by putting Adam into a deep sleep, and then performed the first surgery, a rapid and bloodless removal of one of Adam's rib to form the first woman, Eve.

First bliss, then the fall. Eve ate of the forbidden fruit prompted by the trickery of Satan and then enjoined Adam to do likewise. God's response was thunderous. Death of the body. Expulsion from the garden so as not to allow them to again eat of the tree of everlasting life. God decreed toil, sweat, hardship, and bearing children in pain henceforth, for all mankind.

Then in an act of caring and love, God sewed clothing for each from animal skins, presumably because the fig leaves would not last. Then in a statement directed to Adam, Eve, and Satan, God gave a most remarkable pronouncement: That He would place enmity between the woman and the serpent, and the woman's seed and the serpent's seed, and that the heel of a woman would crush the head of the serpent (presumably at a time in the future). Angels were then placed around the Garden to keep out anyone who might, in the future, venture near.

The story of Eve's first two sons came next. Abel followed Cain; Cain grew into husbandry, while for Abel it was as a shepherd. They each presented gifts to God; Cain gave fruits from the trees, while Abel presented animals, presumably slaughtered, as fat from the animals is mentioned. God was welcoming of Abel's gift, but less so of Cain's. One possible explanation is that God was equally pleased, but that Cain felt that he should have received the greater praise. Cain grew jealous and angry, and persuaded his brother to accompany him out to the field; it was there that Cain killed Abel. God pronounced a curse upon Cain, and put a mysterious mark on him, so that others would not in the future kill him. God was repulsed by the three evils manifested by Cain: envy, anger and murder, and punished Cain subsequently. The case was made that all evil has its source with Lucifer. Satan's enticement of Eve to eat the forbidden fruit would also support this. The implantation of evil by Satan through Eve, and then Adam would potentially affect the entire human race.

During Noah's time God found that wickedness pervaded the earth. Wickedness must have been a mixture of evils that saturated a given group and became so ingrained that a return to goodness was impossible. Remember that God created man with a free will to choose between good and evil; therefore God could not directly interfere with each person's freedom to choose. God was in a bind. At one point, as the story unfolds, God, in remorse, considers destroying the entire human race, and all life forms on the earth.

God found one, and only one, person – Noah – and only one family – the family of Noah – worth saving. God ordered Noah to build the ark. God even laid out the dimensions, and the building materials: timbered planks, and pitch inside and out. When completed, God ordered Noah to go aboard with his immediate and extended family, and also male and female pairs of all the animals and birds, and creeping things on the earth. Everyone who has read these passages sees the impossibility of all of these creatures being crowded into a space three hundred cubits long, fifty cubits wide, and thirty cubits high (a cubit is the distance from finger tips to elbow, about eighteen inches). Remember, the storytellers were not versed at numbers, and they may have easily embellished the number of animal pairs that were put aboard.

The story of the deluge may have a counterpart discovered

from scientific study. As the last ice age, with thick ice covering Europe and Asia, began to recede, the seas rose. The large land-locked inland sea of fresh water, the Black Sea, was affected. Rising Mediterranean waters began to lap across the sill of the Bosphorus, spilling into the Black Sea. With further melting, rivers flowing into the Black Sea reversed course, and flowed into the Baltic Sea.

With time and evaporation, the waters in the Black Sea receded. Science is generally agreed that these events have happened. Then two different processes are invoked to explain what happened next. One, the oscillating theory, postulates a gentle swishing back and forth between the Mediterranean and the Black Sea, beginning about thirty thousand years ago, gradually opened a permanent channel connecting the Mediterranean Sea to the Black Sea.

The other theory is a cataclysmic flood that occurred about 5600 BC. Rising Mediterranean Sea waters breached the rocky sill of the Bosphorus and caused a massive flood of waters into the Black Sea. The flood lasted three hundred days. Sixty thousand square miles of land were flooded. Ten cubic miles of water flowed each day, more than two hundred times the flow over Niagara Falls. The shores of the Black Sea were extended northward and eastward; likewise, anything afloat on the Black Sea would have been carried in the same direction.

Armenia is mentioned as the landing place of the Ark. Current Armenia lies on the eastern border of Turkey, and through history that border has fluctuated from east to west. Current Armenia lies a short distance east of the Black Sea. The Tigris River, mentioned in the scriptural story, originates in eastern Turkey, west of Armenia. Mount Ararat lies in eastern Turkey near the Armenian border, and has been regarded for centuries, by some, as the landing site of the ark. This, while speculative, does much to suggest that the deluge in scripture, and the flood of waters from the Mediterranean to the Black Sea, were one and the same.

As flood waters abated, and the ark settled, Noah sent the raven, which did not return, and then sent the dove twice. The second time the dove returned with a branch from an olive tree showing green leaves. This implies that the deluge did not cover the entire earth, but only a large portion. The mysterious and still unanswered question is that of the ark itself. If indeed it was commanded by God to be built to provide a safe haven for Noah, his family, and his animals, the timing had to be perfect for its building and provisioning, to have all on board before the rains came or the Mediterranean Sea began its catastrophic flood.

50

Noah to Abraham

The epic journey from Adam to Noah, and thence to Abraham continues. The story of Abraham is rich in detail; the narrative touches many places, and is seeped in dramatic events. As the human story continues, it has the feeling of a journey with rest periods reclining on richly ornate Persian rugs within the elaborate tent structures of Abraham's time (as compared to the sand floors and rude shelters during the time from Adam to Noah).

God continues to interact with his people in a direct and personal way. He changes the names of favored personages: Abram becomes Abraham, and Sarai becomes Sara. He announces a pregnancy for Sara at her advanced age of ninety years, and Sara, when by herself, laughs. This is not a direct pregnancy by God; Abraham is the father, but Abraham is ten years older than Sara, and he also laughs; not a laugh of ridicule against God, but rather, a chuckle of incredulity. Abraham never loses faith in his God.

Sin is a concept developed in the Abraham stories in a more detailed manner than previously. Wickedness, as with the Sodom and Gomorrha stories, is a level of sinfulness taken to a new level. The sin-filled men of Sodom approach Lot, who lives in the city, in a threatening way, demanding that the two men (visiting angels) be placed outside of Lot's house to be sexually abused by the sinful mob. Lot then offers his two daughters in their stead, knowing they will be sexually ravished. In a piteous way, that speaks abundantly about the bonds of hospitality; Lot begs that the two men be spared. All are saved when an angel blinds the sinful men so that, having threatened to break down Lot's door, they can no longer find the door opener.

The two angels announce to Lot that he, his wife, and the two daughters need to get away fast and not look back, because they were sent by God to destroy Sodom and the neighboring sinful city, Gomorrha. From thence, the story is familiar; Lot and his daughters escape and make it to a cave, while Lot's wife looks back and is turned into a pillar of salt.

Lot and his daughters are in the cave after the destruction of the two cities, and Lot's daughters concoct a sinful dalliance. They plot to get Lot drunk with wine, and then each sleeps with him on different nights to conceive, in order to preserve Lot's seed (he was old). Both did conceive and added to Lot's lineage. Perhaps the girls felt justified in doing this, however sinful, as stated in the storied account.

Why, one should ask, was the sin of Sodom so reprehensible as to lead to total destruction of the city and all of its inhabitants, whereas God tolerated the sin of the daughters? Perhaps the nature of the threatening mob outside of Lot's door offers an explanation. For those sinful men, sin was so ingrained that they could not be deterred or changed. This was also implicit in an earlier conversation between Abraham and God, involving whether there were even ten just men living in the city, and whether God was willing to spare the city on those persons' account (God would have been willing – Gen.18: 24-33).

There is also the fascinating story of Ismael and Isaac. Ismael was born to the servant girl and Abraham at Sara's insistence, but then Isaac is born later to Sara, as foretold by the angel. Sara speaks to Abraham, and wants Ismael and his mother sent away. This troubles Abraham, but God again intervenes, and says that the lineage will be with Isaac and that Abraham should go along with Sara's request. Abraham gives bread and a jug of water to Hagar, Ismael's mother, and then sends them on their way.

At Sara's insistence, Ismael and his mother Hagar are expelled, driven out into the desert, presumably to die, but God saves both with the promise that Ismael shall establish a great nation (Gen. 21: 17-21). This later is to become the nation of the Arabic peoples, leading eventually to the religion of Islam.

51

Abraham to Isaac and Ismael, Jacob and Esau

The scriptures, starting with the initial storytellers, have lead us on a path from our earliest parents to a major jumping-off time in social-religious development. Despite weaknesses in keeping accurate track of numbers, such as when life started, and the length of life of participants, the storytellers have remained true, providing a pathway leading from earliest times to this major branching point.

These are fascinating stories. They trace lineages, weakly from Adam to Noah, more strongly from Noah to Abraham, and strongest from Abraham to Jacob.

Sinfulness is rife. None of the principal players are seen to be free of sin. Then we see the two great responses of God to unbridled sin: the flood, and the destruction of Sodom and Gomorrha. It is important for us to ponder the difference. Why does God resist punishing all the principals who have sinned, while destroying all of those involved in the above-mentioned two disasters? The difference seems to reside in one's response to committed sin. Often a sin is committed to enhance a future opportunity, such as Jacob's deceit of his father Isaac to receive the blessing and inheritance over the elder son Esau. Principals, including Jacob in this example, seem to be remorseful of their sins afterwards. Maybe this is the key; remorse, with a need to repent after committing sin, compared with an unwillingness to be remorseful and repent.

The branching point, clearly, and almost universally agreed upon in our modern times, is the epoch that plays out from Abraham to Jacob. Jacob's name is changed to Israel, and Israel (Jacob) becomes the father of the Judaic religion and the nation of Israel. The two elder sons provide an interesting background – Ismael was the elder son of Abraham and Esau was the elder son of Isaac. Both elder sons were denied the favored blessing and inheritance from their fathers as a result of deceit and trickery. Some interpret this as being acts of God – that God preferred those chosen, despite the trickery. This seems a weak argument: God could have worked the desired outcome without the deceit. The contrary argument: God allows complete freedom in human action. God does not interfere with the human freedom to choose.

And yet, God still does enter the fray. After human decisions are made, He sends an angel to rescue Ismael and his mother, and promises to make a great nation of Ismael and his descendants. Esau later marries a daughter of Ismael. This nation and their descendants are the progenitors of the Arabs, and later, the founders of their predominant religion, Islam.

Judaism, the religion of the nation of Israel, later gives rise to the religion of Christianity. Thus, the three great monotheistic religions: Judaism, Christianity, and Islam, stem directly from Abraham; all three of these religions reverently refer to "Father Abraham." Abraham thus becomes the forebear of all three.

52

Jacob to Moses

Prior to the Red Sea crossing there were a series of encounters between Moses and a very stubborn Pharaoh. Moses, during each of these encounters, acted at the express command of God. When Pharaoh asked for signs before he would consider releasing the Israelites, there were a remarkable series, including: turning rods into serpents, turning surface water to blood, covering the land of Egypt with a superabundance of frogs, then of flying insects, sickness of livestock, a plague of locusts, three days of complete darkness, and a plague of hail.

Pharaoh resisted each of these signs, until the final sign was given before their release, and this was a declaration before Pharaoh that at midnight all of the firstborn of men and beasts, throughout the land of Egypt, including Pharaoh's oldest son, would be struck dead. Pharaoh agreed to release the Israelites, with their possessions and livestock, only after this happened. The Israelites had protected themselves by sprinkling the blood of sacrificial lambs on the upright posts and transoms of their doors.

It seems amazing that nowhere in Egyptian literature or storytelling do we find descriptions to support those events. Perhaps they were proscribed by a still stubborn, and afterwards revengeful Pharaoh. It is also possible that these stories might be found in the future in still undecipherable hieroglyphs.

Again, the frequent and close association of God and His angels with man is seen; this is in sharp contrast to the near total lack of contact God had with His angels prior to the angelic rift and banishment to hell of Satan and his minions.

53

Moses to David

Angels were absorbed in the events during the life of David: his anointing as the chosen one of God by Samuel, and the dramatic outcome during the battle with Goliath, but especially with David's prophetic words as he lay dying. This man David, who grew up in Bethlehem, tells of a future Christ of the God of Jacob. Who might this be? Would he be descended from David, God's chosen one? And what of the word spoken by God to Satan in the garden: "I will put enmity between you and the woman … she shall crush thy head, and thy shall lie in wait for her heel."

None of the angels knew the answers to these prophetic statements. One angel, the archangel Gabriel, might have had an inkling, but even Gabriel did not know.

The devils in hell were tortured anew, and railed against God and man, their eternal enemies. Satan in particular, suffered terrible torment and consternation. This was for Satan a recurring wound that would not heal, a pain that would not leave.

The angels were captivated. They were used to long stretches of time elapsing as if they were moments. Now these celestial beings, in possession of powerful intellects and seemingly able to predict events into the future, were nonetheless dumbfounded.

For billions of earth years they had managed the developing universe. They managed to maintain the balance of forces within this expanding universe. They were surprised by the implosion of their star, containing the infernal antimatter machine, leaving a mass of neutrons so dense and with such an intense gravitational field, that energy, including light, could not escape; but their surprise was very brief - they quickly perceived all that had happened.

They dealt with the revolt of Lucifer and his defiant angels, and with the dramatic banishment of those angels to a place called hell. They also were aware of the new creation, of beautiful planet Earth, of its atmosphere, seas and land. They were awestruck as life emerged and developed in a relatively short period of time – a few millions of years from the start of unicellular life forms, followed by plants, animals, and then man. Man had existed for a very brief two hundred and fifty thousand years.

They recognized man as special in the new creation. God interacted repeatedly with man, created man with an imperishable soul, with freedom to choose, and with an intellect, inferior to the intellect possessed by angels, but nonetheless, an intellect. Although inferior to angels, man was also different. Angels came into existence all at once. They would continue forever, but new angels would not be formed. Man was generational. From a first man and woman, a series of generations would occur. The expansion was exponential, thus allowing a rapid increase over relatively few generations.

Angels, those sublimely happy with God in heaven, and those fallen ones, now called devils wallowing in hell, watched in fascination the expansion of the human race. They followed the storytellers, aware of the events being revealed, but angels also knew of the weaknesses men possessed in retelling these events. Angels knew all of the books of Holy Scripture even better than humans. They had formable intellects, memories with complete and instantaneous recall, and amazing abilities to link together all of the details.

There was God in the Garden with man, man free to choose; and Satan, corrupting the first woman, tempting her to eat of the forbidden fruit from the tree that would usher in sin and bring death to man. God knew that the evil of sin emanated from Satan and not from man. Accordingly, He, God would stand by man, providing an eventual rescue. And what was the meaning of the statement that the heel of the woman would crush Satan's head? Satan pondered this constantly, in dread, as God had foretold in the Garden.

Then there was the story of man's journey from the garden to Abraham, interrupted, uneven, and including the spectacular flood. God gives to Noah a covenant, a long-standing promise, that the rainbow will be a sign that a flood would never again bring destruction to the human race. Angels marveled at God's interaction with man. God veers! The immutable God varies, from His thought of abolishing the human race before the flood, and again before the destruction of Sodom and Gomorrha, to relenting after His interactions with Noah, and with Abraham.

Man, the inferior, appears to have God's favor. How is it that this inferior being can elicit such a result? And it is not only the occasions of the flood, and the destruction of the two cities: it becomes ongoing. God shapes the course! He anoints a series of persons: Abraham, Isaac, and Jacob. He changes peoples' names, such as Jacob to Israel, allowing a person to become a nation! He then establishes a person, David, as the anointed one, the one that would lead to an inheritance. David's progeny would lead to a rescue. But what kind of a rescue? David was sinful. What then enabled David to become first of the line that would lead to a rescue? What was it about sin that seemed so central? Sin had the capacity to ensnare every human who had ever lived. Angels wondered about this. They were aware of the angelic rift - once rebellion was attempted by Lucifer and his minions, they were banished from heaven forever. But why not man? Satan had confronted God by subverting man's freedom to choose, and thereby had inserted sin into human creation. Why had God not banished mankind to hell, as He had Satan? The angels, those in heaven, and the fallen ones in hell, continued to be puzzled by this.

Then there was the line of prophets. The predictors, following David, spoke in signs of a coming rescue by a Savior. The Psalms, beautiful songs and poems, give a series of these signs. A rescuer coming from God. A rescuer to be born in Bethlehem, the city of David. A rescuer-son, born of a virgin. A rescuer uncomely, not easily recognized by others, and one who would suffer and be unjustly killed, himself innocent, to atone for the sins of all of the human race. How can one death remove the stain of sin from all the men who had sinned? The angels would remain mystified.

54

Limbo

Angels, with the start of the new creation, were given a new mandate by God. The earlier mandate had been to manage the development of the expanding universe. The new mandate was to protect man from Satan's menace, while still allowing man the freedom to choose. Humans could be tempted and drawn toward evil, but angels were not allowed by God to interfere with man's freedom to choose.

Man died – a situation, at first, that was completely new to angels; and yet, man did not die. There was the separation of the imperishable soul from the dead body. What a strange situation faced by the angels! Angels saw the dissolution of the body as it became elements that would return to the earth, a process shared by plants and animals. But what to do with the soul of man? Angels were given the role of shepherding man during life; but life of the soul continued.

Then there was sin. Angels knew that all men inherited, from their first parents, a sullying of their souls, reflecting the original sin of the first man and woman. Furthermore, humans at some time during their earthly lives were sinful. What could angels do? They knew that heaven was closed to sinful men, and that all men were sinful.

Angels were informed that a new and different place had been prepared by God, a place where the souls of men would dwell, not on earth, and not in heaven. A place without pain or suffering. A place of waiting, of longing, of expectation. A place without fulfillment, and without happiness. This place, a limbo, became a holding place for the souls of all humans who had ever lived, and all who were to live in the future. Angels would have a role in carrying these souls from the place of death of the body, to this holding place.

55

Epilogue

What to make of all of this? Angels in heaven, and demons in hell wondered, but they did not know. For once, perhaps for the first time during all of creation, the angelic nature did not have an answer.

Creator God had again demonstrated to angels that He is a God of surprises. Angels and men would not have long to wait. They would soon know!

THE BROTHERS

A Novella

1

Prologue

As a young doctor, I was a Medical Officer with the United States Public Health Service. Seven of those years were spent in the South, three in Claxton, Georgia, two in Chapel Hill, North Carolina, and two in New Orleans, Louisiana. Those were the years 1959 through 1966. They were turbulent times; the landmark Civil Rights Law was signed by President Lyndon Johnson in 1964.

My duties included the design and implementation of an epidemiological field study of cardiovascular disease involving the examination and testing of thousands of Negro and White subjects living in Claxton and surrounding areas. I use the term Negro, with profound respect. It was the name employed then to identify persons now called African American; it was also the name used in the research publications and the medical reports presenting the results of our studies, which were to follow.

My family was totally immersed in the fascinating culture of small town Claxton, and rural Georgia. Two of our children were born at the Fort Stewart Army Hospital just north of Claxton. Many of the events described in the stories to follow were experienced by my family and me. Are these stories real, or are they fictitious? I do not want you, dear reader, to have a clear answer to this question now; rather, I hope that you have an enjoyable read. You will have an answer to this question before you have finished.

2

A Summer Night in Georgia

Buster was on his way home. He walked along the dirt road at two-thirty in the morning, feeling warm inside and comfortable. Outside, the night air was sweltering. The crickets were chirping, the males sending mating signals to attract waiting females. The moon was out making visible his surroundings. As he walked, the dust that kicked up swirled, a mixture of red clay and sand that pervaded the coastal plane of Georgia where he lived and where his family had resided for generations.

As a young Negro man growing up in the south, he had never

been far from home. He had not seen the ocean, fifty miles east, nor been to Florida, fifty miles to the south. It was the summer of 1923; the war in Europe had ended five years earlier, and an economic boom was underway in the country, but had not yet reached rural Georgia where Buster lived.

During much of the year Buster hired on with any of a number of sharecroppers, receiving day wages for helping with the plowing, planting and harvesting of the crops on the owner's lands. He was considered reliable and was able to do the heavy work required on a farm, except for Mondays, when he was often under the weather from a weekend of heavy drinking.

Buster regarded the weekend as his special time. From Friday afternoon until late Sunday or early Monday morning, he was usually away with friends drinking and gambling. His wife Bessie did virtually all of the work at home while caring for their young son Ben and working as a "nanny" for white folks residing uptown.

This night was in the middle of the week, and he was returning from one of his frequent forays to gamble with his friends, mostly losing some or all of his weekly wages, or cavorting with one of several of his women friends. Now he was on the way home.

The road led to a cluster of shed-like houses called "the quarters". This is where he and most of the other "colored" lived in this small southern town. The houses – really just huts – were small, constructed of whatever lumber and galvanized sheet metal could be found. Running water was obtained from a standpipe with a faucet that served several houses. The toilet was an outdoor privy. Most had a small stove for winter heat and for cooking. Buster's house was a little larger. His grandparents and parents had built the house, which contained wooden steps leading up to a front porch.

Buster made the left turn leading into the quarters. His house was down the road on the right. He was feeling tired. Tomorrow would be a full day of work on the farm. He was looking forward to sleeping the rest of the night through.

Soon he was in front of his house. He started to climb the stairs. It was at that instant that he saw his wife Bessie sitting on the porch in a rocking chair and his four-year-old son stepping from the shadows to run and meet him. "Stay back, baby," Bessie said in a loud and menacing voice, catching the little one with her left elbow and throwing him back. At that moment, Buster saw the barrel of the twelve-gauge shotgun swing about and point straight at him. "Don't," he said, as two loud explosions occurred. The first struck him in the center of the chest, while the second struck his neck and lower face.

"Don't," was Buster's last word. His death was instantaneous.

Bessie laid the shotgun down on the porch, and then grabbed and clung to her son. He screamed, "Mama, mama" while he sobbed, clinging to his mother, the tears forming rivulets that cleared the dust in streaks from his small face. Bessie sat motionless, without speaking or crying.

Sheriff Tom DeLoach pulled into the quarters in his sheriff's car. He saw no need to turn on the blinking lights or the alarm. His was an old car, but one of the newest in this small southern town. The county lacked the money to give him more than two deputies. A new car would come every eight to ten years, depending on usage.

The sheriff knew the quarters well, and also almost everyone who lived there. He had received a telephone report of a shooting at Buster McClellan's house. He knew Buster and Bessie, and as he pulled up he saw a body sprawled below the steps and Bessie sitting on the porch. A small crowd had gathered.

Sheriff Tom looked at the body and thought it was Buster, but could not be sure; two large gaping wounds on the front of the body and lower half of the face made identification difficult. He stepped over the body while climbing the steps to the porch.

Bessie sat stone-faced in the rocker. MayBelle, Bessie's sister, was in the background with Ben, Bessie's son. Ben stood erect and had stopped crying. Marks covered both cheeks where tears had washed away the dust. He was stone-faced like his mother, and stood straight without moving.

"What happened, Bessie?" Sheriff Tom asked. He saw the shotgun lying on the porch to the right of Bessie's rocker, and knew the answer to his question without asking.

"I shot Buster," she answered clearly, but in a monotone.

"Why, Bessie?" the sheriff asked.

"He beats me and Ben. I can put up with his beating me, but he won't beat my baby no more." She said this in a slow deliberate manner, while showing no emotion, except a forlorn expression of sadness. The sheriff knew of Buster's gambling and carousing with bad company. He was also aware that Bessie had complained in the past of Buster beating her and their son Ben.

"Bessie," Sheriff Tom said, "I'll take the shotgun, but see no reason to take you to jail. You stay here with MayBelle and little Ben. Stay in the quarters. Do not leave town; it will go very bad for you if you do. Doctor Roger Sales is the county medical examiner. I will call him – stay here until he arrives. He will see that the body is removed. The county will also require an autopsy and a hearing. You will be called to make a statement then."

The call to the medical examiner was placed. Sheriff Tom waited in his patrol car until Dr. Roger arrived. The doctor practiced medicine during the day in this town of two thousand, and also acted as the county medical examiner, a formality that required very little of his time. He had been awakened by the sheriff's call, and said he would be right over. Tom knew Dr. Roger and knew him to be dependable. Shortly after his arrival, the body was taken to a private mortuary.

Sheriff Tom stood in the room while the autopsy was performed. Dr. Roger commented on the two large frontal wounds. The lower was to the chest, partially taking away ribs, lungs, and heart, and exposing the backbone. The doctor mentioned that a shotgun blast at very close range with large buckshot does this, something Sheriff Tom knew very well. The second wound was a little higher. Sheriff Tom suspected this was the second shot, slightly higher because of the recoil from the first shot. The brunt of the shot was at the level of the upper chest and shoulders. The front of the neck and lower jaw had been taken off with the vertebral column showing. "I will send a deputy and a clerk up to obtain fingerprints," said Sheriff Tom.

After Buster's internment, a hearing was held before the local judge, with the county prosecutor, Sheriff Tom, Bessie, and her sister MayBelle present. Bessie was asked questions by the prosecutor and gave her answers. There was no other attorney present. Then Bessie and MayBelle were asked to wait in an adjoining room.

"What do you think, Tom?" the prosecutor asked.

Sheriff Tom provided details of a family with long-term difficulties. Buster was a day laborer primarily employed by farm work. He was also a philanderer and gambled away his wages. Bessie put up with this for a number of years, but then Buster began to beat Bessie and their son, Ben. As Bessie acknowledged, she could tolerate herself being beaten, but not her son. She had come out onto the porch with the shotgun to await Buster's return. Sheriff Tom finished by saying, "The rest you know. Bessie is a good person. She has lived in the quarters all of her life, and has never had a problem with the law."

The prosecutor then turned to the judge. "I don't see a need to prosecute this case. It appears clear that this is justifiable homicide. You could even call it a homicide in self-defense. Tom, is this the way you see it?"

Sheriff Tom nodded, then said, "I was hoping that you would see it that way." They both then turned to the judge who nodded, folded the report, and left the bench.

Sheriff Tom called Bessie and MayBelle into the chamber. "Bessie," he intoned, "the prosecutor and the judge have closed the case. You will not be prosecuted. They have called this justifiable homicide; in other words, you were within your rights to do what you did. Go home now, and raise your son Ben to make you proud of him."

For the first time since the shooting, tears formed in Bessie's eyes, and spilled over to run down her cheeks. She thanked Sheriff Tom before departing with her sister MayBelle.

3

Growing Up

From the outside, the quarters looked like a run-down and shabby place to live. These were ramshackle houses that often resembled sheds. There were no sidewalks or paved streets. About six hundred "colored" Negro men, women and children lived there. They were segregated from white neighborhoods, but not isolated. The quarters was not a ghetto, in the sense of being enclosed. Negroes of all ages roamed the streets and sidewalks outside of the quarters to work and shop.

From inside, the quarters housed families that looked after

one another. Following the shooting, people living in the quarter flocked to Bessie's support. Food was provided. Women, especially women, provided an ongoing presence of comfort and emotional support. Even weeks afterward, neighbors kept a close eye on Bessie and her son. Eventually things returned to normal.

Bessie worked as a "nanny" for several white families, and was paid the standard wage of fifty cents an hour. She had worked for families since before the shooting, and was deeply loved and respected by them. As is so typical of small towns and rural areas, everyone knew nearly everyone else. The families knew in detail the events surrounding the shooting, understood Bessie's role, and accepted the sheriff's and prosecutor's verdict without recrimination.

Bessie helped with the cooking, laundering, and cleaning. She especially loved caring for the children, whether changing diapers, seeing older children off to school with a sack lunch, or comforting the little ones when they were ailing or downtrodden. She had a special grace and tact when with her employers. She knew what to do and when to do it, and did not require instructions; intuitively she knew what was required.

She did the grocery shopping, often taking one of the children along; the grocer would add the amount to the family's running account. The children learned early on that there would be no "shenanigans" with Bessie. She was gentle but firm, and allowed no misbehavior or disrespect. And, of course, the children loved her.

Bessie would rise very early in the morning and make Ben's breakfast. Typically this consisted of mixing a little flour and water to make a batter and frying this as a large flat cake, which was then transferred to the table where Ben, who was washed, combed, and dressed, sat waiting. This was then layered with molasses. After breakfast Bessie would drop Ben off at MayBelle's house, where he would be cared for while Bessie walked to her work as a nanny.

On Sunday, when she was not working, Bessie took Ben to the colored Baptist church for services. Ben did not, at first, understand the readings or sermons, but the communal singing enthralled him. His mother Bessie had a deep and resonant voice, as did many of the others. The rich and vibrant singing of Negro spiritual songs instilled in him a love of music that became lifelong.

Ben started school at age six. This was in a small building, a school for Negro children. His teacher was a lot like his mama, strong and caring but strict, with no misbehavior tolerated. As the years progressed, he learned to read and write, became proficient with numbers, and learned to speak in front of the class. It was an ample schooling, but without frills. He was a good student, not outstanding, but above average.

4

Summer Work

From the age of six, Ben worked in the summertime. This was fieldwork with white or Negro sharecroppers. As a small child he would help with the weeding, and eventually, as he grew older, the harvesting of crops.

Once he was able to do heavier work, Bessie arranged for him to work during the summer for Rufus McDonald, an elderly Negro owner of a small farm. Rufus was tall, lean and strict. He didn't say much, chewed tobacco, and farmed a field of sugar cane.

The cane was allowed to grow and ripen, and then was cut,

stripped and made ready for making molasses, a local dietary staple. Most was sold locally, while the rest was sold at a more distant market, and at a favorable price.

There was much to do on the farm before the harvest. Ben was taught the care of the single mule on the farm. During the spring the mule was hitched to a plow to make rows for the cane to be planted, while after harvest, the mule was used to power the grinding of the cane.

Ben was taught how to feed and water the mule, how to curry, and how to clean out the small stable where the mule was kept; he was also taught how to use the various hitches needed. There was a saddle, used for riding, and Ben learned how to both saddle and ride. Then there were the harnesses. One was for carrying loads on the mule's back, and another for hitching to a wagon. There were harnesses for plowing and a special harness for grinding the sugar cane.

Ben learned quickly,and mastered all of these skills in a short time. He spent time with Rufus, listening as he talked and realizing that he could talk a lot once he got to know you. He learned from Rufus that mules were smarter and more sure-footed than horses, and related situations where a mule could do things that horses couldn't.

"Have you ever thought of a name for your mule?" asked Ben.

"Sure," answered Rufus, as he spit from a quid of moistened tobacco under his lower lip. "He has a name. I call him Sam. He will answer to me when I call his name. I dunno if Sam will answer to any one other than me." Ben spent the rest of the summer trying to get Sam to answer his call.

The cane ripened, and was now ready for harvest. Rufus showed Ben how to cut the stalks down low, close to the ground, while teaching him to be on the watch for snakes. He said that snakes liked the shade provided by the cane, and that most of the snakes were harmless, since they were mostly bull snakes. "They are large, about six feet long," Rufus said. "Don't try to kill one, they help by eating rats and mice." Then Rufus talked about other snakes.

"It's rare to see a rattler, but we do have 'em. They are smaller than bull snakes, but stay away from them – they're poisonous. The real rare ones are the cotton mouths. They are bigger than rattlers, and they like to stay near water, but sometimes we find 'em in the fields after a heavy rain. They're also poisonous, so be careful." Rufus then explained the ways to tell these snakes apart as he spit a stream of tobacco juice out onto the red clay and sandy soil. Ben saw the small cloud of dust rise as the stream struck the ground.

Ben took the heavy knife resembling a machete and started down one row cutting the cane. It was heavy and hard work. Each cane had to be stripped of leaves and the loose outer coating, and then stacked in a bundle. When several bundles had been assembled, they were carried to the press.

Grinding the cane stalks involved a vertical shaft, used for the grinding, that had to be continuously turned. Sam was needed to provide the power. A long pole was used with the thin and longer end used for harnessing Sam. The short thicker end was a counterweight, and the balance point of the pole was fastened to the vertical shaft. Once begun by Rufus, Sam would keep walking round and round in a circle without stopping – all day long if needed – to provide power to the central shaft. Sam was accustomed to this. Rufus had trained Sam well.

While Sam walked and turned the central shaft, Ben would feed stalks of cane, one or two at a time, onto a trough to be pushed onto the shaft where they were ground into a pulp, allowing a thin clear liquid to drain onto a conduit that spilled into a large metal tray. That tray was heated, bringing the liquid to a slow boil. Gradually the volume was reduced, and the color changed to a dark brown; this, the syrup, became thicker, and at a proper time, at least proper to a trained eye, it was poured out as the completed product, molasses.

Ben's wages were slim – just one or two dollars a day. Sometimes he was given a jar of molasses to take home to his mama.

Ben continued to work for Rufus, long summers at a time, between school years. He had become a valued helper for Rufus; in return, Ben had learned about how to live life from Rufus, and be happy and independent as well. Honesty and hard work were the key. Thrift, another valuable lesson, he learned from his mama. His wages, though meager, were kept in an empty molasses jar; he spent none of these on himself. There were other dividends. These came gradually and over the course of years. Ben had grown tall, six foot two, and now he was filling out, becoming muscular and strong. His weight, when leaving high school, was two hundred twenty pounds.

Over the years while Ben was growing up, he and his mother Bessie frequently talked about his future. He loved school, was a model student, and received consistently good grades. He was interested in American history, especially Negro history. Ben had also become well versed in English, literature, music, writing and speaking, with a smattering of math and science. He knew that he wanted to become independent, which he had learned from Rufus. He and Bessie both knew that education was the key, and they discussed college during his second year of high school. Morehouse College, in Atlanta, became the objective. It was a predominantly Negro liberal arts college of high standards, recognized for the quality of its curriculum. But could Ben afford to go there?

And would he be accepted?

Bessie became a catalyst. She discussed this goal with knowledgeable people at her church, and even with the white families for whom she was a nanny. She gradually acquired a trove of information, and then began the process of applying for Ben's college admission. During the winter of his senior year of high school, he received a letter from Morehouse. Expectantly he and Bessie opened the letter. He had been accepted to begin his freshman year the following September! Their enthusiasm and downright joy were boundless. The cost would be covered by some of the money saved by Bessie and Ben, and the rest by a large endowment from the school. Morehouse saw Ben as a worthy candidate, and told him so.

The remainder of his senior year of high school went fast, or so it seemed. There was one more summer of fieldwork, and then it would be off to college. He spent the summer working for Rufus. The cutting and grinding of the sugar cane went smoothly. The molasses seemed to be in larger quantity this year. The growing season had been more favorable and the cut canes were heavier – they contained more juice.

"So you'll be going to college?" asked Rufus.

"Yes," said Ben. "I have been accepted at Morehouse College in Atlanta."

"That's wonderful," answered Rufus. "Not many of us from these parts go to college. I've had my eye on you these past summers. I know you will do well. My wife and two sons have been dead these many years. I have no one else as family. It has been easy for me to hire workers to help with the farm, but I'll tell you what, Ben, you have been the best I've ever hired."

"Thank you, Rufus. You have been very good to me. I have learned so much from you, not only how to cut and grind the stalks, but how I want to live my life."

"I don't s'pose you'll be coming back next summer, will you Ben?"

"I don't know Rufus, I want to come back and work for you in the summer, but it depends on what lies in store in Atlanta."

"Listen, Ben. I have one thousand dollars saved. I have talked to your mama Bessie and told here that if you need any of it, I will see to it that it will get up to you."

5

Morehouse College

In late August, Ben and Bessie took the bus to Atlanta; neither had been there before. Initially they were overwhelmed by the size and bustling activity of the city. Ben quickly adjusted, although Bessie never did. After a few days she was glad to be back on the bus headed for home. Their parting was bittersweet; neither had ever been beyond a short distance from the other.

Ben's freshman year at Morehouse started with courses in English, literature, college algebra, and a foreign language. He chose French and was soon enmeshed in learning. The school work was harder than before, and he was surrounded by smart and serious students. It took about a month for Ben to fully adjust to these difficulties, but soon he was up to speed, learning new things, and making new friends from amongst his classmates.

There was free time during the afternoons, and he began looking for a part-time job. The school administrative office was a great help. They were used to assisting students who needed work to help with college costs, and they kept a list of potential employers.

Ben used the list, and before long found a job bussing and washing dishes in a small restaurant near the school. He quickly picked up the routine, and was found by his employer to be hard working and reliable.

One day while clearing tables he was approached by a middle-aged white man who introduced himself and then asked, "Have you played football, kid?"

"No," Ben answered, "Why do you ask?"

"Your build, kid. You could be a line backer or a big running back. I'm a scout from Clemson University. I know that Morehouse has a football team. Since you are not playing for them I could offer you a tryout with our team during your free time between school terms. If you made the team you would be offered a scholarship for four more years. You could develop into an outstanding player, and then go on to the Pro's and a fine future. Think about it, kid. I eat lunch here once in awhile, and will talk to you again."

Ben had never considered sports, especially football. He knew that he was strong, fast, and agile, and wanted to think more about it. Over the next few weeks he pondered the offer. Then, one day, the scout from Clemson again appeared. "Have you thought more about my offer, kid?" he asked.

"Yes I have. I really appreciate your offer, but I want to stay at

Morehouse and concentrate on my studies."

"As you say, kid. I think you're making a big mistake. I see real potential in you as a great football player." The scout left, and Ben was never to see him again.

Ben was paid what he thought was an exorbitant wage of two dollars an hour, especially when compared to the one or two dollars a day he received while working for Rufus. But this was standard and quite ordinary for Atlanta. Four hours, six days a week provided forty-eight dollars a week. In a few weeks he could save more money than he had earned during a whole summer working at home.

Room and board were provided by the college as part of the admission package that he had received. He lived in a college dorm and took his meals at the college cafeteria. Gradually he got to know other students in the dorm, and found himself drawn into the evening discussions; he listened with enthusiasm, not saying much. Discussions tended to be free-flowing in groups of four to eight students.

He could sit in and leave whenever it suited; that's the way other students participated and he found this to his liking. He liked the measured tones, the respect for other's thoughts and input, and the lack of anger and belligerent talk. He soon learned that such obnoxious behavior was ignored by others in the group. They also shunned the offender during the ongoing discussion.

The subject matter during these discussions ranged widely from favored school courses, favored teachers, interesting eating places, interesting dramatic performances and other artistic events, to deeper discussions involving politics, philosophy, and race relations. He learned from his associates the qualities of effective speaking, and how to carry forward one's point of view. These consisted of careful reasoning, clearly presented rhetoric, invitations for other's points of view, and genuine respect for differences of opinion. He was being educated; he felt it, and savored in it.

6

Home Again

As the first year came to an end he packed his suitcase, and with his carefully saved wages, took a bus back home. Though they had communicated back and forth by mail, this time he would surprise his mama. He rapped on the door and was met by his mother, as wide-eyed and astonished as he had ever seen her. Then she broke down in tears, tears of joy, as she clasped her son, asking a series of questions, one after another, without waiting for an answer. They talked from late afternoon into the evening, while she prepared dinner. She noted the difference in her son. He had grown up and was now a man.

"School has been good for you," she said. "I am so proud of you. Will you be staying the summer? Will you be working for Rufus? Tell me all about your year in college."

Then Ben presented his wages, every penny saved, all three hundred and thirty-six dollars, to his mother. "Mama," he said, "I want you to have this. I earned it working part-time after school." Bessie had never in her life seen this much money at one time, and began to cry again, a brief flow of tears while never losing her composure. She took the money, and put it into a safe hidden storage place, so well concealed that a thief would not find it.

Ben spent the summer at home. He was the proud object of his mother; Bessie extolled her son to all of her friends, and to the white families for whom she was a nanny. He worked the summer for Rufus, again at the prior wage of one or two dollars a day, displaying genuine gratitude while never betraying the difference in wage between his restaurant work in Atlanta and the farm work with Rufus, which was much more demanding.

7

Confrontation

Soon it was time to head back to Atlanta to begin his second year of college at Morehouse. Ben got off the bus in Atlanta, walking with a suitcase, and noticed two persons walking on the sidewalk towards him. One was a middle-aged white man; his companion was a younger white woman.

As they approached, Ben heard the man say, "Move out of the way, nigger." Ben instinctively moved to his right and slowed down. He was preparing to turn to one side and let the couple pass, but just then the white man moved to the side in front of

Ben and said again, "I told you, nigger, to get out of my way." Ben moved back toward the center of the sidewalk as they collided. The white man was thrown off balance, fell backward to the outside, struck his head against the curb, and lay there unconscious and not moving.

His woman companion began to scream and shout, "You hit him!" Passersby's gathered, and a nearby policeman was soon on the scene. Ben did not know what to do. An ambulance was called as the policeman began giving what aid he could. The ambulance crew arrived, found the man had struck the back of his head on the curb and broken his neck. He was dead.

Ben was stunned. The policeman asked what had happened and the woman kept screaming, "He hit him!" The policeman then asked Ben what had happened.

Ben responded, "I was trying to get out of his way. He kept saying, 'Get out of my way, nigger.'"

"Did you hit him?" the policeman asked.

"He walked into me," Ben answered.

The policeman then asked the woman, "Did he say get out of the way, nigger?"

She answered, "No, the nigger hit him."

The policeman then called for a squad car and told Ben, "I have to take you in." Ben was handcuffed, and taken off to jail.

Ben remained in a state of shock over what had happened. He was allowed to contact Bessie, but unsure of what he should say. He did not want to cause her distress, but how could this be avoided? He decided to tell Bessie what had happened just as he remembered it. The telephone rang four or five times, and then Ben heard, "Hello."

"Mama, this is Ben. I'm in trouble. I'm in jail in Atlanta."

"What happened, baby?" Bessie said in a strong voice.

"I was getting off the bus on my way to school when I bumped into a man. He fell and hit his head on the curb and broke his neck. He died, mama."

"Why did you bump into him, baby?" Bessie asked.

"He said, 'move out of my way, nigger'. I tried to avoid him, but he moved in front of me, and we collided, mama."

"Did you hit him on purpose, Ben?"

"No mama, I was trying to get out of his way."

"I will catch the next bus and be up to see you as soon as I can." She said this in strong and measured words with no hint of emotion. Ben recognized his mother's response. She was always strong in a crisis, saving tears for later.

Their meeting was very close, but not an embrace – the glass barrier prevented that. "How are you baby? Are they feeding you? Do you have a place to sleep?"

Bessie would have gone on with her questions, but Ben interrupted, "I'm fine, mama." Ben had regained his composure. "I saw the lawyer they assigned to me, mama. He took my statement and said that he would be representing me at the trial. He didn't have much more to say."

Bessie stayed as long as she was allowed. With faces and palms touching, except for the intervening glass, they whispered their goodbyes as tears began to form in both their eyes. Then it was time for Bessie to leave.

The trial took place in a small courtroom in Atlanta. Ben was asked to plead before the judge; he pled not guilty. The prosecutor presented his case alleging Ben had struck the victim who subsequently broke his neck and died; the coroner's report stated that a high cervical vertebral displacement resulting in spinal cord transection was the cause of death. The defense attorney then called Ben to the stand and asked him to relate what had happened.

Ben then stated the sequence of being confronted by an angry man who said, "Get out of my way, nigger." When Ben tried to step aside there was a collision, the man fell and struck his head. Ben provided further details about the policeman, the ambulance, and his arrest.

The prosecutor then called the woman who had accompanied the victim, to the stand. Her account was different. She was tearful, and related that Ben had struck the victim, causing him to fall and strike his head. When asked if the word nigger was used, she said no, and that the victim did not make threatening gestures. She said it was Ben who had caused the collision.

The prosecutor then pursued his allegation that Ben was the angry one and that there had to be considerable force used to cause the victim to fall the way he had. The defense attorney then questioned the woman. She maintained her version, with tears and anguish, reinforcing the effect before the all-white jury.

The jury recessed, and within two hours returned with its verdict: guilty of aggravated second-degree murder. The judge subsequently sentenced Ben to a life-term in the Georgia State Prison, near Reidsville, Georgia. Both sides failed to find and present evidence that the victim was from out of state, had been drinking, was inebriated, and was in the company of a prostitute.

Ben was transported to prison, where he would stay for the rest of his life for a crime he did not commit. The year was 1939; he was twenty years of age.

8

The Still of the Night

Josh Hampton was a black man, a Negro, and had grown up in rural Georgia. As a small boy he had picked cotton with his mama and daddy, and his cousins. There was little in the way of formal schooling for Josh – he had learned to read and use numbers, enough to count change anyway. That was all he needed or wanted, the practical stuff. Josh's real education came from the fields and the dirt-road, shanty-shed backdrop in which he grew up. He knew when to say yah sir, or yahs'm, with deference and a cheerful face, and at the same time obtain an advantage for himself, often through cunning and deception.

Josh's parents died when he was in his pre-teens; his mother died during childbirth, with the baby also lost, while his father died accidentally while doing farm labor. Josh was left to fend for himself.

While growing up, he roamed the countryside far and wide, One evening, while out in a pine wood forest, he saw wisps of smoke in the distance. He approached and came upon an older black man bent over a strange contraption and stoking a fire underneath. As he approached, the man turned, grabbed a rifle nearby, and raised and pointed it directly at Josh. Josh stood frozen and wide-eyed as the other man asked, while keeping the gun pointed, "What are you doing here, boy?"

Josh responded that he was walking in the woods, and meant no harm. "Where are you from, boy?" the stranger asked.

"I grew up near Statesville," Josh answered.

"How old are you boy?" the stranger asked.

"Fourteen, I think," answered Josh.

"Do you know what this is, boy, do you know what I am doing? Do you know that I could have killed you, and still might?"

"Nah sir, all I know is that I'm scared," Josh answered.

The older man lowered the gun. "Come over here and sit down, boy. What is your name?"

"They call me Josh."

The older man said, "My name is Cedric. This is a still, and I am making whiskey. I either have to kill you, or bring you in with me. I killed one man about three years ago when he stumbled in on me the way you just did. What will it be, boy?"

Josh answered, "I know how to work – I could help you with whatever you want me to do."

"What family do you have, boy?" the older man asked.

"I don't have no family," Josh answered. "My mama and daddy are dead, and I live by myself."

Cedric took a long time staring at Josh, looking him over top to bottom, and then said, "I'll give it a try. You have to stay with me, and do what I tell you. You cannot tell anyone about what I'm doing here, or else I will have to shoot you. Do you understand?"

"Yah sir," Josh answered, "That suits me just fine." Josh knew that he was beginning on a path that was against the law. This didn't bother him in the least; in fact, he rather relished the thought. He was no longer frightened. He knew that he was capable of learning anything. He would learn all about the strange contraption used to make whiskey. This could become an exciting future for him, or at least, so he thought.

9

Making Moonshine

Josh did learn quickly. He first learned to drive the rickety car that Cedric used for getting supplies and delivering his moonshine whiskey to about two dozen customers. Josh joined Cedric in picking up supplies: sacks of flaked corn used for animal feed, sacks of white sugar, and packages of yeast. They shopped a wide range of animal feed stores and grocers to avoid suspicion because what they were doing was illegal.

Josh learned how to ferment the mash in a fermenting barrel, and then, when ready, siphon off the liquid to a copper pot still. He mastered the distillation process to the final product – moonshine or white whiskey. When feed corn was scarce or unavailable, they fermented white sugar in place of the corn, yielding a whiskey just as potent.

Cedric was a famed moonshiner. He knew how to cut the final product, a harsh-tasting whiskey of eighty to ninety percent alcohol, to a palatable product just below fifty percent. The trick was to add water, a little at a time, and then take a teaspoon full and light a match. Whiskey above fifty percent will burn. When it no longer burned, the whiskey was placed into quart jars for distribution.

Fire was used for the distillation. Because of the smoke and the risk of detection, the use of fire was mostly at night. They were always on the alert for the feared revenuers, federal or state lawmen on the lookout for illegal stills. These lawmen carried guns and would shoot. It was a constant game of cat and mouse to stay beyond the reach of the revenuers. Their suppliers, many of whom knew Cedric and knew that he was a moonshiner, would alert him when the revenue men were in the vicinity.

Cedric supplied his white whiskey to about two dozen or more men that had been in his delivery network for years. Some were Negro, others white. Some were politicians and one was a policeman. Cedric also relied on those to whom he delivered for tips on when to shut down activity if revenuers were in the vicinity.

This went on for years. Josh grew into a skilled helper and became familiar with all aspects of moonshining. He and Cedric became close friends; Cedric was even considering making Josh a partner. Josh reached a level of skill and trust such that he could work independently of Cedric on some tasks such as obtaining supplies and making deliveries. Fermenting and distillation were done together. Often Josh was sent to keep watch in the vicinity of the still. He was very good at this – aware of all the footpaths, and the unused single rutted road leading up to near where they worked.

The small shed housing the still was in a wooded recess against a hill and made to blend in with the surroundings. It could not be seen unless someone was directly in front. The car was left a mile down the road on a siding, well out of the way.

Eluding attempts by the revenue agents to find them proved easy. The shed housing the still and the place where they lived were so secluded that they could not be seen except from a dozen or so yards directly in front. Their delivery vehicle, an old car, was kept a mile or so away on a secluded side road or spur, impossible to see from the small fronting road. Whatever cooking they needed to do was done only when the fire was up for the still, and this was invariably in the evening or at night.

They used a staggered system for obtaining groceries for themselves and supplies for the still. Their source of water was a small spring down in the hollow a few hundred yards away; its outflow was a small rill seeping for miles before emptying into a small stream. Toting water, a chore, was one of Josh's duties. They had dug a secluded privy pit far enough away so as not to lead to their shed. Garbage bags and gunnysacks were burned – other garbage was scattered miles away from their site.

The day after the Pearl Harbor attack, which brought the United States into World War II, Josh found himself swept up with a group of men eager to enlist. He underwent the medical evaluation, not wishing to go into the army, and tried to fake the vision test, pretending to be half-blind. Instead, he was rated not fit for duty because of flat feet.

The Selective Service regarded flat feet as a disqualification for going into the army, but why was anyone's guess. Maybe they felt a soldier with flat feet could not march as far or carry big enough loads. Despite his flat feet, Josh was able to carry and walk with the best of them. He could also run fast and far, abilities that more than once had kept him from the clutches of the law.

During the Second World War, Cedric and Josh remained clear of any participation because of their illegal activities. Then one day, Josh heard that the war had ended with the dropping of a big bomb, an atomic bomb. He was glad of that, but did not understand any of it. It was now nineteen forty-five, and he felt good. He was forty years old, more or less, though he really wasn't sure of his exact age.

Cedric had taken sick the year before. First he appeared pale and weak, and then he began to retch and vomit. He would not let Josh take him to town to visit a doctor. As the weeks passed, he grew worse. One day he said, "Josh, I'm dying. I feel it. I don't have much time left. I'm going to leave all of this to you. I have no one else. I want you to promise to bury me here. There is a flat piece to the right of the still. I want you to bury me there. Will you promise me this?"

"I promise," said Josh, tears forming in his eyes.

A month later, Cedric died. Josh dug the grave exactly where Cedric had wanted, placed the body in the grave and then filled it with dirt. Josh was unlearned about religious matters. He knew no prayers, but instead said goodbye to his friend in his own, but nonetheless sincere way.

The working of the still went on after Cedric died. Josh knew all of the small feedlots where he could obtain flaked corn, and knew the grocers for obtaining white sugar, yeast, and occasionally malted barley. The proprietors also knew Josh, and provided him with timely information when the revenuers were about.

Josh was thoroughly versed and skilled in making moonshine.

What he had learned from the master, Cedric, he continued to apply. He could ferment, distill, and bottle as if Cedric had never died. He could also cut the whiskey, using the spoon and the flame taught to him by Cedric, to yield a more palatable product that was every bit as good as what he and Cedric had produced together.

The evening was the time to make deliveries. They were always done at night to escape suspicion and avoid being captured. He would load a dozen quart jars of whiskey in the rickety old car that he and Cedric had used for years. He knew the names of the people to receive deliveries. Names were memorized – never written down – in case of capture.

One summer night he started down the single-lane, rutted road leading to the main dirt road heading to town. It was about one thirty in the morning and the air was warm and humid. He loved this countryside where he had grown up. He had never been anywhere else. His headlights picked up the red clay and sand soil of the road, and he could see the clouds of reddish dust from his car in the rear view mirror.

Suddenly, he saw headlights in the distance. A single car was heading toward him. He was nearing town and figured the car was probably returning from a party. Suddenly, the car veered in front of him, and slammed into a tree just off the road. Josh steered away so as to avoid hitting the side of the car, which was still across the road, but it was too late. Josh struck the other car. The crash caved in the right front of his car; he was thrown against the steering wheel, hit his head against the windshield, and lost consciousness.

He awoke with a flashlight shining through the side window. It was a policeman. Those outside had to pry the door open on the driver's side and help him out. The inside of his car reeked with the smell of alcohol; several of the jars of whiskey had broken with the impact. He was able to walk, although he was wobbly, but he appeared to have no other injuries except a bad headache. Josh was handcuffed and taken to jail.

He later learned that both persons in the other car, a young couple, had been killed when their car struck the tree head on. A statement was taken from him and he was told that he would remain in jail until a trial was scheduled.

He was assigned a lawyer who would defend him at the time of trial. The lawyer was young, asked Josh a few questions, and then left. At the trial, his case was presented. The policeman, first to arrive at the scene, testified that Josh had been drinking. There was a heavy odor of alcohol, and he had a wobbly, stumbling gait when he had gotten out of the car. The policeman further stated that Josh's car was over in the left lane, and it appeared that this caused the other car to veer and crash.

Josh's lawyer made a few comments, but did not provide a good defense. Josh was not called to testify; he had to sit mute while the trial unfolded. Then the jury took the case. It didn't take long before a verdict was presented: guilty of a double homicide while driving intoxicated. The judge then gave him a life sentence at the Georgia State Penitentiary. Josh was stunned. He thought of the jars of moonshine packed inside a carefully built concealed space in his car. They would never have found it. It would do him no good to show them how to open the compartment; it would only add moonshining to his offenses.

Josh knew that he was not responsible for the crash, which had been accidental. He also knew that he was not drunk since he never drank, except to taste a final batch of moonshine. He guessed that the young couple who had died were probably returning from a party, and were themselves drunk.

Josh was transferred to the Georgia State Prison near Reidsville, Georgia. He had received a life sentence, and he would never leave the prison alive. The year was 1946 and he was forty-one years of age.

10

An Early Influence

Scoop Johnson was born in 1923 to parents Jefferson and Hattie, near the seaport and cosmopolitan city of Savannah, Georgia. Theirs was a Negro family, living on the fringes of Savannah; they were rural people, as there were no suburbs in those days. Their house was well-built and comfortable. There was a front porch with several rocking chairs, while inside there was a kitchen with a large wood stove for cooking and heat in the winter – for those few winter days when the outside temperature was uncomfortably cold. Near the kitchen was the dining room with a large wooden table, chairs at each end, and wooden benches on the sides.

Upstairs there was a bedroom on each side of the stairs. Outside, the house stood on an elevated foundation, allowing storage underneath, but, more importantly, also allowing additional cross ventilation during the sometimes unbearably hot and humid days of a Georgia summer.

Scoop grew up with two older sisters, Harriet and Gloria, and an older brother Jeb. Scoop's father was one of a few Negro landowners in the area. He owned a small farm of about sixty acres, and proved to be an efficient farmer, using every part of the acreage to plant crops that could be sold. Near one side of the house was a small peach orchard. On the other side were pecan trees. There was a hen house, providing eggs and meat, and a field for planting other crops.

Jefferson was not just an efficient farmer, but he was also very astute, knowing which crops might in the future stand to yield the most money when harvested. Thus, he rotated his crops between sorghum, soybeans, or peanuts, depending on which of these crops, in the following year, might yield the most money. Jefferson also kept a few acres each year for tobacco. In addition to his own use, he knew that there was always a demand and a favorable market for tobacco.

All of the family would help during planting and the harvest. Jefferson began the year, usually in February, preparing the rows using a mule-drawn plow. As they got a little older, Jefferson taught his two sons, first Jeb and then Scoop, how to plow the field behind a mule. On weekends a family treat was to hitch their mule to the wagon and take the entire family to Savannah, a distance of about ten miles. They often had a picnic along the banks of the Savannah River, where they could relax under large oak trees interlaced with Spanish moss, providing a canopy of shade on hot summer days, while watching ocean-going ships come up the Savannah River to riverside piers. Sometimes Jefferson's older brother Wilbur would join in the picnic activities. Wilbur had no family, but he always gave the appearance of being well-off, wearing fancy clothes, or showing a hefty wad of bills when something was purchased.

Scoop was seven when the first effects of the Great Depression began to reach Savannah and the surrounding areas. The adverse economic effects at first were small, with little effect on the price of crops. The economic downturn seemed to come in waves, but the full-blown Depression didn't hit their area until 1933. Some farmers in the area were heavily mortgaged and lost their farms to the banks because they could not keep up with mortgage payments. Jefferson was more fortunate. His was a family farm, fully paid for, and in his family for at least three generations. Jefferson was also inherently thrifty, and had not been taken in by farmland speculation during the boom period of economic growth, which followed the First World War.

Scoop was not a good student. He didn't like school – he found it boring. He also hated the farm chores. While his older brother Jeb took to farm work like a duck takes to water, Scoop knew, from an early age, that he would avoid it in the future, if he could manage it.

During summer picnics in Savannah, Scoop found Uncle Wilbur a fascinating person to be around. Uncle Will, as everyone called him, proved to be a mysterious and flamboyant presence, and Scoop was naturally drawn toward him. During the summer of 1940, at the age of seventeen, Scoop took the bold step of asking Uncle Will if he could spend the summer with him. It was between planting and harvest time, and he figured that his father might allow it. He was surprised and elated when Uncle Will eyed him severely, and then said sure.

It was a summer Scoop would never forget. The Second World War had just started in Europe, and ship traffic from the Atlantic had picked up along the East coast ports, including the port of Savannah. Scoop had been staying with Uncle Will for about a week, but still had no idea what Will did for a living, until one day when they were walking along the quay of the harbor, Will was approached by a young white woman, heavily made up and scantily dressed. The conversation was hushed, and then she went off.

11

The Bull Pen

Will then leaned over and spoke into Scoop's ear so that he could barely be heard: "This is the bullpen. I'm the bull, and she's in the pen. She will work the street near the ships, looking for sailors who are coming ashore. She will provide the sex, extract the money, and then give it to me."

"You mean, Uncle Will, that you are a pimp?" Scoop asked.

"Some would call it that," answered Will.

This was Scoop's first exposure to the shady world of pimping. During that summer he was immersed in that world, and all of its seamy currents. There were girls, white and black, that worked under Uncle Will's control. He took their money, gave them a small share, and maintained an active surveillance of all activities including the cheap nearby flophouses where sex was exchanged for money. Work was brisk along this busy port. Uncle Will had a few others whom he paid for their silence, including the policeman walking the beat and a higher up official.

Sex was offered, though Scoop refused. Sex was of interest to him only as a way to make money. He was asexual, if indeed there is such a category. He knew he was not homosexual. If, at a future time in his life, sex was needed, he knew he would engage in sex for its other purpose, producing children; but now, his sole interest was using sex to make money. Scoop avidly pursued Uncle Will, and that summer, learned everything that Uncle Will could teach him.

He stayed with Uncle Will through the summer and into the winter of 1941. Jefferson allowed this, as Scoop was at best a poor farmer, while older brother Jeb took after his father and was in line to inherit the farm after his father was no longer able to work it.

Pearl Harbor came as a shock to the United States, and to Savannah. One day after the attack Scoop announced to Uncle Will that he wanted to join the Navy. Will said to him, "The only thing they will let you do is wait tables on a ship. There is the color barrier for other jobs. Are you sure that is what you want? There will be a draft, but we can find ways to keep you here, and I will have need of you."

Scoop answered, "I'm going to join the Navy. When the war is over I would like to come back and help you out."

"I see," Uncle Will responded, "You've got a patriotic streak in you. I used to feel that way, but now I'm too old. Good luck to you, Scoop."

The next day Scoop went to the Navy Recruitment office

in Savannah. He noted the long line that extended around the block. He stood in line for what seemed like hours as the line slowly moved along. Then he was face to face with a recruiter. The usual information was taken. He was eighteen and appeared to be able-bodied. There was a need for Negro men in the United States Navy to do stevedore work, wait tables for officers, or do mechanical work. He was given an appointment for a medical examination the next day, which he passed; then he boarded a bus with a full load of recruits headed for the naval training station.

His training included an assessment. He was found to be highly endowed with mechanical skills, perhaps as a result of his earlier farm chores, which, strangely, he had loathed. Scoop was sent to mechanics' school where he underwent a short but intense course in mechanics. He learned quickly and passed the examinations. He was assigned to a cargo ship, helped in its lading, and then began his career as a sailor in the Navy outbound, to pass through the Panama Canal and into the Pacific Ocean bound for Pearl Harbor.

They arrived and had to be guided by a harbor tug past the twisted superstructures of warships that had been sunk during the attack. Soon they docked and he went ashore. The ground was a beehive of activity. Work teams were going in every direction, some on salvage boats to dismantle the ships that had been sunk, others to shops that fronted the waterways to participate in the rebuilding of the harbor. Scoop spent the entire war at Pearl Harbor on the island of Oahu. He worked eight to ten hours a day, five or six days a week in a large machine shop, custom making parts for ships that came in for repairs. There seemed a long backlog so that his team was always busy. For the big jobs that required a dry dock, ships moved under their own power, or were towed stateside for needed repairs.

After hours, Scoop roamed the seamy world of sex for hire,

not for his own use, but to observe how it was done on Oahu. He found that the main factors were the same in downtown Honolulu as in Savannah, Georgia: girls to ply the trade, an area to concentrate customers, such as an active seaport, a pimp to oversee the girls and take in the money, and hush money paid to the local policeman, and sometimes to a supervisor. The girls tended to roam from place to place, and had to be replenished as needed. It was also necessary to enforce strict rules so that the girls would not pocket money that would otherwise go to the pimp.

Then one day the war was over. Most of the warships were put in mothballs, so to speak, and military manpower was rapidly downsized. Scoop found himself with an honorable discharge, a ship to take him to San Francisco, and train fare to take him to Savannah. He took the bus to the farmstead and greeted his parents Jefferson and Hattie, his older brother Jeb, and his two older sisters Harriet and Gloria.

They had all changed. Mom and dad were graying and slowing down, Jeb was running the farm, and both sisters, now in their late twenties and early thirties, were not yet married. He had a respect, even a reverence, for marriage, learned from his parents while growing up. He must never let on to them that his plan to make money was to become a pimp.

He stayed at home a few days, answering the flurries of questions about his life in the Navy, and what he was planning to do now that he was home. He answered that he liked Savannah and in a few more days would head there and look up Uncle Will.

"Why not wait till Sunday, that way we could all go to Savannah, and have a picnic in the park, just like olden days," someone said.

"Sure, why not?" Scoop said.

They drove, not by mule and wagon, but in a car, an old rust bucket that Jefferson had pooled their money to buy. They drove, three in front and three in back, a much quicker trip than by mule and wagon as before. Scoop learned that wartime on the farm had gone well for the Johnson family. Jeb had received a deferment from selective service because of the necessary work on the farm, and the farm had prospered with better payment for crops.

Soon it was time to head back to the farm. Scoop was to stay in Savannah; he had brought his duffle bag along. They said their goodbyes, tears forming in his mother's eyes. He watched the car drive off until it was out of sight, and then headed towards downtown. He would find a cheap room and contact Uncle Will in the morning.

Will was staying in his old digs, a small room in one of the numerous flophouses just uptown from the wharfs. He stayed close enough to the action to keep tabs on his girls, to know that he was not being cheated, and to settle disagreements, which might crop up between his girls, or between a girl and a customer.

Scoop knocked on the door, and was met by Uncle Will. They both stared with uncertainty and disbelief – they had both changed. Will seemed a shell of his old self. He had a cough and had lost weight. They exchanged hugs, and Scoop entered and looked around. The room was neat and sparsely furnished. A hot plate was on the shelf near the sink. A radio was on playing classical music. Classical music? Something must be wrong, or at least different.

Scoop, strangely, while at Pearl Harbor, had been exposed to classical music, played by one of his team members when they both worked in the naval machine shops. Scoop had never given it much thought, but did learn to like it and had acquired a familiarity with the major composers. "Uncle Will, why do you listen to that stuff?" Scoop asked.

"Because I like it," Will answered. "One of my former girls, while you were in the Navy, played violin in the local symphony orchestra. They didn't pay much, and she would earn extra money by turning tricks. She used to listen to classical music on the radio, and I came to like it."

There were two ash trays in the room, one on the sink counter near the hot plate, and the other on the side table near his bed. Both were overflowing with cigarette butts, smoked down as far as they would go. A waste-basket near the sink was half-full of smoked-down butts. There were three packages of Camel cigarettes on the shelf, one torn open and mostly empty.

"Uncle Will, why do you live here? You must be making enough money to live uptown in a better place. I see you are smoking a lot, and have a bad cough. How long has that been going on?"

"Listen, Scoop. I have saved a lot of money. A lot is hidden here where no one can find it. I don't need much room. Besides, I want to be down near my girls. It's still the Bull Pen you know – I'm the bull, and they're in the pen. I do smoke a lot, a nervous habit I guess. My cough has been with me a long time. It's called a smoker's cough. I don't eat much; I don't have much of an appetite. But I'm doing all right."

"You look like you've lost weight."

"Maybe so, I don't weigh myself, but I look thin in the face when I shave in the morning. Listen, Scoop. You showed up at the right time. I've been thinking of cutting back. You could help me. We could work together, bring in more girls and more money for you. I think I'm fair. I don't, and never have, cheated my girls. I always give them one-third, or close to it. I play by the rules, and make sure they do too. They know me and stay in line. It's always a cash transaction; the girls check in advance to make sure the customer can pay. I've known some real slime bags, who cheat their girls, give them only a pittance to get by on, and some that beat up on their girls. They're real low lives."

Scoop and Uncle Will nodded in agreement. Scoop found lodging nearby – close enough that he could stay in daily contact with Will. Over the next few weeks they were able to find more girls. This meant expanding their area of doing business, a complex arrangement that involved Will's girls, other pimps working nearby areas, and the girls controlled by other pimps. This expansion was done gradually. Abrupt muscling in was to be avoided – it could lead to hard feelings, or worse.

Scoop solicited and employed girls to expand his part of the joint enterprise. He laid down the rules, and made certain that he was understood, and that he would be in control. When he was offered sex, he refused. His interest was in making money. He also knew that he would exercise greater control if he did not participate in sex with his employees. He followed Uncle Will in sharing proceeds: one-third for the girls while retaining two-thirds for himself. He did not share Will's method of hiding money. It was not safe to hoard large sums of money in living quarters or on one's person. Why do this when there were banks? Uncle Will was old-fashioned. He had grown up when there were few banks and they weren't always trustworthy. There were three local banks. Scoop would open accounts at all three.

Business slowly picked up, and money was accumulating. He was able to make regular deposits into his three bank accounts. There was hush money to be paid; he was experienced in this important part of the shady enterprise. He lived frugally. He had learned this from his own upbringing, and from his prior pre-war association with Uncle Will. He did not smoke or use alcohol. From the outside he seemed to others to be a model of virtue, a young man with his feet on the ground, successfully employed, becoming moneyed, an exemplar with no bad habits, a paradigm for others; but he was a pimp.

12

Fortune's Turn

He heard the scream, and the loud banging from the room facing the street. It was mid-afternoon; he was nearby, keeping an eye on his enterprise. The sound came from the flophouse where his girls worked. Scoop lost no time entering and going to the door of the room from whence he heard the screams. The door had no locks, which was a precaution he had installed so that doors used for business could not be locked from the inside.

Scoop opened the door, and was met by the sight of one of his girls being beaten by a burly middle-aged white man. The girl was scantily clad, her clothes having been ripped off. Her face was bloody, swollen, and her nose was broken, flattened to one side from a heavy blow. The man continued to pound her with both fists, unaware that Scoop had entered the room. He appeared to be enjoying the fight, one-sided, as the girl was lying on her side in a semi-fetal position, trying to protect herself from the flurry of heavy pounding.

Scoop grabbed the assailant, pulled him away from the girl, and slammed him against the wall. They tussled, both landing blows, and then went down to the ground, with Scoop underneath and the assailant on top. Scoop was able to turn them both to the side, each having a tight grasp of the other. Suddenly the assailant shrieked and loosened his grip. Blood was issuing from the left side of his chest, with a knife deeply embedded, and he went limp. Blood was soaking into Scoop's shirt as he tried to extricate himself. Instinctively he withdrew the knife and laid it aside, and then tried to gain a footing and stand.

The noise had been heard outside, and someone called the police. Two police officers entered the room. They quickly assessed the situation, motioning for Scoop and the girl to step to the far side of the room under the gaze of one of the officers, while the other gave aid to the stricken man on the floor. The man was actively bleeding and appeared limp and unconscious. "What happened?" the officer standing near Scoop and the girl asked in a loud voice. Then the stricken man came awake.

"The dirty nigger did this to me," he said and then lapsed again into unconsciousness.

"Call an ambulance," one of the policemen said. They tried to apply pressure to the wound, but the bleeding continued. When the ambulance arrived the man appeared to be dead. They loaded him into the ambulance and sped off.

The two officers took statements from Scoop and the girl. As he stood there, bruised and battered with a bloody shirtfront, he told of responding to screams and noise, and finding the girl being beaten. He made no mention of the knife, not sure where it had come from. The girl was in shock and gave no coherent statement. Both were taken away – the girl to a hospital for treatment and Scoop to jail. Scoop sat in his cell after cleaning up and being given jailhouse clothes. It had all happened so quickly. What would happen to him now?

Uncle Will arranged for an attorney to represent Scoop at the trial. The evidence was presented: oral testimony by the deceased victim before he died indicated that Scoop had caused the knife wound. Scoop's fingerprints were found on the knife. Scoop's shirtfront was soaked with the victim's blood. And there was the testimony of the two police officers, who were first on the scene.

Scoop was brought to the witness stand and gave his testimony. He told of being outside and hearing screams, then going inside and finding the girl being beaten by the victim. He and the victim then got into a fight. They fell to the floor and he then noticed the victim bleeding. He did not know where the knife had come from. He denied using the knife, saying that his only involvement was responding to the girl's cries of distress. When cross-examined by the prosecutor and asked about how he happened to be in the vicinity so close to what was happening, his answer was vague; he did not want to divulge that he was pimping, not only for himself, but to protect Uncle Will's enterprise.

The girl had been found, and was called to the stand to testify. When asked what she had been doing in the room, she replied that she was staying in the room and found herself being assaulted. She was still badly bruised, especially about the face and head. Her answers were slow and halting. She did not distinguish who had assaulted her, only that she found two men, one white, the other black, fighting. When asked, she said she knew nothing of the knife. The defense attorney tried, but could not elicit any further testimony.

After being recessed, the jury returned a verdict of aggravated second-degree murder. The judge sentenced Scoop to life in prison at the Georgia State Prison in Reidsville. Before being transferred, Scoop had one last farewell talk with Uncle Will. Scoop was still shaken and bewildered, but was aware enough to notice that Will was sick. He was weak, had lost more weight, had a worse cough, and was spitting up blood-streaked phlegm. They embraced and not much was said – they both were teary-eyed, knowing this would be their last embrace.

Shortly afterward, Scoop was placed on a bus headed for the prison. He was handcuffed and in leg irons. The year was 1947; he was twenty-four years of age.

13

Georgia State Prison, Reidsville

When opened in 1937, the Georgia State Prison at Reidsville was a state-of-the-art, maximum-security facility. Most prisoners were sent there after a sentence of life in prison. Few inmates were ever paroled during those early years. It was considered a model prison; the American Medical Association gave its first accreditation for quality medical services at prisons throughout the United States to the facility at Reidsville.

The prison warden was a professional. He maintained a strict environment inside; the guards were carefully trained, and periodically instructed on how to maintain order under varied circumstances. They were also taught to avoid racist behavior; failure to do so would be punished. The warden was considered to be top notch, strict but also fair.

Ben McClellan got off the bus with a group of prisoners, ambling along single file. There were about a dozen in the line, all with leg irons and a short chain to keep them from bolting and running off. Each was also handcuffed from the front, a limited but not too uncomfortable position on the bus ride to the prison. Ben and the others were led through the prison gate in 1939, two years after the prison opened.

They were ushered into a waiting area where they sat on benches. Each in turn approached a window where they were questioned, prior paper reports were scrutinized, and then each was led down a corridor to another room where leg irons and handcuffs were removed. There were now guards, two for each new inmate. One at a time, they were told to strip and shower with the guard standing by. Each prisoner then donned his prison garb and was led into another area where they underwent a brief medical examination with guards present.

After the exam, they were moved into another waiting area, and wait they did, until all of the new inmates had made it through the processing. Seated on benches, all in prison garb, they were given a set of instructions as to what to expect in prison. They were told that they were all "lifers", and as such they should expect to spend the rest of their lives in prison. "Behave yourselves and don't cause trouble" were to be the watchwords of this new discipline. "You will be treated fairly, but if you get out of line or cause any kind of trouble, it will go very hard on you.

"There will be two to a cell with upper and lower bunk beds. You are to decide between you who sleeps where; if you can't decide, a bunk will be assigned to you. There will be no loud commotion or fighting in any of the cells. Three times a day at seven in the morning, noon, and five in the afternoon, cell doors will be unlocked, and you will walk single file into the dining room. You will walk down a line with a tray and be given food. You will be given a cup, fork and spoon. Knives are not allowed. You will sit on benches at a long table, and have about fifteen minutes to eat. After eating, leave the silverware and cup on your tray. The silverware will be counted and taken away before you are allowed to leave.

"Troublemaking will lead to immediate removal of the inmate. The offender will be placed in a small solitary cell without light or heat. Food will be provided twice a day through a slot in the door. There will be no silverware, and only water to drink. If troublemaking continues, you will be placed in solitary confinement in the hole, for a month at a time.

"Each cell has a toilet and a sink. Do not try to dismantle the plumbing; it has been tried before, and it doesn't work. Do not try to stop up the sink or toilet – it might result in a month in the hole. About every two weeks you will be allowed out for a shower, and a change of clothes. If you play by the rules you will be allowed outside for exercise two or three times a week. We will not start this for a month or so until we are sure that none of you are troublemakers.

"Don't try to escape. It has been tried a few times, but no one has escaped from this prison. The guards nearest you are not armed. They are always within eyesight of other guards who are armed, expert marksmen, with orders, if necessary, to shoot to kill. That is all."

14

Why Am I Here?

Ben was still in a state of disbelief and shock. It had been one month since the trial, followed by the tearful separation from his mother, Bessie. Now he found himself contained, like a sardine in a tin, never to get out. He pondered his situation almost constantly, but could not forge a coherent picture. He was in the maximum-security prison for the state of Georgia. He recognized that, and knew that he needed to adjust to the routine.

Ben had been raised on routine, almost a daily repetition of what some would find boring, although it had not been boring for him. He was used to humdrum, and had even throughout his life found it satisfying. The terrifying incident when he was a small boy, when his mother Bessie had used the shotgun to kill his father Buster, was now an almost faded memory. His father had beaten him, and also had beaten his mother. He held no love for his father, but retained a strong affection for his mother; she had protected him from another beating. The strong family and community connections in the Quarters where they lived also supported his mother's action; even the sheriff, Sheriff Tom, had called it justified, and in self-defense.

In his spare time, and he had ample of that, he ruminated on his past life, trying to find meaning for what had recently happened to him. He had been raised in the slow quiet life of rural Georgia. He loved the summer work on Rufus McDonald's small farm. He recalled the hard work of chopping sugar cane, then using the mule Sam to grind it and begin the process of converting it into molasses. He remembered Rufus offering to advance his life savings, all one-thousand dollars, to help with expenses at Morehouse College in Atlanta.

He had loved the college life at Morehouse. With completion of his first year he had gained a perspective that was new and exciting. He had known that he could go far. He had been confident that with completion of three more years and then graduation, there would be many doors opened to him for advancement. And then the horrible incident occurred that led him to this dreadful place – the state prison with a life sentence for a crime that he did not do.

He felt disoriented. He had learned a long time ago to bottle up any sadness he felt, any somberness, behind a stoic face. Maybe his stoicism started as a four-year-old when he witnessed his mother kill his father, standing by until the sheriff, and his aunt

MayBelle came. He had also learned this from his mother as she stood strong but silent, awaiting what was to come next.

Still, Ben could find nothing in his own behavior that had propelled him into prison. An anger began to well up in his inner soul. He was angry at the system and the set of circumstances that had put him here, or more precisely, allowed him to be here. Then he stopped. He must not let anger rise up – it could only destroy him. He had learned this from his mother. She was not angry, only deliberate with a plan of action that was clearly thought through. No one could say that Bessie was a victim of her own anger. Ben could and would strive to put his anger down. He must keep a clear head. He needed to think through his new situation and find ways to cope – he learned this while growing up in the Quarters and the fields of rural Georgia – but he had also learned this in the classrooms and informal group discussion sessions at Morehouse College.

Since becoming an inmate, Ben had been the sole occupant of a cell meant for two. He slept on the bottom of a double bunk, only because it was easier to get out of bed late at night or early in the morning to use the toilet. This was about to change.

One day the guards unlocked his cell, inserted another inmate inside, and locked the cell door again. There were no words spoken.

Ben noticed that he was an older Negro man, gray around the temples, and that he had a limp. The cells were racially segregated, which was understood, accepted, and not questioned. "My name is Ben McClellan – what's yours?"

"I go by the name of Amos Murphy," the new man said. Amos appeared to be in his late fifties; he was short and thin. Ben had noticed that Amos had a pronounced limp, and that he appeared to be in pain when he walked.

Ben decided at that moment that he would offer the lower

bunk to Amos. He did so without other words being spoken. It was then that Ben felt a sensation, which he had not felt since before being sent to prison; a feeling of peace, a feeling that he had done the right thing, a good thing, and that he would, henceforth, be better able to put up with the struggles of prison life.

Gradually a friendship between Amos and Ben unfolded. Neither of them asked questions about the incidents that had led them to prison. Prisoners, Ben had learned during this early period of being incarcerated, did not ask questions that were personal, or that might be hurtful. This was a bridge that most would not cross, and added a nobility of sorts to prison life, at least for some.

Ben went over the prison routines with Amos, even though he knew that these routines had been explained in detail by the guards beforehand. He mentioned the meal times, the kinds of food to be expected, the dining room with its long tables and benches, the periods allotted for exercise, and what to expect from the guards. He mentioned the guards who tended to be nearby. He pointed out that from what he had seen the guards were strict, yet fair. He had not witnessed name-calling or racist slurs by any of the guards.

Life, sharing a single cell with Amos, went on for eight years. Ben and Amos developed a friendship over those years that included mutual respect and esteem; there were even times of sharing humorous stories and events from each of their past lives. As a pair of prisoners required to share the same small cell for prolonged periods of time, they were fortunate, and they both grew to recognize this and to appreciate it.

Then things began to change. Amos started to slow down. His lame gait became more noticeable, and his walks to and from the eating room were becoming more taxing. He appeared weak and short of breath, and was limited during their outside exercise periods to alternating intervals of slow walking and then sitting to rest.

Ben asked if he would like to be seen by the prison doctor; Amos said no.

Then one morning when Ben got out of bed, he noticed that Amos was just laying there in bed, not moving. Ben went to rouse him for the morning walk to breakfast, but Amos did not respond. Amos was not breathing, had no pulse, and had a glazed look in his open eyes. Amos was dead.

Ben rattled the cell door, got the attention of a guard, and shortly thereafter two guards, one armed with a shotgun, entered the cell. Ben was ordered to move to one corner of the cell, and when questioned by a guard, explained that he had found his cellmate dead in bed.

The body was removed. An inquiry established that death was from natural causes. There was no evidence of violence, so Ben was absolved from any responsibility. Ben was again alone in his cell. Amos had come to the Georgia State Penitentiary in 1939, shortly after Ben had arrived, and had died in 1947. Ben later learned that Amos was sixty-three years old when he died. As he sat in his cell, alone again, tears slowly welled up in his eyes and flowed down his cheeks in rivulets, similar to those tears he had shed, at the age of four, when he witnessed his mama use a shotgun to kill his father on a summer night in Georgia so many years before.

About a week after Amos died, Ben's cell door was again unlocked and two guards brought another prisoner in to share Ben's cell. This was another Negro man, older than Ben, and smaller in stature. This was not unusual. Ben was more than six feet tall and weighed more than two hundred pounds. At an earlier time, while in college at Morehouse, he had been approached by a scout from a different southern university encouraging him to tryout for football, dangling the possibility of a four-year college scholarship if he were able to make the team.

Since Amos' death Ben had continued to use the upper bunk bed. He eyed the new cell occupant, and then introduced himself as Ben McClellan.

"I'm Josh Hampton," the new inmate said, without adding anything more. There was no further conversation until Ben mentioned that he had been using the upper bunk, and left it at that. Josh then said that he would accept either bunk; he felt that Ben had been in the cell first, and that he, Josh, would take whichever was left. Ben began to like his new cellmate after this brief exchange.

As with Amos, years earlier, Ben began reviewing the routines of prison life. Josh listened without interrupting, and when Ben had finished, mentioned that he had heard all of that just before he was led to his cell. Ben found his new cellmate to be quiet at first, with Ben having to initiate conversation. Gradually this changed. It took many weeks before Ben learned that Josh was talkative. Josh began regaling Ben with stories of his earlier life, how as a boy he had picked cotton with his cousins. Later he had dropped out of school and roamed the countryside on his own. Ben found Josh to be not only talkative, but at times noted him to talk up a storm, so to speak. It might in the future prove to be an irritant, but at this point Ben was enjoying it. Silence and quiet had been his usual companions over so many years.

One day Josh began telling Ben that he knew how to make whiskey, really good whiskey – moonshine whiskey, that is. Josh told the story about walking in the woods as a fourteen-year-old boy and seeing smoke in the distance. As he had approached, he saw a gun pointed at him and was told to come forward by a man named Cedric. Josh related how he was nearly killed, but that Cedric took him in, taught him to make corn whiskey, the finest moonshine whiskey in the region, and gradually brought Josh in as a partner.

Josh, over the span of weeks, told how he and Cedric had made moonshine together, how they had managed to evade the revenuers, and how they had had a dedicated clientele to whom they made deliveries. Then Cedric had become weak and unable to shoulder the heavier work. Josh mentioned Cedric's last months and how he had wanted to take Cedric to see a doctor, but that Cedric would have no part of that. Then one day Cedric had said that he was dying, and would leave all of the business to Josh, but made him promise to bury him in a designated small plot of ground near the whiskey still. Josh had done exactly as he promised, and then went on to make and deliver whiskey as before.

Josh then told of the incident that eventually resulted in his being put in prison – how he had been on the way to a delivery early one morning, and had been hit by a car coming from the other direction. Two young people had been to a party. Their car had swerved, collided with his, and then struck a tree. When the police arrived they found the odor of alcohol in Josh's car, from broken jars of moonshine in a hidden compartment, and claimed in court that Josh was drunk. He was convicted of vehicular homicide while driving drunk. Josh went on to say that the irony was that he had never used alcohol, and that the driver of the other car was probably drunk from partying.

15

A Bus Load of Prisoners

The bus left at ten in the morning and traveled on mostly rutted roads. It was summertime, and the fields were dry; it had been weeks since the last drenching rain. Outside, clouds of red dust were being kicked up by front and rear tires, grinding the sand and red clay soil into finer powder. Scoop Johnson sat, handcuffed and in leg irons, with about a dozen other prisoners. They were all "lifers", men sentenced to life in prison for serious crimes; most were murderers.

Hands were cuffed in front, making it much easier to bear the long trip compared to being cuffed from behind. The leg irons were not too uncomfortable. They were ankle bracelets, much like handcuffs in size, but connected by a short length of light chain. They allowed normal walking, perhaps with a slightly shorter stride, but would prevent running. Three guards sat with the prisoners. Two were unarmed, while the third sat behind a heavy wire screen armed with a shotgun.

Scoop Johnson, one of the prisoners, looked out the window at the fields of sorghum, peanuts, corn and occasional tobacco. There were also cotton fields, though not as numerous as when Scoop was a boy; newer strains of cotton, such as pima from Egypt, had glutted the market just before the start of the Second World War. Scoop thought of the war. He had enlisted in the Navy the day after the bombing of Pearl Harbor, and had served the entire war stationed at a large machine shop there. During the downsizing of the military, after the war, he had been given an honorable discharge from the Navy.

Then he pondered his present situation. He was being sent to prison, a life sentence for a crime he did not commit. True, he had engaged in petty crime, especially pimping; it was also true that he might have effected the jury conviction by telling the jury of his role as a pimp, but he had refused to do this, not wanting to implicate his uncle Will. As he mused on these things, a heavy sadness settled upon him, as heavy as the fog that filled San Francisco Bay the day his ship returned from Pearl Harbor.

Then they were at the gate. The sign read "Georgia State Prison, Reidsville, Georgia". The door of the bus swung open and the prisoners were led out one by one through the gate. There were other guards; those with guns were within eyesight, but far enough away so that they could not be reached.

The induction station included filling out a questionnaire, a photograph, a brief medical examination, a shower, and the donning of prison clothes. Then the new prisoners were given a lecture on prison routines. Scoop was then led to his cell, occupied by one other Negro prisoner. He was told the top bunk was his. The cell door slammed shut, and Scoop heard the key turn and the bolt shift into place. It was the summer of 1947 and he was twenty-four years old. Scoop would spend the rest of his life in prison.

His cellmate was an older man, at first sullen and menacing. Scoop knew such feelings and considered how he might respond to any of a number of threatening situations. Scoop introduced himself, but the other man did not respond. Over time there was a silence, a grudging awareness of the other's presence, like an armed truce, though with nothing to be bargained for. During all of the time that he shared the cell, Scoop was not to learn the name of his cellmate.

16

A Crime of Hate

The years dragged on. Scoop learned, early on, that if you "keep your nose clean," prison life, while boring, is usually not menacing. The days, then the months, went by having their own routines. Days were spent between the meal routine, in the cell, and the hour outside for exercise three times a week. Every two weeks was time for a shower, and a change of prison clothes. Food was plain and not appetizing, but appeared adequate to allay hunger and keep from losing weight. The seasons were recognized by the shorter and cooler days of winter, and the longer warmer days of summer. Spring, with its emerging flowering, and fall, with the change in color of the leaves, were not a part of prison life. The prison walls separated these changes from the sensibilities of the prisoners.

One day while in line heading for the noon meal, it happened. Kyle Springer, a white prison trustee, was dry mopping the floor near the wall alongside the line of prisoners heading for the dining room. Suddenly a prisoner ahead was seen to fall. His feet had become entangled in Kyle's mop. Scoop left his place and positioned himself between Kyle and the fallen prisoner. Kyle was still holding the end of the mop, which was entwined between the ankles of the fallen prisoner. Kyle had a triumphant look, even a sneer on his face, but did not speak. "Drop the mop," Scoop said in a strong and steady voice.

Scoop expected the trustee to twist the mop, maybe even to use it to strike the prisoner, but this did not happen. Two guards approached as Kyle was releasing his hold on the mop. One of the other prisoners in the line had bent over and was ministering to the one who had fallen. One of the guards addressed Kyle, "I saw what you did, Springer, I'm going to bring you up before the warden."

The fallen prisoner was not seriously hurt. The line reformed and proceeded to the dining area. Each prisoner grabbed a tray and went through the cafeteria line. As Scoop was leaving the end of the line he heard a voice asking him to come over and sit down. It was Ben. He introduced himself and Josh Hampton, and mentioned that it was Josh who had fallen. Scoop Johnson then introduced himself to the others.

"It was a brave thing you just did, Scoop, coming and placing yourself between the trustee and Josh. If it had not been seen by one of the guards, you could have been in for a heap of trouble."

"How so?" asked Scoop.

"I know about Springer. He is a racist, one of the worst kinds. He would claim that Josh came out of the line toward him, and that he used the mop to ward off an attack by an enraged prisoner. They might have put both of you in solitary, or in the hole, for a month or longer."

That afternoon there was a meeting in Warden Hale Winston's office. In addition to the warden, Kyle Springer, the guard, and Scoop Johnson were present. The warden spoke, "Prisoner Johnson, what happened?"

Scoop told how he saw the mop being used to trip the prisoner. He placed himself between the person holding the mop and the fallen prisoner. "Why did you do that?" the warden asked.

"Because I thought the guy with the mop was going to hit the other guy."

"Not so," Springer interrupted. "He came at me like he was trying to strike me."

The guard was then asked to speak: "From where I was standing, I saw Springer use his mop to trip the prisoner."

"Was the prisoner out of line?" the warden asked.

"No, sir."

"Did the prisoner say anything or do anything to taunt Mr. Springer?" the warden asked.

"No, sir."

Then Warden Winston addressed Springer: "Your days of being a trustee and having special privileges have come to an end. I will not tolerate behavior that reflects racial overtones. This will not be allowed in the prison that I run."

Then the warden addressed Scoop: "I commend you on your action. If not seen by the guard, it could have been told in a different way. It might have gone badly for you. That is all."

Scoop was then led back to his cell. The meeting with the warden occurred during the winter of 1953.

During eating hours, Scoop was often singled out to sit near Ben and Josh. Over the course of many months the three got to know each other during meals in the dining hall. They sat on benches, Josh next to Ben, while Scoop would scurry to the other side to sit opposite his two friends; for truly, they were becoming fast friends, sharing events of each of their past lives, and even sharing humorous stories that would elicit laughter, a response that was rare during the humdrum of prison life.

After dinner one late afternoon the three sat, having completed their meal of pork, rice, thin gravy, collard greens and sweetened tea. There were ten minutes left before they would have to stand away from the table, while trustees came to count the silverware on each tray before depositing it into a large container on a wheeled cart, all under the watchful gaze of guards. Prisoners soon realized they could not get away with trying to steal silverware – it would not work without bribing a trustee or a guard; in all the years that Ben had been incarcerated, he had never seen such a stand down, though he knew it was always a possibility.

And so they sat, enjoying each other's company. Joy? Such a word! A word so foreign to a penitentiary for hardened criminals for whom there was no joy. Joy? How could there be joy in this place of confinement, of concrete and steel, of high walls and barbed wire, of guards, some with guns, and of so very little light and no freedom? Joy was foreign to this place. And still they sat, genuinely enjoying one another's presence.

Other prisoners nearby had seen the growing camaraderie that was developing between these three, and tended to wonder about it, sometimes with an inner envy that was not easily understood; the joy was not contagious – far from it, it tended to be resented. The guards were also aware. They were inclined to pass it off as some kind of anomaly of prison life. Guards dealt with prisoners who tended to be sullen, suspicious, and sometimes dangerous. They had to be always on their guard. Yet, here was this anomaly, which was not threatening nor dangerous; rather, these three were compliant and easy to deal with.

17

A Study Group?

Conversation was light and engaging. All three participated. Then Ben asked the question, "We could all three of us study together; would you like for the three of us to form a study group?"

He was met with silence, an incredulous penetrating silence. Then Josh chimed in, "What are you talking about, Ben?"

"The prison has a library. It is a small locked room available to prisoners. It is seldom used. We would need the permission of the warden."

"But would the warden allow the three of us to be there all at once?" asked Scoop.

"We would have to ask, but I don't see why not. We might be allowed an hour or so at a time. They would keep a guard outside, and it would be just as easy to guard three as to guard one; the door would be locked from the outside, just like our cell doors are locked."

"Ben, you have been to college, while the two of us left school at an early age," said Josh. "You are so far ahead of us, I don't see how it could work."

"Look Josh, you and Scoop can read, and each of you has a fine mind. On the outside, both of you were successful businessmen, though admittedly outside the law. I know it could work if we picked a subject to study, then continued at a pace that all three understood before moving on. Would you be willing to give it a try?"

"I'm willing," countered Scoop.

"Count me in," said Josh, "but what would we study?"

Then Ben answered, "How about God?" The three looked, slack-jawed, at one another, eyes betraying uncertainty as they slowly regained composure; they then joined hands and all said, "Let's do it."

Days later Ben asked one of the guards about study time in the library. "It would have to be approved by the warden," the guard answered.

"Would you ask the warden for us?" Ben asked.

"How many would there be?" asked the guard.

"Three of us," answered Ben.

A few days later Ben was led into Warden Hale Winston's office. "What's this about three of you wanting to study together," the warden asked, "and who are the three you have in mind?"

"Myself, Josh Hampton, and Scoop Johnson," Ben answered.

"Was it prisoner Hampton that was tripped by a trustee, and prisoner Johnson who came to his aid?"

"Yes, sir," answered Ben.

"Why do you want to do this, and what would you be studying?" asked the warden.

Ben answered, "The three of us have become friends. We eat together when we can. We have thought about studying together. We want to study and learn all we can about God."

The warden was surprised. He sat back and looked intently at Ben, looking into his eyes. "I have previously reviewed your record including the jury proceeding. I see that you had a year of college at Morehouse, a fine Negro college. There were also irregularities in your trial that I am not at liberty to comment on, or do anything about. You have been here for fourteen years, and have been a model prisoner. I'm going to let you and the other two prisoners use the library an hour after lunch three days a week, Monday, Wednesday and Friday.

"Father George M. says Mass twice a month here; I will ask him if he can find Bibles and other study materials for you. But you and the other prisoners need to know that there can be no secondary gain from doing this. You will not be allowed other privileges, and this will not open an avenue to be released from prison before you have served your time; and for all three of you, your sentences are life in prison."

"Thank you, sir," Ben answered.

The next day, after lunch, the three of them were led into the library, a room with table, chairs, and shelves with old magazines and a few books. They heard the door being locked behind them. Ben explained that the warden was allowing an hour of study three days a week. He also mentioned the warden would ask a priest who said Mass twice a month at the prison if he would supply Bibles for all three.

"What now?" Josh asked.

"While waiting for the Bibles, we might talk about God, and what each of us thinks," Ben said. "I will start."

Ben told of the death of his father, killed by his mother when Ben was four years old. It was considered by the judge to be justifiable homicide at the time. Ben told of his early upbringing, and how he had gone with his mother to Sunday worship services. He had been struck by the beauty of the songs, which the women sang, deeply spiritual and emotional songs, bringing out a love for music but not much else. He hadn't thought often about God until beginning his first year at Morehouse College. The college had religious affiliations, but was non-denominational. During free time, all kinds of subjects were discussed, sometimes including religion. But he had never gone further.

Josh went next. He mentioned leaving school at an early age and being on his own. He related how he stumbled upon a moonshiner making whiskey one evening and could have gotten himself killed, but instead the moonshiner took him in as a helper. He mentioned how he had learned to make good whiskey, becoming involved in all aspects from obtaining supplies, paying off persons who could tip them off when the revenuers were in the area, making the mash, using the still, diluting, pouring into quart jars, and delivering.

It was an exciting life, Josh recalled. While he was involved in a delivery there had been an auto accident that was not his fault. Two persons in the other car were killed. He was convicted of vehicular homicide while intoxicated, even though he had not been drinking. The evidence was based on a strong odor of alcohol in the old car he was driving due to hidden jars of whiskey that had broken. He decided not to tell of the hidden compartment as he did not want to have moonshining added to his charges. He was shocked to receive a life sentence for being involved in an accident he did not cause; he had expected a lighter sentence. He had never thought much about God, nor of any religion.

Scoop then spoke. He related leaving school and teaming up with his Uncle Will in Savannah. Uncle Will was a pimp, but treated his girls fairly, and would never beat them, or cheat them from a fair split of the money earned. He related how he had served in the Navy at Pearl Harbor during the Second World War. This was when he had his first exposure to religion from chaplains that were in the military service during the war. He had attended Mass a few times, and he had been impressed, but never stayed with it. After the war he again teamed up with his Uncle Will. He then related how he had been accused of a murder he did not commit. At the trial he avoided bringing up his pimping because he did not want to implicate his Uncle Will.

It was nearing time for their hour to come to an end. Ben added some closing comments. He pointed out how each of them had been sentenced for a crime they did not commit. He also noted that each of them realized there was no chance of being released from prison; they were all convinced that they would never get out of prison alive. Despite this, they all found joy in each other's presence, so unusual during incarceration, and this was noticed by other prisoners and also by the guards.

Ben also pointed out evidence of goodness possessed by each of the three; they had all performed acts that could be considered generous, even heroic, including the way that they had protected others during their trials. "This is something we should keep in mind as we go further in our search for God."

Then they heard the sound of the key in the lock. It was time to return to their cells. Ben was thirty-four years old and had been in prison fourteen years; Josh was forty-eight and had been a prisoner for six years; and Scoop was thirty and had also been in prison six years.

These three would spend the next eight years studying together. They never missed a study hour in the prison library, and they never proceeded further during a study session until all three were satisfied. There was also a tacit understanding, never verbalized, and never committed to writing, that any future action resulting from their study would be made in unison; all would agree to take that step, whatever it was, or none would.

Ben had learned the art of civil discourse during his year at Morehouse College. This required respect for the opinions of others, learning how to get one's mind around an idea, formulating a response or reply, and also recognizing phoniness or absurdity whenever they occurred. He was good at this; but he also knew that these were skills that had to be developed. Josh and Scoop were street-smart, able to sense the circumstances they might face, and respond quickly. Ongoing discussion of ideas was another matter. Slow-going would be necessary, but of course they had time, much time.

18

No Priest Land

During the 1930's, an Order of Catholic priests and brothers based in Cincinnati, the Glenmary Order, pointed out that of three thousand or so counties in the United States, fully one thousand had no priests. These counties were in Appalachia and the deep South. They called the area "No priest land, U.S.A." They organized a Mission, to provide priests and working brothers to as many of these counties as possible. That is how the Glenmary Missions began. Typically a priest and a brother would be assigned to an area. The area usually involved more than one county. The

Glenmary priest and brother, together with a few local Catholics, and perhaps with a few converts, would start a small church. Then brother and priest would assist with obtaining materials and building the edifice. Gradually other churches would spring up, all small, and relatively inexpensive.

Father George M., a Glenmary priest, served four churches in a multi-county area, including the chapel at the maximum-security prison at Reidsville, Georgia. Fr. George was a man in his mid-thirties; his services were stretched thin. He traveled from church to church and said Mass on Sundays every two weeks, driving back and forth to provide regular services at the other churches he served. He said Mass twice a month at the small prison chapel for the few prisoners and guards who would attend.

During the week, Father George would participate in local activities, meeting with other Christian ministers and helping with acts of charity for those in need. Over the years he became a beloved figure in the many communities he served. He was a humble man who loved the people he served, and gave unstintingly of himself.

After one of his Sunday Masses at the prison chapel, he was met by Warden Winston. "Father, strange as it sounds, I have three prisoners who want to start a study group to learn about God. I have allowed the three to use the prison library three days a week, but I'm wondering if you might be able to arrange Bibles for each of them?"

Father George replied, "Warden, it is so good of you to allow them to study together in this way. I'm sure I can obtain the Bibles. It may take a little time, but I will deliver them to you when I have them. I am also available to meet with them and answer any questions they might have. They are also free to attend Sunday Masses. They don't have to be baptized to do that. I think it is wonderful that they intend to do this. It would be best to let them follow their own direction as they go along. Be assured, warden, that I would never proselytize, or force my religious beliefs on them, or on anyone else for that matter."

"I know you well enough, Father," said the warden. "You would not do this. I will also ask you to give the Bibles out in person. That way you can meet them, and arrange to answer their questions if needed."

Father George said Mass at the prison the following Sunday. He brought a Bible for each in the study group; more precisely two Bibles for each, the larger Old Testament, and the smaller New Testament. He gave them out, and also said that he was available twice a month after Mass to answer any questions. He also mentioned that he was not going to influence them one way or another, but encouraged them to continue on with the study of God.

The three, at their next study session, decided that they would go slow. They would start with the Old Testament book first, reading a few pages at each session. They would take turns reading, and then stop to discuss what they had read. They weren't in a hurry, and made light of the fact, which for them was a very important fact, that they had "all the time in the world". They would look for natural beginnings and endings for each hour of their study time. The first day they covered the creation of the world. Reading, at first, was difficult for Josh; he was the least schooled of the three. With patient support from the other two and with repetition, Josh eventually became more comfortable and more proficient with his reading. Josh's reading speed and comprehension slowly improved.

Discussion was carried out in the same way; each was by now tolerant of the views expressed by the others; after all, they had become friends. They had learned during past life experiences what friendship was all about – a preservation of the bond that had brought them together as friends in the first place. When the six days to create the earth came up for discussion, Josh was the first to suggest that the word "day" was used differently back then, and that it could have meant something else. They accepted this without reservation or further questions, and passed on to other things to discuss.

At the next session for study, they were impressed with the story of Adam and Eve and of their fall from Grace. Ben was especially touched by the story of the murder of Abel by his brother Cain. It recalled to him the killing of his father by his mother when he was four years of age, and brought a momentary lump to his throat.

They covered Genesis in five weeks, having read as a group each word, and having discussed all that they felt they wanted to. The story of Abraham resonated with all three. Scoop recognized the lust that spelled the doom of Sodom and Gomorrah, seeing similarities in his earlier life as a pimp, while Josh, for whatever reason, loved the story of Isaac, and his near sacrifice by his father Abraham – perhaps reminding him of his near-murder at the hands of Cedric, the moonshiner, a man who later became like a father or brother to him. At the end of this early period of study, they all felt an enthusiasm for what they were accomplishing. They felt captivated and drawn to further study together. The love of learning, learning something good for its own sake, had seeped into each of them, a love that would never leave.

The three spent much of their time together – the formal time during the library hours, but also the informal times during and after dinner, musing and talking about life, human life, and how during those earlier biblical times it appeared so similar to the lives each of them had lived.

They mused about the garden, how life must have been so

pleasant before the apple. God had created the garden of Eden for Adam and Eve, and they were to go on and live forever. And what was it about the apple? "Was it the apple itself or some other symbol that led to their fall?" Scoop asked.

"No," replied Josh, "it was because Eve did not obey God. Remember that God commanded them not to eat the fruit of one of the two trees, the tree of good and evil."

Ben chimed in, "I think God was trying to protect them, letting them be free, and knowing that to eat the apple from that tree would be a disaster."

"That must have been where sin came from," mused Josh. "Remember that God told them that they would die if they ate of the fruit of that tree. Sin is mentioned, and came first. Then death."

"Josh," said Ben, "you are amazing. You have figured this out on your own. I have had more schooling than you, but I don't think I could have figured out what you just said."

"God talks about the devil as a serpent, and how he tricked Eve," Scoop joined in. "Does it mean that the devil was behind it all along? In my earlier life as a pimp I knew all about tricks, I used them all the time."

Ben then entered the discussion: "I think you two have figured it out. I have learned things from you that I would never have learned on my own. Evil came from the devil. God tried to protect Adam and Eve from evil, but was not successful. Sin came, and sin brought death. Something else has just occurred to me: the sin and death that we all experience have come to us from Adam and Eve, our first parents."

Later on, when the above sequence of discussions was related to Father George, he was seen to shake his head and mutter, "Profound thoughts from the mouths of babes. Even theologians quibble over such."

19

They Were Just Like Us

Noah was a source of interest during their next session. They marveled at the widespread sinfulness of people during Noah's time. They wondered about the boat, noting that God defined the exact dimensions for its building. "Apparently Noah and his family were the only good ones living then," quipped Josh.

"There must have been a lot of shenanigans going on, and some real bad stuff," said Scoop. They did not question the size of the boat, or how pairs of the different animals and birds would fit together with Noah and all of his family. If such questions came up in any of their minds, they tended to dismiss them as inconsequential; there were more important things to be learned from the accounts that they were reading and discussing.

The rain, the rising of the waters, the death by drowning of all the people that were left, the eventual grounding, and then the bow, the rainbow, used by God to seal a covenant with Noah, were discussed in awe by all three. "What does the covenant mean?" asked Josh.

Ben said, "It is a compact. God said He would never again use a flood to destroy His people, and He left a rainbow as a sign of this. We still can see it today. God seems to be telling His people to behave, otherwise He might get angry again, but He would no longer punish His people by a flood."

The story of Abraham was just as riveting as they studied on. Abram, before his name was changed to Abraham by God, and his wife Sarai, whose name was changed by God to Sarah and who was barren, were approached by God. God established a covenant with Abraham saying that his progeny would be numerous, and be a people formed by God.

"This seems to have been a very important moment," noted Ben. "God has several things to say. In their old age God promises Sarah that she and Abraham will have a son. Meantime, Sarah, knowing she is barren, has arranged for her maid servant Hagar to become pregnant by Abraham. There is a lot going on here. Both Abraham and Sarah appear to giggle in disbelief that Sarah, at her advanced age, could conceive.

"Hagar is the first to give birth to a son named Ismael. Sometime later Sarah is found to be pregnant, and gives birth to a son, Isaac. Usually the oldest son is handed the inheritance, but God intervenes and says that it will be Isaac who is to be the favored son. Sometime later, Hagar and her son Ismael are banished.

They are given a little food and water, and sent into the desert to fend for themselves. When food and water are gone, they stop and await death. Hagar prays for deliverance, and God sends an angel to open up a well of water and to otherwise provide for Hagar and her son. The angel also promises that God will make a great nation from the descendants of Ismael."

"It looks like God is establishing two separate groups of His special people," says Josh. "Isaac is the one first selected by God, then later Ismael. They are two different groups, but why?" The three pondered that question, but could not come up with an answer.

"There is God and angels; but people are behaving just like us in these accounts," said Ben.

"Angels must be special," ventured Josh. "There was a mention of angels guarding the garden after Adam and Eve were expelled, and several times we have read of angels accompanying God as they met with Abraham. Sometimes they appear like men, and other times more like spirits; we can't really tell."

They were caught up in the dramatic doings of Abraham, commanded by God to take his son Isaac up the mountain as a sacrifice. As they read on, fully expecting Isaac to be killed by his father, they were relieved that God had sent an angel at the last moment to save the boy. There was indeed a sacrifice, that of an entangled ram in the briars, but not Isaac.

"They were just like us," quipped Scoop.

"How do you mean?" asked Josh.

"But don't you see?" answered Scoop. "They made mistakes; they committed sins, just like us."

20

Circumcision, Yipes

They were entranced when God reestablished his covenant with Abraham and Isaac, their descendants to be as numerous as sands on the seashore, or stars in the sky. They did not stop to ponder a one-for-one single descendant with a single grain of sand or a single star. They would have labeled such questioning as trite and even ridiculous.

But then God did a very strange thing. He demanded circumcision – that the foreskin of all male infants be removed at eight days of age, and that uncircumcised males of any age be circumcised. This was to apply to all future generations. They each questioned, "Have you been circumcised?" None of them had, though they each had been aware of others who had.

Now the covenant of circumcision was established before Ismael and his mother Hagar had been expelled. The three were spellbound when they read of Abraham circumcising Isaac, then Ismael, and then all of the males in his extended family. They were even more astounded when they discussed the obedience of Abraham to God's word, and of the high degree of faith and acceptance of circumcision by all of Abraham's sons.

At another afternoon session in the prison library, the three chuckled over the story of the twins, both the sons of Isaac and Rebecca, and how Jacob grabbed the heel of Esau, still in the womb, apparently aware that he wanted to be the firstborn. Nontheless, Esau was the firstborn and thus eventually entitled to be blessed by Isaac, and thus to be the leader of the special people of God. As they grew, Esau became the outdoorsman, the archer, while Jacob, the second son, seemed more homebound. As they followed the story in their study, Isaac grew older and became blind. The story was full of delight for the three students, because it abounded in trickery and deceit, known so well by Ben, Josh and Scoop. All along, Isaac favored Esau, while Rebecca favored Jacob. Isaac sent Esau far afield to hunt and bring back venison meat for a stew. Rebecca covered Jacob with lamb skins, used the lamb's meat to make a stew, and presented Jacob dressed as Esau. After Isaac ate the stew, Jacob faked Esau's voice and asked for the special blessing. Isaac was initially suspicious, but after calling Jacob and feeling his hairy exterior, he gave Jacob the blessing. When Esau returned he was furious. He told his father of the ruse, and asked Isaac to rescind Jacob's blessing, and to give the blessing to him instead. Isaac, when learning of the deceit, said no. The blessing had been given. It belonged to Jacob.

There was much bad blood subsequently between the two twins, Jacob having to leave under a threat of death from Esau. While Jacob was away, Esau married a daughter of Ismael, solidifying the second line of progeny set up by God, and again discussed by the three during a study session. They found this fascinating, but could draw no further understanding from it.

They followed Jacob's wanderings, his dream of a golden ladder from earth to heaven with angels ascending and descending, and then, during his dream, a call from God that his descendants would spread out in all directions, and become as numerous as the dust of the earth. Still later, God appeared to Jacob and changed his name to Israel, and again made him the head of a favored people.

"They are just like us," Scoop said.

"What do you mean?" Ben interjected.

"Why, they lie and cheat, just like we do. None of the three of us would be in prison today except for the deceit and tricks that were played on us."

"I get your drift," said Ben, "but if we weren't here together, we wouldn't be studying the things we are learning about God."

With that they all fell silent, a silence that lasted and was accompanied by a feeling of peace, a peace that they all shared.

The trio of students next began to read and ponder the story of Moses. As before, they took turns and read slowly, a page or two at a time, and then paused to discuss anything that caught their fancy. They had developed an ease with one another and had learned a great deal. There was no longer the need to await slow or staggered reading, or to be embarrassed to participate during discussions. There was now a flow of information and ideas that would have been the envy of any college discussion group. They, without being aware, were using the Socratic method, but without a Socrates! The poser of challenging ideas was the Scriptures! They were guided in their discussion of ideas by the Holy Book itself!

They read of Moses the shepherd tending his flock near Mount Horeb, when Moses spotted a burning bush. Approaching, he noted fire but no burning; then he heard, "Approach no further, this is holy ground. Take off your sandals. I am the God of Abraham, the God of Isaac, the God of Jacob." They noted that God had heard the cries of the enslaved people of Israel, and that He intended to do something about it.

They were very interested in the enslavement episode. They were steeped in their own history of enslavement, but did not know that others had also been enslaved.

They closely followed the attempts by Moses to convince the Egyptian Pharaoh to free the captive people of Israel, but without success. They hung on every word of the Exodus, the use of the blood of lambs to mark their houses, the death of all the Egyptian firstborn, both human and animal, by the avenging angel, and the flight of the people of Israel away from Egypt.

As they continued reading, they were mesmerized by the account of Pharaoh's chariots, his whole army, in pursuit of the fleeing people, and the pillar of fire and the darkness that caused Pharaoh's chariots to halt. They were struck by the awesome spectacle of the parting of the Red Sea. They imagined what it must have been like to walk on dry ground between two massive walls of water, one on each side of a column of people with their animals, walking to freedom.

Then came the resumption of Pharaoh's pursuit. The chariots and foot soldiers followed between the walls of water and were gaining, but then the vanguard of the approaching chariots began to slow, as their wheels became entangled in the soft sea bottom. This allowed the fleeing people with their animals to cross unharmed. Finally, the sea rolled back to engulf and destroy all of Pharaoh's army.

They sat in silence looking at one another. They were caught up in the drama of something none of the three had known before. Here was a story of slavery under very harsh conditions, with back-breaking labor and a struggle toward freedom. Here was a flight away from the oppressors, the Egyptians, dramatic miraculous events, and sudden death occurring on a massive scale. They read, then reread the descriptions, and discussed all of the varied aspects. They were left in a quandary. How could God kill those thousands of pursuing soldiers, soldiers who were simply following orders from superior officers? They decided to pose the question to Father George.

They petitioned Warden Winston for permission to attend Sunday Mass, and it was granted. It would be more than a week, since Mass was offered only twice a month. Scoop had attended Mass a few times when he was in the Navy and he explained to the others, as best as he could remember, what it consisted of. Mass began at 9:00 am, and the three joined the small gathering of guards, prisoners and civilians in the prison chapel. They were curious and respectful. They saw Father George enter wearing strange robes they later learned were called vestments.

They took their cue from others when it was time to stand, sit or kneel; and kneel they did; they were not at all adverse to this. Theirs was an attitude of inquisitiveness. Just as with their studying, they wanted to learn as much as they could.

They sat and listened to the first reading, a passage from the Old Testament. It was about Abraham, and they recognized the reading immediately as something they had previously studied.

Then they stood for the gospel. This was about Jesus, a name they had all three heard before, but knew hardly anything about. After the reading of the gospel they sat down again and listened to the homily delivered by Father George. This was short, taking probably no longer than ten minutes to deliver. Father George spoke clearly and in a manner that caught the attention of his small congregation. The homily dwelt on the gospel, pointing out that Jesus was the Son of God, born of the Virgin Mary, who gave His life to atone for sins, and allow heaven to once more be opened for sinful man.

After Mass they approached Father George, reintroduced themselves, thanked him for supplying their Bibles, and gave a summary of where their studies had gone so far. They presented their quandary about Pharaoh's soldiers being killed by the returning waters of the Red Sea. Since the soldiers were following orders, why were they killed? And what would happen to them? Father George gave them a surprising answer, one that led to repeated discussions the following week. They were told that no one prior to Jesus Christ was able to enter heaven. The souls of the dead were kept in a place without suffering, but deprived of the happiness of heaven. "As you study further, you will find predictions of a Savior who is to come. That Savior is Jesus. You will learn all about Jesus when you get to the second book I gave you, the New Testament."

21

The Predictions

They continued their study of the Old Testament, noting the Ten Commandments, the Prophets and the Kings, and were especially intrigued with the stories of David. They were riveted with the account of the young boy David slaying Goliath, the giant Philistine warrior. They noted that it was David, selected by God, and anointed by the prophet Samuel, who was to be the progenitor for a future Savior. They also noted that David was from the village of Bethlehem. They searched, especially as they progressed, for mention of a Savior who was to come in the future. David's last words before he died spoke of he being the man to whom it was appointed, concerning the Christ of the God of Jacob.

They found reference under the words of the prophet Micah:

> *"And thou, Bethlehem Ephrata, art a little one among the thousands of Judah; out of thee shall come forth unto me that is to be the ruler in Israel; and his going forth is from the beginning, from the days of eternity."* (Mi. 5)

They found under the prophet Jeremiah:

> *"Behold the days come, sayeth the Lord, and I will raise up to David a just branch; and a king shall reign, and he shall be wise; and shall execute judgment and justice in the earth. In those days shall Judah be saved, and Israel shall dwell confidently; and this is the name they shall call him; The Lord our Just One."* (Je. 23)

Then Zacharias said:

> *"Rejoice greatly O daughter of Sion, shout for joy, O daughter of Jerusalem: Behold thy King will come to thee, the just and savior; he is poor and riding on an ass, and upon a colt the foal of an ass."* (Za. 9)

It took the three, studying in the library, month upon month, year upon year, to slowly make their way through the Old Testament, reading and then discussing. Whenever a quandary came up, they would save it and present it to Father George after the next Sunday Mass. They were thoroughly engrossed in their study, and were also becoming attached to the Catholic Mass being celebrated by Father George.

Soon they were into the Psalms. They found them to be beautiful, much like a series of lyrical poems – a lot like music, which they all loved and could relate to. They were still focused upon predictions of a savior to come.

The Psalms spoke of the son of God being born in Bethlehem, ruling with justice and being rejected by men, with a future of suffering and death. The Psalms mentioned his tormentors casting lots for his garments just prior to his death. They spoke of God's covenant with David, confirming his posterity for all future generations.

Ben, Josh and Scoop continued their studies. When they finished reading and discussing the Psalms, they became convinced that a clear prediction was being given of a savior, a redeemer, a son of God, a descendent of David, and one who was to be born in Bethlehem. They then went on to Isaiah and the rest of the Old Testament.

22

Reflection

Ben, Josh and Scoop had spent more than five years on a slow and gradual study of the Old Testament. At first it was getting used to a new way of expression – to a quite different way of using words. They took time after each hour of study to discuss what they had just covered. They were, by now, fast friends, relying on each other's insights to forge the way ahead. Despite initial difficulties of studying about a different time and place, expressed often in a quaint and sometimes a puzzling writing style, they persisted. Impatience was not a detriment. They each cherished the hour three times a week that warden Winston had allotted to them. So what if it took them years of plodding away; they had all the time in the world to spare.

Over the last year, they were especially taken with the predictions of a savior, a mysterious person to save the nation of Israel, and beyond Israel, the gentiles, from their sins.

They had studied the time lines, learning that Abraham lived around 2000 B.C., Moses around 1500 B.C., and David around 970 B.C. The Psalms were written around the time of David and his son Solomon. Isaiah lived around 790 B.C., Zacharias around 753 B.C., Micah around 737 B.C., and Jeremiah around 642 B.C. But what did B.C. mean? They were intensely curious, and asked Father George what this meant, and he explained. Pope Gregory VIII in the year 1582 revised the old Roman Julian calendar, put forth by Julius Caesar. The new Gregorian calendar would be centered upon the birth of Jesus Christ. For those years before the birth of Christ, English was used; they were called Before Christ, abbreviated B.C., while for those after the birth of Christ, Latin was used. Those years were called Anno Domini, abbreviated A.D.

They were about to enter a new study – a study of the New Testament; one that would eventually connect all of the predictions found during their five years of Old Testament inquiry, but now connecting to a concrete person, Jesus Christ. They would spend nearly three years on this next phase; and there would be life-changing consequences for Ben, Josh and Scoop; changes that none of them could have foreseen when they began their study of God.

23

The Gospel of Saint Matthew

They were now avid, and on a mission of discovery. All that went before had been thoroughly reviewed, discussed and digested. They were three friends, seemingly with one mind, or more precisely one aim. They were like bloodhounds, on the trail of scent, not willing to stop until their quarry was found.

They were fascinated to read in Matthew's prelude about the coming of the Savior and the genealogy of Jesus, traced from Abraham, through David and then the Babylonian captivity to the birth of Jesus. There were forty-two generations, and they recognized several of the names, for they had spent the prior five plus years studying them.

Next they read of the virgin birth. Mary, a young virgin, was with child by the Holy Spirit. They sought details, but could not find them until they took up the gospel of Luke, perhaps a year of study away; but Scoop said, "This is the virgin birth predicted by Isaiah; it had never happened before – it was a miracle." Next, they read that the baby, named Jesus, was born in Bethlehem, as predicted seven hundred years earlier by Micah.

Matthew's gospel went quickly to the public ministry of Jesus. When John the Baptist was delivered up, they read that Jesus withdrew into Galilee. Leaving the town of Nazareth, he came and dwelt in Capernaum, which is by the sea in the territory of Zabulon and Nephthalim, fulfilling the words spoken by the prophet Isaiah:

> *"Land of Zabulon and land of Nephthalim, by the way of the sea, beyond the Jordan, Galilee of the Gentiles: The people who sat in darkness have seen a great light; and upon those who sat in the region and shadow of death, a light has arisen."* (Is. 9)

The three marveled that this was predicted more than five hundred years before the birth of Jesus. They saw in Matthew the mission of Jesus being fulfilled by preaching and miracles. They were astounded to read the Beatitudes. They noted that the persons being honored were the poor in spirit, the meek, those who mourn, those that hunger and thirst for justice, the merciful, the clean of heart, the peacemakers, and those being persecuted for justice's sake. They discussed these qualities over several days, and all came to the conclusion that life would be better for everyone if people could live like that.

They followed the course of Jesus as he selected his Apostles. They were ordinary persons, fishermen and a tax collector, persons of little or no education; they also noted that when called by Jesus, they came and followed without delay. They also took note that Jesus called these early followers the salt of the earth, and the light of the world.

They read that Jesus discussed the old law and the new: that he did not come to abolish the old law handed down through Moses, but to fulfill it. He contrasted the old law, "thou shalt not kill", with his admonition against anger with one's brother (instead of first offering a gift at the altar, go first to be reconciled with thy brother).

Jesus talked about chastity of mind and body when he contrasted the commandment not to commit adultery with his new command that anyone who so much as looks with lust at a woman has already committed adultery with her in his heart. This reading resonated strongly, especially with Scoop who had been a pimp before going to prison.

Jesus contrasted the old law of justice that spoke of an eye for an eye, and a tooth for a tooth when he said:

> *"I say to you not to resist the evildoer; on the contrary, if someone strike thee on the right cheek, turn to him the other also; and if anyone would go to law with thee and take thy tunic, let him take thy cloak as well; and whoever forces thee to go for one mile, go with him two. To him who asks of thee, give; and from him who would borrow of thee, do not turn away."* (Mt. 5)

The three, as they read and pondered, had much to think

about and discuss. They recognized Jesus as someone special, someone who bridged the gap between the Old Testament that they had so thoroughly studied, and the New Testament that they had recently begun. They recognized that the New Law, while being an extension of the Old, had some starkly different concepts. It would take them awhile, with thought and discussion, to come to grips with the concept of turning the other cheek; they were unsure if they could ever accept this.

They continued to read, study, and discuss the gospel of Matthew. Reading on, they came to Jesus' words about the power of prayer:

> *"Ask, and it shall be given you; seek, and you shall find; knock, and it shall be opened to you. For everyone who asks, receives; and he who seeks, finds; and to him who knocks, it shall be opened."* (Mt. 7)

Ben was the first to comment, as the three sat stunned and in awe, from what they had read. "Jesus is truly someone very special. His words strike me to the heart. He teaches lessons that apply to everyone. He speaks with an authority that comes from God Himself. He speaks of the heavenly Father as his own Father. He speaks as the Lord Himself, when he says: 'Not everyone who says to me, Lord, Lord, shall enter the kingdom of heaven.' Jesus also speaks of judging 'on that day,' indicating that he has the power to decide who of us will be able to enter the kingdom of heaven. I am in awe of this, and don't know what else to say."

Josh and Scoop kept looking at him, unable to speak. Finally, Scoop spoke, "All that you have said I have also felt in my heart. Jesus is someone very special. We have seen how he fulfills the predictions we have studied in the Old Testament. The way he teaches those around him touches my inmost self. We have just started studying the life of Jesus; we need to continue our studies; they are like a journey we are taking, a very exciting trip."

Still avidly reading and discussing the Gospel of Matthew, they turned a page and were confronted with a series of miracles. The first was a leper. He also cured a man with a withered hand while teaching in the synagogue on the Sabbath. When criticized by the Pharisees for performing this on the Sabbath, Jesus responded by asking "what man would refuse to lift his sheep having fallen into a pit on the Sabbath?"

Jesus cured the blind, the lame, the deaf and the dumb; and when it was whispered by the Pharisees that he casted out devils by the power Beelzebub, the prince of devils, Jesus responded that any kingdom divided against itself cannot stand – if Satan casts out devils, then he is divided against himself.

Jesus went on to cure many who were possessed, curing all of the sick brought to him, taking to himself their infirmities and bearing all of their ills.

Josh then stopped reading, searched for his Old Testament Bible, and looked up Isaiah, chapter 53, and there it was, as it had been stated nearly eight hundred years earlier: "Surely he has borne our griefs and carried our sorrow." When he found the passage, he read it to his companions, and they were silent, and in awe for many seconds.

The three student-prisoners were greatly impressed from what they had just read. Here was Jesus confronting two disturbed men, so fierce that others stayed away from them. And they spoke, not as men, but as evil spirits. Ben said, "Jesus commands evil spirits, and they obey. They also refer to Jesus as the Son of God." Ben then went back in his Bible to the Old Testament, and found the reference in Psalm 2, that he was searching for: "The Lord said to me: 'You are My son, this day I have begotten you.' " He slowly read this passage to the others, and mentioned that it was a prophecy told about one thousand years before the birth of Jesus, and yet it seemed to apply to Him.

None of the three, as they discussed this further, had a contrary opinion. They were of one mind. At some point during their eight years of study about God, faith made an entrance into each of their lives. They recognized a new sensation, later described by Father George as the beginning of faith. But on this particular day, none of them spoke about it.

The three students of the Testaments continued to have much to discuss. They kept reading about Jesus, and then would search the Old Testament for the prediction that fit each circumstance They found several, including the last words of David, several of the Psalms, and many from Isaiah, Micah, Zacharias, and Jeremiah. The more they brought these up for discussion, the more they were in awe, and the more they believed them. They spent time discussing each of the miracles recorded in Matthew's Gospel, and came to accept them as being authentic. They recognized the miracles of healing and casting out of evil spirits as beyond human powers, and knew that God Himself had to be the cause.

They dwelt at length on discussions of the initial twelve apostles: how simple and unlearned they appeared since many were ordinary fishermen, repairing their nets, and cleaning their boats on the shores of the sea of Galilee, which their families had done for generations. They recognized the apostles as ordinary men, men in possession of all of the weaknesses that other men possessed. The ordinariness of the apostles made a great impression upon the three students, who regarded themselves as ordinary too, albeit unfortunate to be kept as prisoners.

The three, bent on this eight-year study of God, were amazed again and again as they read these passages from Matthew's Gospel. They talked more of their own lives – ordinary men caught up by unforeseen and unfortunate circumstances. They all had undergone a similar progression, from confusion and anger, to eventual resentment and finally acceptance of their fate. Most of the prisoners they saw day to day were dispirited; they seemed beaten, men who had given up; men who saw no hope.

The three student-prisoners were not at all like that. They possessed an inner peace, and a striving for answers to what each considered as becoming central to their lives, namely: just who is this God we have been studying, and especially, just who is this Jesus Christ who is regarded as the Son of God, and the Savior of the world?

They pondered the mission handed to the apostles – to spread the words that Jesus had spoken to them. They trembled a little as they reviewed Matthew's passage concerning their future enemies: they were "like wolves in sheep's clothing" ready to devour them, and took comfort in Jesus' statement to the apostles to "be not afraid", that he would always be with them.

They were in awe of the conflict that arose between the Pharisees, a part of the priestly elite, and Jesus, over the miracles Jesus was performing in the synagogues, and on the Sabbath. How could the pharisees not accept the evidence of miraculous cures by Jesus? This happened not once, but numerous times. They were puzzled by the pharisees' reaction to Jesus – plotting ways that they could capture Jesus and put him to death.

They found fulfillment in the prophecies of the Old Testament when reading the forty-second chapter of Isaiah, as being yet another of the many references pointing to Jesus as the Messiah, the Son of Man, the Son of God, the Savior.

They were amazed in reviewing the mercy of Jesus. They puzzled over Jesus' reference to sin, when he stated that every kind of sin and blasphemy will be forgiven of men, except sin against the Holy Spirit. They, in their discussions, could come to no understanding of this.

But one thing that was happening to each of them was a beginning awareness that the Holy Spirit was special – special like Jesus. Therein was the beginning notion for them of a trinitarian God: The Father, the Son of God, and the Holy Spirit of God. They were not there yet, but were close to seeing this; and this became another something, in their ongoing studies, that they would ask Father George about.

They also began to sense a new and different understanding of the mercy of God. To be saved must mean to be allowed to enter heaven. This seemed to be the purpose of Jesus, the Savior. But in referring to sin Jesus was noted to say that every kind of sin and blasphemy committed by men can be forgiven. This was important to them; they went on to discuss that all men, not just a few, could be saved; the only exception seemed to be blasphemy against the Holy Spirit.

24

The Kingdom of God

Several parables that pertained to the kingdom of God were then taken up. They would use their allotted hour in the prison library to take turns reading a portion, and then stop to discuss what they had read. They were astounded when reading the parable of the sower whom they recognized as God, the good seed as those belonging to the kingdom, and the weeds as evil spirits or persons. They were just as surprised by the conclusion – that both the good and the bad seed would be left undisturbed and not separated until the harvest – the good grain would then be carried into the barn, whereas the weeds would be burned.

They marveled at the parable of the woman adding leaven to flour and watching it spread and cause the dough to rise up. They recognized in this parable that the kingdom of God would spread everywhere.

Josh spoke up, "These parables told to the Apostles by Jesus are like stories. They are similar to the stories I listened to, told by my elders when I was growing up."

"Yes," said Ben, "They carry a power, these stories about the kingdom of God; and they tell of the separation of good and bad people at the end of the world. To believe in Jesus means to accept that the world will come to an end, and that bad people will go to hell and be punished in fire."

Scoop added, "I don't want to go there. I want, instead, to go to heaven. I think we will be reading about Jesus and how he saves us. I am learning from these readings in the Old and New Testaments that we are all sinners." They discussed the various ways that Jesus taught about the kingdom of God, and that each story told in an amazing way how the kingdom could be understood.

Next in Matthew's gospel they covered the Passion, Death, and Resurrection of Jesus. They began with Jesus predicting his death, but then promising to rise from the dead after three days. They dwelt on the betrayal of Jesus by Judas, one of the apostles. They marveled at the details portrayed at the Last Supper – how Jesus broke the bread and offered the wine as the New Covenant of his body and blood.

They were amazed when reading of Jesus' agony in the garden, when the son of God asked that the coming burden of suffering be lifted by his Father, but that his Father's will should be followed regardless. They discussed the weakness of Jesus' humanity that was on display. Then Josh commented that "he was just like one of us".

They were saddened as they read and then discussed the details of the Passion and the Crucifixion. They could understand how the apostles ran and hid in fear, except the apostle John who stood by the cross with Mary, the mother of Jesus.

Then they reviewed the burial of Jesus and the resurrection, the glorious centerpiece of what was to become the Christian religion. After the resurrection, Jesus stayed with his apostles and many other disciples another forty days, eating with them, teaching, and finally commissioning them to go forth to the ends of the earth, baptizing in the name of the Father, and of the Son, and of the Holy Spirit.

With the end of the Commission by Jesus to the Apostles, the Gospel according to Saint Matthew came to a close. There was much to discuss. Ben started by stating that Jesus had foretold his death and resurrection on three separate occasions. Scoop mentioned the triumphal entrance into Jerusalem and how the obtaining of the ass and its foal, used by Jesus to ride into Jerusalem, had been foretold in the Old Testament.

They then talked about the Last Supper. They were astounded to review what Jesus had said as they all gathered at table. They recognized the importance of Jesus' use of bread and wine, and how he stated that they were his body and blood: Eat and drink to be saved, and do this in remembrance of me. Scoop was the one to comment, "Jesus meant it when he said this is my body and blood; otherwise he would have said this is bread and wine. This was meant by Jesus to be a miracle, which would continue to our present time."

Ben remarked, "Scoop, you have nailed it! I did not pick up on the power of this until you just said it. Another thing, when Father George says Mass, he repeats the exact same words that Jesus used. We should ask Father George about this the next time we attend Mass."

The three spent one whole hour in the library discussing the death, burial, and resurrection of Jesus. Ben spoke first, "This is central to the belief that Christians have. Jesus brings the two Testaments together. We have seen that the Old Testament mentions someone to come, a Savior. We have also found many predictions about the Savior in the writings of the Prophets, and the Psalms. At the start of our study of God, we purposefully focused on these predictions; and we have seen that they all point to one person, and that is Jesus, as being the Savior."

Josh then spoke, "Jesus predicted his own death and rising from the dead in three days; it happened, exactly as he foretold. There was a guard placed at the tomb, ordered to keep watch to prevent anyone from coming to steal the body. We know about guards. They won't let anyone get away with anything. They were struck down afraid when the angel came and rolled back the stone."

Then Scoop spoke, "Jesus even predicted that Judas, one of his disciples, would betray him to the Chief Priests for thirty pieces of silver; and it happened exactly that way. Judas then repented and went to the Chief Priests to give back the thirty pieces of silver; but they refused to recind the bargain. Judas was so upset that he threw the silver pieces onto the temple floor and went out and hung himself. The priests picked up the silver pieces, but decided that it was blood money so they used it to buy a Potter's field for the burial of strangers. The Old Testament, hundreds of years earlier, had predicted the thirty pieces of silver, and that they would be used to buy a Potter's field."

Ben was the next to speak, "I feel that I am ready to accept Jesus as the Son of God, and my Savior; but now I don't know what the next step should be."

Josh then spoke, "You have been our leader since we started. I am with you. Jesus is truly my Savior, and my Redeemer, as demonstrated in both the Old and the New Testaments."

Ben spoke again, "We started this together, and together we should continue. I would not want to take another step forward, unless all three of us agree. We have been at this for nearly eight years now, and we have the rest of the New Testament to cover."

Then Scoop spoke up, "You have both said what I feel. I too would not want to take a next step, whatever that would be, unless both of you were with me. Maybe we should ask Father George what the next step should be. I know that I have been impressed when we have gone to Mass. He says exactly the same words that Jesus spoke at the Last Supper. I would like to ask him more about that. Do you think we should ask Father George where we might go from here?"

They, all three of them, always together in their years of study, placed their hands together in the same affirmation they had used when their study began. They would move forward together, or not at all. So ended their study of the Gospel of Saint Matthew.

25

The Gospel According to Saint Mark

They covered the Gospel of Mark in a relatively short time. They noted that it was shorter than the Gospel of Matthew, but otherwise quite similar. One difference, an addition actually, was at the end. Matthew made no mention of the ascension of Jesus, but it was mentioned by Mark:

> *"So Then the Lord, after he had spoken to them, was taken up into heaven, and sits at the right hand of God. But they went forth and preached everywhere, while the Lord worked with them and confirmed the preaching by the signs that followed, Amen."* (Mk. 16)

26

The Meeting with Father George

They asked Father George if they could meet with him after the next Sunday Mass. He said yes, but that he had one other church to attend to that morning; he had four scattered small churches, including the chapel at Reidsville Prison, and offered Mass twice each month for each. "What do you want to talk about?" asked Father George.

"About our study of God, and some questions we have about the Mass. We have completed all of the Old Testament, and the Gospels of Saint Matthew and Mark in the New Testament," said

Ben.

"I am greatly impressed with your efforts," said Father George. "Could we schedule another time, maybe next Saturday afternoon, to give us more time? I feel certain the warden would approve. I will ask him before I leave; wait here."

As the three waited in the prison chapel, a guard outside the door, Father George returned – next Saturday, at three in the afternoon, here in the chapel. The warden had no problem with that.

The following Saturday they met again with Father George. Ben began by outlining how far they had gone in their studies and discussions, and how from the beginning they had moved as a group, wanting all three to agree before taking the next step. They had had a recent one-hour discussion of the Last Supper, and had noted the words used by Jesus in offering the bread and wine were exactly those used by Father George during the Mass. Scoop was the first to point out that Jesus referred to the bread and wine as being his body and blood and if He had not meant this, he would have just called them bread and wine.

Then Father George spoke: "The three of you have uncovered a great truth, one that has been accepted since the start of the Christian Church by Jesus, and spread by the Apostles, even until now; that is, that the bread and wine are truly the body and blood of Jesus. I applaud you taking any additional steps together. I could join your discussions in the prison library anytime you would like me to, and review with you anything dealing with God and your study of the Holy Scriptures. I will ask the warden if he would allow this; I feel that he will."

27

The Gospel According to Saint Luke

The three students of the Testaments, Old and New, were eager to explore the Gospel of Luke. They especially liked that Luke dealt with the birth and early life of Jesus – a time in the life of Jesus barely touched on by Matthew, and not mentioned at all in the Gospel of Mark.

Luke's Gospel spoke of the appearance of Archangel Gabriel to a young girl named Mary. Mary was initially startled, but then was reassured by the angel not to be afraid. The angel stated that Mary was to have a son, being overshadowed by the Holy Spirit, and that her virginity would be retained. Mary responded that she would be the handmaid of the Lord. Then Mary was told by the angel that her cousin Elizabeth, aged and previously barren, had been pregnant for six months, and would bear a son to be named John.

Mary visited Elizabeth, and was greeted by Elizabeth, who recognized that Mary was to be the mother of the Lord. Mary then recited one of the great prayers given in Luke's gospel, referred to as Mary's Magnificat.

Soon it was time for Mary to give birth. This is the Christmas story, so well known, even to these three prisoners. Nonetheless, they marveled at the happenings. They commented on the Virgin Birth, foretold in the Old Testament predictions, and the subsequent narrow escape of Mary, Joseph and the Baby Jesus on the trek to Egypt, barely ahead of Herod's murderous soldiers.

The three students were in awe of Zachary's pronouncement. They recognized references and exact predictions – what they came to identify as prophecies – from hundreds of years earlier in the Old Testament. These were from the prophets Zacharias, Micah, and Isaiah, whom they had studied before. These guideposts from the past reinforced for all three their emerging faith.

The three continued their studies three times a week for one hour. They went to Father George's Mass every other Sunday, and asked him questions concerning what they had studied. Father George made it known that he had asked the warden for permission to attend some of their study sessions, but the warden had refused, indicating that he wouldn't feel right having to lock up a priest. The warden suggested some time in the chapel after Mass, and if more time was needed, it could be scheduled in the chapel on a Saturday afternoon.

The rest of Saint Luke's Gospel was continued to its end. Ben was especially impressed with the account of the two thieves crucified one on each side of Jesus. On the next occasion of meeting with Father George, Ben asked about the two robbers crucified with Jesus, especially the one regarded as the good thief. Father George responded that his name was later determined to be Dismas.

28

The Gospel According to Saint John

As they began the study of John's Gospel, they noted it was different from the other three. They asked Father George about this, and they were told that the gospels of Matthew, Mark and Luke are referred to as synoptic, because they tell the same stories. John's Gospel shows the Divine nature of Jesus. The three students were especially impressed with the way John began his gospel:

"In the beginning was the Word,
and the Word was with God;

and the Word was God
He was in the beginning with God.
All things were made through him,
and without him was made
nothing that has been made." (Jn.1)

They read on, through all of the rest of the gospel of John, continuing to be amazed at what they were learning. Then they moved on to the Acts of the Apostles. They read of the ascension of Jesus into heaven, and of the two men in white garments, whom they recognized as angels, asking in a very ordinary way:

"Men of Galilee, why do you stand looking up to heaven? This Jesus who has been taken up from you into heaven, shall come in the same way as you have seen him going up to heaven." (Acts 1)

They saw how Judas' replacement, a man named Matthias, was selected as the twelfth apostle by drawing lots. They read about the days of Pentecost, and the descent of the Holy Spirit upon the Apostles as a violent wind, and then as tongues of fire settling upon each of them. The apostles began speaking in foreign tongues, went outside the house where they were staying, and began baptizing new believers by the thousands. The three prisoners continued to read, discuss, and be amazed, finishing the Acts of the Apostles and then covering all the epistles of saint Paul, the other letters, and finally, the apocalypse.

29

What Now?

They were done. Finished! Their eight years of study were now at an end! What they had set out to do was now over. It was a powerful journey for all three. They had had a goal to study God – a daunting task that they approached timidly at first. They had had many doubts: Could they study together? Would they stay together given the vast differences in schooling between all three? How to begin? Would the warden allow them to use the prison library as a place of study and discussion?

They had overcome these obstacles by recognizing their recently formed friendship; and the need to proceed slowly, so as not to leave anyone behind. When Ben had suggested a study of God, they were stunned. It took awhile to orient their minds around this; a study about God? Would this be too much for them to handle?

Ben was the first to suggest that they review what they had learned. "Let's all take a turn and tell the others what seems important. I'll start. Everything starts with God. He is the Creator of everything."

Scoop then added, "I liked the story of the Garden. Though Eve took the apple and brought sin into the world, it was the devil that tempted her. Sin, and maybe all evil, comes from Satan. After that, we saw sin everywhere. Eve's two sons Cain and Abel got into it, and one of them became a murderer, just like most of us here in prison. The flood was all about saving the few who were good people from the rest who were evil."

Josh came next, "The story about Abraham was amazing. God made Abraham the father of a whole lot of people. There was Jacob who came through Isaac, and whose name was changed to Israel. He seemed to be the forerunner of the Jewish people. But there were others of Abraham's descendants, Ismael and Esau, who were fathers to another group. I think these must have been the Arabs. I wish there had been more in the Bible about them."

Ben said, "When I was in college at Morehouse, we had discussions about the Jews and the Arabs, and how they seemed to be fighting each other over the centuries. I was surprised to read about the way people fought each other in the Old Testament. The story of David fighting Goliath, and the armies of Israel and the Philistines come to mind. Also, the chariots of Pharaoh chasing after Moses and his people crossing the Red Sea. We were all caught up in the drama of that episode. I remember we asked Father George how God could have allowed soldiers following orders to die in that way."

"Sin and death seem to have been everywhere in those ancient times, just like now" said Scoop. "It goes back to the Garden. I remember sin came from Satan and the apple, and then came death, a sentence given to everyone. Everyone who sins dies, so everyone who dies must be a sinner. This seems to have carried through because it applies to all of us."

"God is interacting with his people throughout the Old Testament," said Josh. "He leaves space for people to commit sins, but He asks for people to repent before He is willing to forgive. He is forming His people; we see many references to the God of Abraham, the God of Isaac, and the God of Jacob."

"We have all been impressed with the predictions in the Old Testament of a future Redeemer," said Ben. "We have taken special note and made it a part of our discussions to focus on these predictions. We have many prophecies from the prophets and the psalms that provide specific information about a coming Savior. Then, when we get to the New Testament, hundreds of years later, these predictions all turn out to be true."

Josh said, "The New Testament is all about Jesus. He is the true Redeemer. I especially liked the stories about Jesus from the Gospel of Matthew. He was an ordinary man, like us; poor, like many of us; but He was also the Son of God. He came to redeem us, and he did it by dying on the cross; once for all of us. Then, as He predicted, He rose from the dead, stayed around another forty days, and then ascended up to heaven."

"We have also learned that Jesus promised to send the Holy Spirit to be with each of us, to guide us on the path to salvation," said Josh. "And we read about Pentecost, when the Holy Spirit came upon the apostles with a loud wind and tongues of fire, and they were miraculously changed, speaking in tongues, curing diseases, and baptizing thousands of people, as Jesus had previously told them, in the name of the Father, and of the Son, and of the Holy Spirit. Father George, at some of the Masses we have attended, has made mention of three persons in one God; these are the Father, the Son, or Jesus, and the Holy Spirit."

They continued taking turns reviewing what they had learned during their eight-year study of God. Ben chimed in, saying, "'Do not be afraid,' is something that has turned up over and over again. I remember in the book of Kings in the Old Testament when the prophet Elijah met the starving widow and asked her for a cup of water and a little bread. She was gathering sticks for a fire to bake the last of her flour and oil for a small cake for her son and herself, before they were to starve. Then Elijah said to her: 'Do not be afraid.' He stayed with them for a year; she continued to bake bread, and the jar of flour and the jug of oil never ran out.

"In the New Testament we have seen many times that Jesus also says, 'Be not afraid.' There is something going on here; something that God wants us to know. I think it means that we should not be afraid of whatever happens to us in this life; our true happiness will come later. The three of us have had our share of misfortune, as we live out our lives here in prison. 'Do not be afraid' should have a special meaning for us."

Now it was Scoop's turn. He faced the others and said, "The story of the Last Supper stays in my mind. We first saw it in Matthew's Gospel, but again in all of the other gospels, and also in the letters of the apostle Paul. When Jesus, the night before his crucifixion, stood before his apostles, and said; 'This is my body', he didn't say, "This is a piece of bread.' Likewise, when Jesus lifted the cup, and said: 'All of you, drink of this; for this is my blood of the new covenant, which is being shed for many unto the forgiveness of sins.' Jesus did not say: 'Drink of this cup of wine.' I have to believe that the bread and wine that Jesus offered were really and truly his own body and blood." Scoop stood before them solemnly, as if in prayer, and then there was silence.

Scoop continued, "When we started this we were uncertain. Now, I am certain. Jesus is my Lord and Savior. He is the Son of God. When he says, 'I and the Father are one,' it must mean that Jesus is also God. We have attended Mass with Father George. He also says during Mass: 'This is my body' even though he is raising up a piece of bread."

"I am ready to go further," Scoop said, " but I won't do this unless the three of us do this together."

Josh then said, "I have felt exactly this way for a long time, but I was afraid to be the first to say anything. Scoop, I'm with you, but only if Ben joins us."

Now it was Ben's turn to speak. The eyes of the other two were gazing intently upon him. He began by saying, "It was I who suggested we study together, and it was I who suggested we study God. After a period of uncertainty and uneasiness, we made progress. It was our unfailing friendship that has carried us through this. It was slow at first, but we agreed to move ahead only when we were all ready.

"It has been eight long but enjoyable years that we have been doing this. We have moved along as if we were of one mind. By that I mean we have not had a single disagreement about what we were studying. We have all participated in the discussions, and asked questions. We were, all of us, eager as we went along – eager I will add in a search for truth – the deep and abiding truth that these Old and New Testament books have brought to us.

"Scoop, you have said these things so beautifully. You want to go further – so does Josh, and so do I. I too have felt this way for a long time now. Since I was the one that proposed these studies, I did not want to be the first to speak. I am happy that we all agree. I think that as a next step, we ask Father George after the next Mass if he would be willing to give us further instruction. What would you think of that?"

They all joined hands. This would be their next step.

30

The Next Step

They went to Mass the next Sunday with renewed interest in the Mass itself, but especially what it portended. When Father George raised the host at the Consecration, and said the words, "This is my body", and later raised the cup and said, "This is my blood", they knew what was being said; it reinforced what they had studied, and what they had previously said to one another.

After Mass they met with Father George. They told him that they had finished studying, and that they were interested in taking a next step. Would he be interested in giving them further instruction?

Father George responded, " I am delighted that you feel this way. It was eight years ago that I brought Bibles for you to use. I have also seen you together at Mass, especially during the last two years. I will be happy to instruct you further about God, about Jesus, about Christianity and about the Catholic faith if that is what you are interested in." They responded positively, even eagerly, that this is exactly what they were hoping for.

And so it started. Father George had obtained permission for an hour on Saturdays, from one to two in the afternoon. A guard would be stationed outside of the chapel door.

The first Saturday was spent reviewing what the three had studied. They talked, while Father George listened. Father George was amazed not only with their knowledge of the Testaments, but also of the zeal with which all three participated. He mused, cheerfully to himself, that these three were already better prepared with the foundations of faith than most others that he had baptized.

The following Saturdays were spent in discussions about Jesus and Christianity. Father George pointed out that he was Catholic, one of several Christian denominations. He also spoke of Peter the Apostle as being the first Pope, and that the Catholic faith extended from Peter down the centuries to the present. Then Father George asked if they wanted to go further. "Do you wish to be baptized?" he asked.

They all said, "Yes."

Then Josh spoke: "I remember what Saint Matthew said at the end of his gospel. 'Go, therefore, and make disciples of all nations, baptizing them in the name of the Father, and of the Son, and of the Holy Spirit'; I memorized it."

Father George questioned all three further to ensure their statements were genuine. He was convinced, but would not leave a stone unturned when it came to such an important step. He went over the seven sacraments of their new faith. Baptism was the first, and in some respects the most important. With baptism by water and oil, all prior sins are removed. The newly baptized person immediately is in possession of the Holy Spirit, to be with them for the remainder of their lives. He then reviewed the other sacraments as special channels of grace: Reconciliation, Eucharist, Confirmation, Matrimony, the Sacrament of the Sick. and Holy Orders, which enables the consecration of new priests. He also went over God's grace, which is given to each one of us; the need for and the power of daily prayer; and the benefit of giving one's self to Jesus. He also explained the special place that Mary has in the Catholic faith.

It was then that Scoop interjected and said, "You know, Father, it's no secret, but before I came to prison, I was a pimp, and abused women. When I read the words that Mary said to Elizabeth, the tears came into my eyes. I knew immediately how wrong I had been. I will always have a special feeling for Mary, the mother of Jesus, the mother of God."

"You know, Scoop," Father George said, "She is also our mother; the mother of all who have ever lived. Jesus gave her to us as he hung on the cross just before he died."

Father George then told them that they were spiritually ready for baptism, that each of them could select a baptismal name, and that he would like to select a godfather for each of them.

Josh answered first, "David is my choice. He was a major person in the Old Testament. He was also a great sinner. Maybe there is hope for me."

Then Scoop spoke, "Joseph will be my name. It was in Saint Luke's Gospel that I first became aware of the birth of Jesus, and of Mary his mother. Joseph was the husband and protector of

Mary; and Mary remained a virgin after Jesus was born. As I have already mentioned, I have abused women during my earlier life. Maybe this name will help when it comes my time to face judgment."

Then it was Ben's turn. "I will take the name Dismas. He was the good thief, crucified next to Jesus, who defended Jesus against the taunts of the other thief. I know that Jesus will forgive me, since he forgave Dismas."

Conversation then went on to the godfathers. Father George pointed out that for Catholic baptisms it is customary to select a godfather for boys and men, and a godmother for girls and women being baptized. These are persons that are available to help assure a continuing spiritual education if it becomes necessary. He said, "I would like to select one for each of you. My parishioners are all white; do you have any objections if I find a white godfather for each of you?"

"No, not at all," they answered.

Then Ben chimed in, "Maybe they would object."

Father George then said, "I'll see what I can do. I would like to bring them by next Saturday for you to meet with them."

The following Saturday afternoon, Father George drove into the prison parking lot and parked his rusting old sedan. He had three young men, all white, as his companions. They were admitted to the prison, and then escorted to the chapel.

Inside were the three black candidates waiting to meet the strangers who were to be their godfathers. At first there was silence as they looked at one another. Then they introduced each other, and began conversing.

Father George had chosen his subjects well. He had told them that he needed three volunteers to become godfathers for three prisoners at the Georgia State Prison at Reidsville. He pointed out that the prisoners were black, and that they were all serving life sentences. He reviewed the duty of a godparent, to be available to support the spiritual education of the person being baptized. This duty usually applied to children being baptized when the parents were no longer able to do this. Since the prisoners were adults, and in prison serving life sentences, this duty did not really apply; even so, Father George wanted each newly baptized person to have a godfather.

Then Father George appointed a godfather for each of the prisoners. He noted the age differences. The prisoners were older, considerably older. Then he said, "I see that you three to be newly baptized are quite a bit older than your newly assigned godfathers." This brought chuckles and laughter from those being addressed. Then he said, "I think it would be better for you to regard each other as brothers." This brought looks of incredulity from black as well as white members.

"How can this be?" asked Scoop; "We are black and they are white."

Father George answered, "With baptism there is a new life. All previous sins are forgiven. There is a new bond formed between the person being baptized, and the godparent. The bond is from God. Race has nothing to do with it. I just think that because of the age differences, 'Brother,' would be more appropriate than 'Godfather.' Are there any questions? Are you all comfortable with this?"

There were no questions, only grins and knowing glances of understanding. Then they all embraced with heart-felt murmurs of brother, one to another.

Father George went on with his explanation. "The baptisms will take place next Saturday afternoon at one o'clock. I have already talked with the warden and have his permission. Immediately following the baptisms, we will have Mass. This will enable the newly baptized to receive Holy Communion; they have already received instruction as to how to receive and reverence the Host; and they are fully aware that what they will be receiving will be the Body of Jesus, as Jesus Himself instructed at the Last Supper. If there are no further questions, I will leave now, and take the white brothers with me, unless they wish to stay in jail until next Saturday." There was laughter. The brothers, black and white were finding out that Father George had a sense of humor.

The next Saturday they all gathered as planned. A few unarmed guards were there and so was Warden Hale Winston, though Warden Winston was not Catholic. Josh Hampton went first. "And with what name do you wish to be baptized?" intoned Father George.

"David," Josh said.

"Okay then," Father George said. "Step over here while I bring this pitcher of water over and have you bend your head over the basin. David, I baptize you in the name of the Father, and of the Son, and of the Holy Spirit." David was then given a towel to dry himself off.

Next Father George selected Scoop Johnson to step forward. "With what name do you wish to be baptized?"

"Joseph," Scoop said.

Then Father George said, "Joseph, I baptize you in the name of the Father, and of the Son, and of the Holy Spirit."

Last to step forward was Ben McClellan. "And with what name do you wish to be baptized?" asked Father George.

"Dismas," answered Ben.

"Dismas, I baptize you in the name of the Father, and of the Son, and of the Holy Spirit."

Mass followed. All of the brothers, black and white, together with one of the guards, received Holy Communion. After Mass there were congratulations and well wishes that made the rounds. Father George and the white brothers then left.

David, Joseph and Dismas were led back to their cells. The year was nineteen hundred and sixty-two. David was fifty-seven years of age, Joseph was thirty-nine, and Dismas was forty-three. All three subsequently served out their life sentences, and died in prison.

31

Epilogue

This is a work of fiction. Or is it? Buster, his real name, and all of the details of what occurred that summer night in Georgia, are presented exactly as they happened, although the time frame is different. Most of the other names are fictitious.

Three Negro prisoners, with life sentences for murder and their eight-year search for God, are real; and so is their baptism at the Georgia State Penitentiary at Reidsville.

The name of Dismas, taken by one of the prisoners, is true. I know – I was there – I was the godfather and brother of Dismas.

THE SMILE

THEN

Ashif ibn Shihab walked slowly along with his group of companions. They were in single file, spread about ten yards apart. It was midday and the sun bore down on the group as they made their way across the desert sands. Then they came to a stop. In front of Ashif was a prisoner, arms behind his back, held in place by ties around his wrists. Ashif stood to one side and behind his prisoner, forced him to a kneeling position, and told him to say his prayers. Each of Ashif's companions had a prisoner, clad in orange robes. Ashif reached for the long knife in a scabbard at his side. This was a heavy knife that he had sharpened that morning on a grinding wheel, and then on a whetstone for an extra-sharp edge.

Ashif felt the hilt in his right hand, and on a pre-arranged signal, brought the knife down quickly to sever the head of his prisoner. The head rolled onto the sand, while the body collapsed lifeless onto the ground. There was no movement. He observed hardly any blood draining from the head, while blood was squirting in rapid pulses from the four neck arteries, the two large carotids at the front of the neck, and the two smaller vertebral arteries at the rear. After several more seconds the spurting red arterial blood came to a stop, while purple venous blood continued to ooze and puddle from the body, before sinking into the desert sand.

Ashif pondered the clean beheading which he had accomplished and also how beheading was a swift and virtually painless way to die. He had learned this as a medical student in Paris some years before, knowing exactly where to strike just below the skull, but also above the shoulders to achieve a clean severance. He noticed that one of his team had struck a prisoner on the skull, but the prisoner had fallen to the ground and multiple hacks were needed to sever the head. Another member hit his victim high on the shoulders below the neck. That victim also fell, but cowered and then convulsed as further hacking took place. Dumb clucks, Ashif thought, I instructed them just yesterday as to where and how to strike.

After finishing his grizzly deed, Ashif wiped the blood from his knife and hands with a special cloth that he carried. This cloth, with its dried blood, would be kept in his possession as a trophy and a reminder of this special day. They walked back in single file. He thought of the exhilaration he had felt during the execution. His jaw muscles tightened, and he could not suppress a triumphal smile of pleasure. Then he remembered what his prisoner said to him just prior to the fatal blow: "I forgive you for what you are about to do." His smile slowly faded.

As Ashif marched back from the site where he had beheaded his victim, he berated the two dumb clucks who had botched their executions. Death, but not additional suffering, was to be their purpose, but they responded that they wanted to prolong the executions for the sheer joy of it.

THE EARLY YEARS

Ashif was born in Syria in 1983. His family were refugees from Palestine where they had been farmers and orchardists for generations, but they had been forced to leave during the Arab-Israeli war of 1948. Initially they lived in a Syrian refugee camp, but with the aid of extended family members, they were able to settle in a suburb of Damascus, where Ashif's father started a small business, and gradually began raising a family. Sadly, one conflict after another unsettled the civil tranquility that so many longed for. During 1967, Syria joined Egypt in the six-day war only to have the Syrian Golan Heights taken by Israel. In 1973, Syria attacked Israel in the Yom Kippur war, and more Syrian territory was annexed by Israel. When Syria began a thirty-year occupation of Lebanon in 1976, the family decided to move too. They settled in Beirut where Ashif's father again opened a small business in support of his family. Gradually the family thrived. Ashif was sent to private schools where he was found to be a quick learner and a serious student.

A RUDE AWAKENING

In 1993, two powerful truck bombs exploded in Beirut. One targeted the barracks housing United States Marines, the other the barracks for French Paratroopers. There was enormous loss of life.

Later, an obscure group calling itself the Islamic Jihad claimed responsibility. Ashif was ten years old at the time. Though curious, he had little or no sympathy for those who were slain. Israel had invaded Lebanon in order to destroy the Palestine Liberation Organization, which was headquartered there. The United Nations brokered a cease-fire and foreign soldiers from the United States and France had been sent to maintain the truce. Ashief had sympathies for the PLO, as his ancestral family was from Palestine, but he did not form allegiances then. His interest was in pursuing an education.

Ashif graduated from school with honors, and was fluent in Arabic, French and English. His family had become affluent, and they arranged for college studies abroad in Paris. He drifted during his first year of college, and then entered a pre-medical curriculum. After four years of college he was accepted into medical school. In 2005, at the age of twenty-two, he began medical studies.

PARIS

His friends while living in Paris were mostly former refugees like himself. They tended to be from families who had fled Palestine, with periods of life in refugee camps in Lebanon or Syria where some of his friends, like himself, had been born. Conversation typically focused on the turmoil in those countries, and events as they changed were followed daily. Gradually they began to share a conviction that they and their families had been treated most unjustly. They blamed Israel. They also blamed the countries that had allowed, and even fostered the formation of the State of Israel. These entities were more and more regarded as foreigners occupying Arab lands. A smoldering anger began, very subtle at first, expressed by one or another in the group of friends, then gradually taking the form of group hostility. Despite these feelings, Ashif pursued his medical studies with enthusiasm.

In 2007, an event occurred which was to have a profound effect upon Ashif and other members of his group. Israel, in a surprise attack, bombed a site in Syria suspected to be a nuclear reactor being built with the assistance of the North Koreans, who themselves had possession of the A-Bomb. Why, they asked themselves, should Israel be allowed to bomb Syria since it was well known that Israel also possessed nuclear bombs? A seething resentment leading to hatred of Israel, and all of Israel's allies, especially the United States, but also France, Britain, and the United Nations, became a galvanizing force for members of this group.

A NEW FORMULATION

At the end of his second year, Ashif decided to drop out of medical school. When asked by his French teachers why he was doing this, he gave vague answers, such as a desire to see more of the world. He never discussed his political ideas with anyone other than his Palestinian friends; when asked about his views on Israel and turmoil in the Middle East, he became noncommittal. He dropped out of school, and then seemed to drop from the face of the earth. He left Paris after another year for destinations unknown. He did not return to his family in Lebanon, and had no further communication with them. Gradually he was forgotten by his family, out-of-sight, out-of-mind. When he was discussed by family members, they assumed that he was traveling the world, and leading a life of leisure somewhere.

He and the other members of his group decided to strike out on their own as activists to achieve the rights that they felt had been denied them. They kept to themselves, though gradually meeting and befriending other young men with views similar to theirs. They frequented cafes for food and conversation, and then began attending mosques, though Ashif and his friends had not considered themselves to be particularly religious. One day they were approached by an older bearded man who invited them to a place for food and further fellowship. He expressed views, though initially reserved, similar to theirs. Gradually a friendship was formed, and other bearded men, mostly older, joined in. Conversation slowly became more focused on what was being said about the common enemy, namely Israel, the west, and the UN. This was a topic Ashif and his friends could readily agree with; they felt an expansion of solidarity and unity with the group, and a gradual feeling of belonging developed.

At some point the conversation veered toward action. This was subtle at first, not directed and not spelled out as to what form the action might take. This resonated with Ashif and his friends; they had on their own decided to become activists. The need to cause small areas of damage to the common enemy was then discussed. They bit, like a trout to a fly. Why not, Ashif and his friends responded. The first stage of their preparation was now complete.

Ashif was recruited to join with a small cadre of like-minded young men. They were all strangers. None of his friends were in this group; they were elsewhere; in fact, Ashif was never to see any of them again.

He arrived at a camp. He was not told where they were going. Activity began in earnest. Ashif and his new companions were told that absolute obedience to the leader was required; any lapse would receive immediate and severe punishment. They were up at dawn and went immediately to calisthenics and a slow run in single file. Prying eyes seemed everywhere. They had two daily meals and shaving was not allowed; they were told to let their hair and beards grow. There would be no changes of clothes. Bathing was infrequent, sparse, and without soap.

Soon the lectures began. These were conducted in the afternoon, and started with a reiteration of the common enemy and the need to prepare for warfare wherever this enemy was to be found. Thematic material was always the same: find, attack, destroy, kill. Ashif knew early on that this was indoctrination; but fear, the strong urge to succeed, and strict orders for silence, and therefore not being able to discuss any of this with others, proved to be stronger than any feeling to resist or to slow down. Gradually he became hardened and unquestioning.

Ashif's trainers found that he was intelligent and had advanced schooling. Most of the others had no schooling at all, or only an early smattering. Some could not read or write, but here was one that could do both. He was shoved upstairs.

He was taken in silence to another place, a small village, with a journey, sometimes by car, sometimes on foot, lasting a few days. There he was turned over to another person, more senior, and to whom he was to maintain strict obedience. His travel companions left; he never knew who they were and never saw them again. At first there was nothing to do except to be at certain places at certain times. He felt he was being observed, and by others besides his master. Gradually he was oriented to duties that mostly involved communications. He was shown a computer, a familiar piece of equipment, and instructed on its use; he was taught several codes, and the need to keep messaging short and infrequent. He was also briefed on the ever-present surveillance, especially by known satellites, and instructed to transmit only when they were beyond the horizon. These rules also applied to the use of phones.

Ashif did what he was told. Life was slow and leisurely, but he had to be admonished more than once not to engage in conversation with any except his master and his master's close associates.

He was not used to so much leisure time on his hands as he had always been busy during his earlier life. He was also found by his superiors to sometimes veer outside the limits of procedure, using a wrong code or transmitting a bit early or late. His superiors put up with this for about two years but then started to consider Ashif a risk since everyone's safety depended on strict adherence to protocol. One day he was told he would be going elsewhere. The next day he left again on a long journey, without any idea of his destination.

The camp to which he was dispatched was small, but quite different from where he had been indoctrinated. He joined others in carrying out small acts of destruction. His initial work was in finding others to act as martyrs in detonating bombs. These were poor destitute men or women, uneducated and unable to read or write. These persons were brought to the camp and given a rapid course of indoctrination. They were told about the positive effects of martyrdom: sainthood, and monetary benefits for their families, which was often all that was needed to persuade. Those who could drive, or be taught to drive would be trained to deliver car or truck bombs to designated targets. Other mules, as they were called, were instructed in the use of explosive vests. Those unable to be taught, or unwilling, were executed at night and at a distance; they could not be released as they would pose a danger for the camp.

This kind of activity went on for three years. Periodically the camp was moved for safety and security reasons. Ashif found himself in a different place with different companions, but carrying out the same work as before. Then one day this all changed.

Ashif knew very little of Islamic Jihad, except the name. But Islamic Jihad was also rapidly changing. Power vacuums were developing throughout many of the Arab countries. Northern Iraq adjoined eastern Syria and was a rich area to exploit. Instability also occurred in Yemen and Sudan. Potential Jihadi fighters were also showing up in large numbers from foreign countries, even from those countries considered to be enemies. These fighters would have to be trained, but already appeared indoctrinated. Training for war would not take long.

Soon Ashif found himself in a larger camp. He was to be one of those training others to fight. With his years of experience this would be easy. He was given a briefing about methods, especially the need for strict discipline. After two months the first group under his command was ready for war. Other raw recruits were brought in. He noted a difference in these foreign recruits. They were unruly, often with criminal convictions. They were harder to train initially. Sometimes strong punishment had to be meted out in the form of severe beatings. Occasional malcontents, recalcitrant and unmanageable, were taken out of the camp at night and executed.

Someone higher up declared himself to be Caliph of the Islamic State of Iraq and the Levant, or of Iraq and Syria; and this designation was shortened to ISIL or ISIS, and then further shortened to IS. The resources for its rapid formation came from somewhere, but Ashif had no idea where. There was great enthusiasm for the future. Ashif found himself in a large group of fighters that moved from eastern Syria to northern Iraq, then south toward Bagdad. They moved rapidly in cars and trucks down the well-maintained roads. Before long, they found themselves approaching the northern outskirts of Bagdad.

Resistance was non-existent. The Iraqi army was unwieldy, inefficient, and uniformly corrupt. Most of the officers shed their uniforms and ran in the face of the advance. Others who were not so lucky were rounded up, then marched in single file into the desert and executed. Ashif and his companions had been instructed to show no mercy. Brutality was to be their method. It was felt, higher up, to be a strategy, a way to strike fear into the hearts of enemy countries.

NOW

So when did it happen? Ashif began experiencing doubt. He had become inured to the slaughter, but who were they slaughtering, and why? These were not enemies, but other Arabs. Persons from enemy countries had joined their ranks and were slaughtering Arabs. This did not seem to make sense.

His thoughts drifted back to another time, a time of relative peace in his life. He thought of medical school in Paris, and the girl. She was also a medical student, quick to learn and skillful in the anatomy laboratory. One day in class they sat at adjoining seats and he caught her gaze. He was startled at the beauty of her face, the black hair and those deep blue eyes. Those eyes, so open, so innocent, so joyful, so strong, left a lasting impression. Gradually they struck up a conversation. He introduced himself as Ashif, originally from Palestine. She gave her name as Jeanne, and said that she had lived all of her life in France.

His thoughts ranged back to the times he had spent with Jeanne. They sometimes had lunched together at an outside cafe in Paris; at other times, they had walked together along the Champs-Elysees, and under the Arc de Triomphe. One Saturday, she asked him if he would like to accompany her to church the next morning. He responded that he was not a very religious person. He thought more about it, and because he was becoming fascinated with this girl, he said yes.

They took the underground to Notre Dame Cathedral. Before entering, Ashif studied the architecture. He was fascinated by the high arches, flying buttresses, and even the gargoyles. Inside he was struck by the immensity and the beauty of the stained-glass windows. He was awkward during the service with the postures of kneeling, sitting or standing, and took his cue from Jeanne, though he did not kneel. He watched while she went to the altar for communion.

Later they stopped at a cafe for brunch. He asked for an explanation of the bread and wine, and was told that Catholics believed it to be the living body of Jesus, but in a different form. Ashif knew enough of his religion of Islam to respond that Jesus was a prophet, just before Mohammed, the last prophet. Jeanne responded that she knew a little of Islamic faith, that there were a series of prophets including Abraham and Moses that were shared in faith between Moslems, Christians and Jews; she also knew that Moslems accepted the virgin birth of Jesus from Mary.

Over time Ashif had other troubling thoughts. If Moslems accepted Jesus as a prophet, why had they not been taught anything about his life? They knew Abraham, and regarded him as Father Abraham. They also knew of Moses, but why not Jesus?

Doubt deepened. Ashif cut his hair and shaved his beard. He was shaken in his beliefs, and greatly disturbed. One day he was asked why he had cut his hair and shaved his beard. He had no reply. His superior noted that he had been acting strangely. Ashif said he did not want to participate in further killing because he found himself killing other Arabs and not the enemy. All he saw in return was a scowl in silence.

The next day he was taken and placed in a small room, locked from the outside. He was briefly visited, and told that he would be given a few days to rearrange his thinking and come to his senses, but that they could not let him go. He thought about all of this repeatedly and deeply. He realized that he had stopped short of a precipice, but that there was no turning back. Though deeply troubled, he found himself strangely at peace. As the days went by he continued to rethink the predicament he was in. He could save his life by recanting, but knew that he would have to lie. He also knew that he could not, and would not play a deceitful game. The door was unlocked and his superior with two others came into the room. They were hard-faced men. He was asked if he was prepared to change his mind. He said no. He was then told he would be executed the next day.

The following day he was given a mid-morning meal, then ordered to don an orange jump-suit. An hour or so later his door was opened, and he was escorted to the outside. His executioner approached, a man he had not seen before. While his wrists were being tied, he engaged him in conversation, explaining that he had beheaded a prisoner before. He said a quick stroke from behind between the skull and the shoulders was best.

Then they proceeded to walk single file to an outer desert area. There were three or four other prisoners, all wearing orange suits. They stopped. He was told to kneel, lean forward, and say his prayers. His last words to the executioner were: "I forgive you for what you are about to do." Then the heavy knife descended quickly to lop off his head.

The executioner gazed intently at the inert body and the pooling blood. Then he looked at his victim's head. The hair was short, and there was a stubble of returning beard. The head had fallen into a position to look back at the executioner, but the eyes were closed. Then he noticed the faint smile on the victim's face.

DIVVY UP

GROWING UP

Boris grew up in a village near Vladivostok. As a boy he became a pickpocket and was skilled enough to have never been caught. Rubles and kopeks he pocketed; watches and other fleeced goods he pawned. The petty-crime underworld was so efficient that he was able to evade apprehension during all the years that he was growing up.

His family noticed early on that he was self-sufficient in that he never seemed to lack for necessities. They wondered about this, but never appeared to catch on to his life of petty crime. He did attend school and became an avid student, especially in mathematics and social studies. His teachers were impressed and concluded that they were dealing with a student who could be advanced. They placed him in an advanced grade with special course work, which he quickly mastered, then advanced him again. He completed the required eleven years of secondary education in nine years.

MOSCOW

Tertiary education was at the Moscow Engineering and Physics Institute, where after four years, he was granted a doctorate in science (Doktor Nauk). Then Boris branched out into Industrial Research and Development where he excelled in telecommunications.

He worked for several years with a small team of subordinates in the shadow world of industrial electronics research. He carefully allocated tasks to subordinates so that no one under his supervision could see the outline or progression of a major project. His interest was encryption methods for coding messages such that only authorized parties could read them. His team developed many encrypted codes.

He regularly travelled to conferences and industrial fairs outside of Russia. He was keenly focused on new techniques that might have an application in his work. His approach to others was that of a mendicant, giving the impression that he lacked advanced knowledge in his field, and fawning obeisance for any favor offered by another. He also had an unusual awareness of personal weaknesses in the people he met, especially peculiarities of character that might suggest or underlie deviant behavior of a criminal nature. He sought out such individuals whom he thought might be of some benefit to him in the future.

At one such meeting in New Delhi he met Ezra, from Tel

Aviv, very up-to-date in the telecommunications field, and one whom Boris perceived as a definite crook. He would keep Ezra in his repertoire of persons of possible use to him in the future, but would keep a mental asterisk. Because of the antagonistic attitudes between Israel and Russia, he would have to be very careful in approaching Ezra in the future.

Then there was Dekg, from Nairobi, a first-class crook, but not at the forefront of industrial development. He was a lightweight and would be of no use in the master plan that was slowly incubating in the recesses of Boris' mind. Hwan from Seoul was first rate in telecommunications, but suffered a deficiency. He was too honest. Maybe with time and suitable inducements he could be turned, though the prospect seemed unlikely.

DUBAI

At one such Industrial fair and conference sponsored by the United Arab Emirates, he met Raghib from Dubai. One of the topics at the conference was the insidious working of malware in telecommunication networking. Raghib presented a paper on recognition techniques for dealing with viruses, worms, and trojan horses, which laid out a very detailed approach to understanding and dealing with these types of infections. Boris introduced himself to Raghib after the presentation. This time Boris did not take on a fawning attitude. Instead he presented himself as the brilliant scientist that he indeed was. The two began a conversation that included cutting-edge details of encryption and malicious software. Both found themselves in the presence of a fascinating other, someone they could learn from. Thus began a friendship that was to have lasting and unforeseen consequences.

Boris was invited to Raghib's apartment in one of the high rises in Dubai. Raghib, like Boris, was a bachelor, and appeared to be an adventurer, a person fond of fast and expensive living. They left for dinner at an upscale restaurant where reservations, at least by Raghib, appeared to be unnecessary. The meal was sumptuous with many courses suggested by Raghib. They each had a before-dinner cocktail, which Boris noted, as most Arabs do not use alcohol. Boris took his traditional vodka, while Raghib drank a martini. Boris took note of no olive, and asked about this. Raghib answered that olives spoilt the flavor and taste of an otherwise excellent gin martini, and that he preferred a twist of lemon rind. There was wine with the meal. The meal and alcohol had a familiarizing effect with both talking of their varied forms of leisure, and of their backgrounds. Boris provided only enough conversation to encourage Raghib to further disclosures. Raghib noted that while he had grown up in the oil-rich environment of the Middle East, his family did not directly benefit from oil's riches. His schooling was subsidized, and because of innate ability he was able to advance rapidly.

Then the conversation shifted, or was directed by Boris, to financial matters. Raghib indicated that although he was well paid, he lived most of his life from paycheck to paycheck, and was in considerable debt. Boris sensed an opportunity, but did not press forward at that time. The conference was to last another three days. After thanking Raghib for the splendid meal and fine half-day of their developing friendship, Boris took his leave, but before leaving he made it known that he wanted to return the hospitality: would two days hence, late afternoon and evening work out? To this they agreed.

After revisiting the hardware booths and checking the round of papers, Boris met again with Raghib. They went to a modest bar; Boris did not want to appear ostentatious. There they began several rounds of drinks; Boris started with two rounds of vodka, then an imported German beer which he was quite capable of handling. Raghib stayed with mixed drinks, and after two hours began showing signs of exuberance, and early inebriation. That was the point when Boris changed the subject of their conversation back to money.

Boris pointed out that business in Russia was most often conducted with a handshake, and a wink. Corruption was rife, and though he did not agree with the system, he had to play by others' rules. It was simply the way business was conducted. Then he asked about business in the Emirates. The hook was in. Boris could feel it. It was unmistakable. Raghib began to spout. His speech was a gush of pent-up feelings. He had been involved in many such dealings, but always seemed to come out with less than he expected. He felt that sometimes he was unfairly taken advantage of, but was not at all adverse to behind-the-curtain deals. The next steps would be easy.

Boris laid out the outline of a plan that involved using a bank's own computer programs to siphon off money into a separate account. He said he was certain this could be done without being detected, but that he would not proceed unless Raghib was willing to be a participant. Boris did not want an answer at this time; he wanted Raghib to ponder it, and he would review it with him later. Then they went to a modest restaurant for a meal that was devoid of further alcohol. When the dinner was over, and before dropping Raghib off at his high-rise apartment building, Boris asked him whether he could say if he was in or out. Boris could tell by the enthusiastic response that Raghib was in. He then told him that future communication would be by encrypted messages on the internet, and provided him with an encryption key.

The months went by, while Boris and Raghib communicated back and forth using encrypted messages. Boris was essentially non-informative with these messages, wanting to make certain that Raghib was familiar with the codes, and was being up-front. Boris also took his time to search the back avenues of the internet to see if there had been any detectable leaks. He knew that their encrypted messaging could be intercepted, but that they could not be deciphered by anyone except one in possession of his key. A leak would point the finger at Raghib, but none was found.

Gradually more information was exchanged. It was pointed out that a third person was needed, someone involved with large bank transactions; someone who would have to be brought into their scheme. They stated the need and that both would be on the lookout for such a person; however, any approach would be delicate, and perhaps the most perilous point of their joint enterprise. Both would review possible persons of interest, but make no contact. Careful discussion and further study of a possible candidate was mandatory.

SINGAPORE

Then it happened. Just how it came about did not at first seem apparent. Boris and Raghib attended a telecommunication conference in Singapore. Their joint appearance had less to do with the program content than the opportunity to again meet in person, and exchange a new encryption key for continued messaging. Raghib left for Dubai the next day citing the need to be back on his job. On the second day, Boris, while standing at a refreshment table during an intermission, found himself next to a short and thin middle-aged Asian gentleman. He introduced himself, and the Asian gentleman gave his name as Hairie. Boris asked how he was enjoying the conference; Hairie answered that he found it dull and boring; his interest was banking, but none of the papers or displays were relevant. Boris sensed an important contact, and said that he too was bored, and then suggested that they both go out for a drink. Hairie agreed, but said his drink was tea; alcohol made him sick.

They found a teahouse and a booth where they could be alone. Boris told of his background, his doctorate in science, and his current work dealing with telecommunication industrial research. He did not divulge that encryption was his special area of interest. If pressed, he would lie and give another field.

Hairie listened and then gave his background. He was a Singapore native raised and schooled in the British tradition. He was involved in banking, a mid-level executive of a large international bank headquartered in Singapore. He lived in a small house and was divorced. He was Malaysian, was distrustful of the government, and had an unsettled anxiety about his future because of a perceived political instability in that part of Asia. He talked freely, perhaps too freely, Boris thought; but Boris encouraged him to go on.

The waitress came to pour more tea, and left some small cakes. Hairie said he was bored with his job, that he wasn't paid enough, and saw no possibility of advancement. Then Boris asked about business practices in Singapore, especially the banking sector, and whether Hairie had ever known of kickbacks, noting that this was a common practice in Russian banking circles. Hairie said he had witnessed such practices, and suspected them to be common but didn't know. Then Boris, avoiding his usual caution, boldly asked Hairie if he would like to work with a small group to make more money. Yes, was Hairie's quick reply.

They met again the next day. This time Boris was more circumspect, wondering if he had moved too quickly the day before. But what he found was avid greed - a willingness on Hairie's part to participate even if it meant engaging in shady deals. Boris let another day go by.

Once again they met at the same teahouse in a secluded booth; Boris took time to evaluate his quarry. He asked if Hairie had access to the bank's computer files, particularly names and access methods for any of several accounts. Hairie said yes, this was his main responsibility. If he showed any hesitancy, Boris could not see it, and Boris considered himself an excellent judge of another's character; indeed he had based his career on that talent.

EASY MONEY

Then Boris sketched out his plan, discussed encryption, which the two would use for communicating, and gave him an encryption key. He made no mention of Raghib, and gave Hairie a key that had a different encryption code than the one he had given Raghib.

Once again Boris returned to Moscow, to the small flat where he lived, and his laboratory. His communications with Raghib continued, but less frequently, and with less content. He did not mention Hairie. When Raghib wondered about progress in recruiting someone, Boris would respond with the need to keep looking, and the need for extreme caution.

There were frequent encrypted communications with Hairie over the next several months. Once again Boris was cautious. He provided only enough information to be tantalizing, and to act as bait. Would the fish strike? And strike Hairie did. He proved avid in his thirst for information and in going ahead with the master plan. Boris also used his contacts with specialists in Moscow to comb the back eddies of the cyber world for leaks; but again, as with Raghib, no leaks were found.

Boris then made a detailed request. Select six of your large accounts. Each must have balances in excess of one hundred million US dollars. Do not include accounts that belong to any government. When you have made your selections, send me the account numbers and all access codes.

Within two weeks Boris had the selections in hand. Quick work, Boris thought. Hairie was turning out to be better at this than he had hoped. Boris then turned his efforts to devising a worm for each of the six accounts. His laboratory subordinates were assigned segments. No subordinate had overall control. It took several months to develop a worm that would divert one million dollars from an account and simultaneously leave the account not knowing that it had been hacked. Furthermore the worm was designed to render all computers in the account network blind to the transfer. A separate worm was designed for each of the six accounts, then each was exposed to a series of rigorous tests. Eureka! They were ready! They all worked!

Boris then fed the worms back to Hairie. Within another week the encrypted message from Hairie confirmed that the insertions had all been accomplished, and that six million US dollars had been removed and transferred to a new account at Singapore's branch bank in New York City. Why, Boris messaged back, had he choosen this method? He could have made the transfer to any of a number of private banks in Moscow. The answer back was cautionary. They need to keep their tracks covered. They should let this new account rest for three to six months before making withdrawals. Boris was satisfied with this explanation, even giving Hairie credit for better judgment than he had expected.

NEW YORK

Six months went by with no suggestion that any of the hacked accounts had been discovered. Hairie messaged that he felt it safe to proceed; there was a telecommunication conference scheduled in New York City two months hence in April, and that would be an ideal time for the two of them to meet.

Springtime in New York City; what a delight. The city was always vibrant and now the flowers were starting to show; it was nice to get away from the dismal winter of Moscow. He met Hairie at the meeting. Both men were excited and full of anticipation. They decided to get away from the conference to go over their plans in private. Hairie mentioned that there was no good teahouse in New York and that he would settle for coffee. They found a Starbucks.

When settled at a private table, Hairie mentioned that the six million dollars was theirs for the taking. He had already decided what he was going to do with his half. Oh my friend but wait, said Boris. Hadn't he told him that his share was not half, but twenty percent? Since Boris had devised the master plan and brought Hairie into the enterprise, Hairie was therefore the junior partner. But, Hairie said he had expected a bigger share and that he thought Boris was being stingy in the way he was divvying up. Boris told Hairie that he would have to get used to it. After all, he would still clear one point two million. Besides, there would be more of these enterprises, and he would cut him in for a bigger share.

Hairie nodded his acceptance. He did not appear too disturbed. He even showed signs of being satisfied. Then Hairie said he had gotten tickets for the New York Metropolitan Opera for the following night for the two of them. Mussorgsky's Boris Godunov was playing, and he thought Boris would enjoy the work of this Russian composer. Yes, Boris said that he would like that very much. This was Mussorgsky's greatest work, a true masterpiece, revered throughout all of Russia, He would like that very much!

After a late afternoon dinner they went early to be ahead of the seven-thirty opening curtain. Boris was surprised when they were ushered into a private box. How, he asked, was he able to land such choice seats? Hairie answered that he had quite a bit of pull with the bank branch managers who had obtained the seats. But a private box, Boris intoned! This will be delightful.

Following the prologue and the first two of the four acts of Boris Godunov, there was an intermission Hairie asked how Boris was enjoying the opera. Boris said it was a sheer delight, one of the artistic highlights of his life, and to see it performed so sumptuously in New York City at one of the world's great opera houses, was truly memorable.

Then refreshments were brought into the box. Boris was handed a glass and a canister of vodka. Hairie received a cup, saucer and a pot of tea. Hairie remarked that at last he had found a good cup of tea in the city. But Boris was puzzled; there was another glass on the tray. It appeared to be a martini, and on closer inspection contained a twist of lemon rind. Suddenly, Raghib appeared and took a seat.

Hairie began to explain: Hairie and Raghib were Interpol agents. He cautioned him not to try to bolt and run as there were detectives from the New York City Police Department outside the box. It was sheer happenstance that Boris had recruited Raghib. Their cybercrime unit frequents telecommunication events to keep up with technology. Raghib was also advanced enough to have been invited to give a paper on malware. It was also happenstance that Boris had run into Hairie in Singapore at one of the conferences. At any rate as soon as Raghib was on board, they knew they had him, they only had to let the plot play out to find enough evidence for a conviction. Boris's master plan was brilliant and might have succeeded, except for an unlucky turn of fate. Now Boris, the second half of Boris Godunov is going to start. Don't you think we should stay to the finish?

Because finally, in the end, you really weren't, Boris, good enough.

62927202R00209

Made in the USA
Lexington, KY
22 April 2017